THE HEART OF A PIRATE

Book 4

THE HEARTS OF ADVENTURE SWEET ROMANCE SERIES

CHLOE FLOWERS

DEDICATION

To my husband. I love you.

DESCRIPTION

IF YOU GIVE A PIRATE A TREASURE

*NOTE: This is the stand-alone, *sweet version* of the novel *If You Give a Pirate a Treasure*, (Book 4 of The Pirates & Petticoats Series By Chloe Flowers).

Captain Conal O'Brien's *Seeker* has just been overrun by the most unlikely band of pirates to sail the seas. When he discovers that they work for his sworn enemy, he develops a scheme of his own. But these nutty brigands aren't who they seem to be, and if Conal's not careful, he's going to lose his heart as well as his ship to a lady pirate determined to possess both.

Stevie Sauvage is on a quest to find a hidden family treasure. When her eight-year-old twin siblings are kidnapped by the pirate, Captain Gampo, and the ransom demand is a merchant ship, she must find the courage to conquer her fears and fight for those she loves *before time runs out* for the twins.

The Heart of a Pirate is a high seas, historical, pirate romance filled with action and adventure, mystery and intrigue, and a quest for hidden treasure (with a few laughs along the way).

AUTHOR'S NOTE

A note on Anne Bonny:

There are many stories about Anne Bonny, one of most notorious female pirate in history. There is no solid documentation of her entire life, in fact, there are large gaps as well as a debate on when she actually died. Some say she was smuggled out of prison, some say her father's bribes freed her.

Some say she married and moved to Charles Town (today's Charleston, South Carolina) and lived under the name Burleigh and had several more children.

Some say that Mary Read faked death in prison and escaped, hidden under a shroud, and she and Anne eventually moved to New Orleans and lived out the rest of their days together.

No one seems to know the entire story of Anne Bonny.

Perhaps it's best that way.

DISCLAIMER

THE HEART OF A PIRATE

The Hearts of Adventure
Sweet Romance Series

Book Four

PROLOGUE

As usual, I left a gift for you at the end of the book. The recipe for Citrus Beach Pie is both easy and delicious!

June 1811
New Orleans

S tanding among the charred debris of his family's boarding house in New Orleans, Bernard Sauvage lifted a blackened marble box from the rubble. Nearby, his sons as well as his late brother's children were salvaging what they could, shifting bricks and burned beams.

The smoke-scented morning was hushed by tragedy; they'd lost everything.

Bernard shifted the box in his hand well enough to remove the lid, then sucked in his breath. Two roughly cut emeralds rested on a stack of letters. He stared for a moment before brushing them with his fingertips, half expecting them to dissolve into dust.

They were real.

He fingered through the yellowed parchment. The first letter was dated almost 100 years ago. He scanned it and raised his eyebrows in shock at the signature.

It had been written by the notorious, female pirate, Anne Bonny.

Bernard moved to an upturned water trough and sat to read. A short time later, he replaced the letters in the marble box along with the emeralds. The lady pirate hinted that she'd hidden a fortune in jewels just before she and the crew of the *Gallant* had been captured.

It was a risk, but if he could find this secret treasure, he and his family would be able to rebuild what they had lost.

His late brother sired five children. He looked up as the youngest, eight year-old twins, approached. Julian lowered a box of blackened silverware to the ground, and Jacqueline placed a bent serving tray and three blackened dice on top of it.

"What did you find, Uncle Bernard?"

"Can we see?"

Bernard smiled and rubbed the cool marble. "Our past. And our future. Get the others. We're going on a journey."

CHAPTER 1

The first letter from Anne Bonny to her father William Cormac:

3 March, 1718

Dear Father,
I bid you farewell. I know you disapprove of my choice for a husband.
True, he is but a simple sailor. However, I refuse to marry any of those
milksops or fortune hunters who continue to darken our door. I love James
Bonny and he has sworn his life to me. I ask nothing more from you than
your prayers for my health and well-being.

Your daughter,
Anne

July 1811
Harbour Town, South Carolina

Captain Conal O'Brien leaned forward and felt for the linen cloth draped over the foot end of the tub. After wiping his face, he braced his hands on the rim and began to push himself to his feet. He mustn't dawdle if he was going to make it to his sister's wedding on time. His cousin Brendan would learn that he could also dress for an occasion in polished boots and finery. They'd carried on this good-natured rivalry since they were boys.

Conal raised his head, and his nose nearly clipped a pistol barrel. The faint acrid odor of gun powder assailed his nostrils. Focused on the cold, grey metal, he was careful to avoid any sudden movement as he eased himself back into the water. He raised his gaze to peruse the person holding the weapon, a brigand wearing a wide-brimmed hat pulled low. Beneath the hat, a brightly colored scarf covered his hair. Behind the gun bearer stood a second figure.

"You have my attention," Conal said evenly. Naked and unarmed, what choice was there other than negotiation? Although talking his way out of a situation like this wasn't his strength. He was better at negotiating with his fists.

The one holding the pistol stood between him and the lantern, but from what he could ascertain, the intruder was tall, but slight in build. All that prevented Conal from going on the offensive were their weapons.

The closer man must have been thinking along a similar line of thought, because his pistol shook slightly. "This ship has been taken," he said. "If you value your life and the lives of the crew that remain, you will yield."

Crew that *remain*?

Conal's stomach twisted. How had he missed the sound of battle aboard? Granted, all but the watch and a handful of men still making repairs had been allowed to go ashore to attend the wedding celebration, but he should have heard a warning shout or a pistol shot even down here in the galley. How many of his men had lost their lives? He ground his teeth, a silent vow of vengeance burning his throat, guilt trapping it there.

"Do you yield?" The intruder tightened his hold on the pistol.

Conal cursed under his breath. "I yield ye black-hearted spawn of a tavern whore. What are your demands?"

"You will take us and this ship to Jamaica," he said. "Immediately."

Conal tilted his head and narrowed his eyes. The voice sounded too...fragile. A woman, perhaps?

STEVIE SWALLOWED and gripped the pistol handle more firmly. Her arm was beginning to tire from holding it for so long, but she didn't dare lower it. The mountain of a man in the tub looked as if he could crush her head like a grape with one hand, and her young cousin's with the other. More often than not, she could look an average man straight in the eye. However, with this one, she doubted her head would reach his nose.

Stevie and her family had spied on the *Seeker* for hours.

"Look," Uncle Bernard had finally pointed. "Most of the crew is heading to shore. There's only a small watch left behind." He rubbed his chin and peered through the thick fog in the direction of the sun, which was up there somewhere in the late afternoon sky. "This fog bank will provide perfect cover. Let's go. The quicker we get this ship to that devil-pirate Gampo, the quicker he'll return the children to us."

The memory of the pirate's men ripping her little brother and sister from her arms and taking them into the belly of a vessel called the *Dragon* had Stevie checking the priming of her pistol.

Thankfully, she hadn't needed to use it. The remaining crew of the *Seeker* had gathered around an upturned crate and played cards, enabling Stevie and the rest of the family to surround them.

The men had surrendered with barely a word.

It had been a foolhardy plan.

Ridiculous.

Dangerous.

Crazy.

Yet, an absolutely imperative one to execute with success.

THE MAN in the tub arched his brows, still awaiting her answer, then his eyes narrowed before sliding down to her soft doeskin boots and back up again. She cursed her stupidity. They should have stayed further in the shadows; it might have given them more of an intimidating appearance.

"Stevie," her young cousin whispered from behind her, bringing her attention back in line. What was the question? Oh, yes. Demands.

"You will relinquish your freedom and possessions," she said, barely able to keep the tremor from her voice. Her gaze paused at the gold signet ring on the man's finger. If they were going to become pirates, she might as well start acting like one. She took a deep breath and drew her shoulders back a little. "Beginning with your ring," she said, holding out her hand.

The man's jaw clenched and the knuckles gripping the tub's edge whitened. He was contemplating his chances of overpowering her and taking her pistol; she could see that in the way his gaze shifted back and forth between her and Gabriel. If he'd had a weapon, and if it had been a one-on-one situation instead of one against two (with guns), he likely wouldn't have paused to contemplate it this long. He would have defended himself by attacking them. And he'd have won. Even now, she sensed he was still calculating his odds.

She was far from her cozy little room off her brother's gaming house kitchen. Handling a weapon was only slightly more foreign to her than wearing her cousin's britches. Uncle Bernard had given her a brief lesson on managing a pistol, but it still terrified her to hold it.

She eased a step back, careful to keep her pistol well within a lethal range. "Please don't try it," she said. "I'd prefer to save my shot."

His eyes widened and his brows raised in surprise. She'd been right in her assumptions, then. She usually was. Her intuition annoyed her brothers no small amount, and they always avoided her when they wished their thoughts to remain hidden. Only one of them could hide from her, but he was a gambler and so it was expected, otherwise he wouldn't be a very good gambler, would he?

The man twisted the ring from his finger and tossed it to her. She caught it and placed it on the only finger it would it—her thumb.

Keeping her focus on their hostage, she moved behind him to the stack of clothes on the galley table and removed the dagger and pistol next to them. She'd keep a close watch; he looked like the type of man who'd rather fight against the odds than give himself over. They needed to get him up on deck with the rest of her family before she fainted from the trauma of this whole episode. She came down to the galley to see what stores they had. Finding a man taking a bath was *not* what she'd expected to discover.

"Get dressed," she said, with as much authority as she could muster.

With the oily movement of a cat, he stood then reached for a linen rag. Stevie felt her eyes widen. She was wrong. *Very wrong.* The top of her head would barely reach his chin, let alone his nose. Wide, thick shoulders rippled as he moved, and took up most of the space in the galley. A long scar trailed across his ribcage. A fighting man. A very strong, very muscular, very handsome, very *naked,* fighting man.

She should shut her eyes, avert her gaze, *something*, but that would be foolish right now. She'd never seen a naked man as perfectly proportioned as this one. To be honest, she'd only seen one other naked man (other than her terribly immodest brothers while growing up). Her cousin, Gabriel's mortified expression from the doorway prompted her to roll her eyes and give him a pointed look he interpreted perfectly. She'd changed *his* diapers when she was eight. Besides, she was no dainty maiden.

She'd lost her virginity after falling foolishly in love with a gambler who'd promised her a life of love and luxury, then left her the next day. After losing everything he had as well as several hundred dollars in credits to the house, he disappeared and never returned.

He'd crushed her heart. Ruined it. Ruined her.

Worse were the looks of thunderous anger and then pity from her brothers and male cousins. Especially her brother Tristan, who'd tried to warn her, but she'd defended the snake, and refused to listen. It had been a painful lesson to learn.

Men told a woman anything to sway her attentions to the bedroom, even profess their love and ask for her hand in marriage and persuade her to give him the most precious gift she had.

Their captive turned toward her and reached for his clothes. Her tongue stuck to the roof of her mouth and she could barely swallow. He had a chiseled chest with a faint layer of fine, light brown hair that darkened to a burnished auburn as it trailed past his navel.

Oh, my.

"Satisfied, little rabbit?" he asked. A cocky brow quirked up toward his damp hairline.

So he'd already guessed she was a woman in men's clothing. She assumed he was talking about her perusal, which she wasn't about to address. No need to give him a burst of confidence right now. Besides, her mouth was still dry. Instead, she licked her lips then asked a question. "Little rabbit?" She looked nothing at all like a rabbit. Her ears, along with her hair, were covered.

"You look as if you're ready to jump out of your skin. Perhaps you're afraid of me?" He leaned toward her.

Yes.

"No." She barely managed a response. Her attempt at laughter was pathetic at best.

"Well...little rabbit," his voice was lower than a growl, "you *should* be."

Her heart jerked in a panicked beat and she stepped back.

He dressed. A pair of shiny cordovan boots stood next to the tub, and he pulled them on while muttering obscenities about someone named Brendan. That task complete, he straightened, crossed thick arms over his very impressive chest and glowered at her. His eyes were a grey-green with a golden band around the pupil, reminding her of a tiger she'd once seen in a traveling show. She wanted to swallow, but was paralyzed. Was this how its prey felt just before it became the tiger's dinner?

He'd already determined she was female. Now, he was studying her, calculating the odds on a successful confrontation. If he charged her right now, she'd probably squeal and tumble into a terrified heap on the floor, but he needed to believe she'd shoot him.

She pulled back the hammer of her pistol until it clicked to help him with his decision-making process, and hopefully to fortify hers. Still, her heart pulsed and throbbed in uneven beats. Running the kitchens in her family's boarding and gaming house was a far cry from being a brigand. Pirating was not on her modest list of talents. In fact, she was rather pleased she'd pulled the hammer without accidentally discharging the gun.

Stevie called over her shoulder to her cousin, inwardly cursing at the way her voice trembled. "Gabriel, if he makes a move toward either of us, shoot him." His hammer clicked behind her.

Good.

Pointing toward the door with the pistol, she gestured for her prisoner to go topside.

Almost soundlessly, he moved in long, sinuous strides through the passageway and up the ladder. He smelled of soap, new leather boots, and a musky scent she knew was all him. The vision of that tiger from long ago crept into her thoughts again as she eyed his movements.

Her thoughts jumped to her family up on the main deck, probably thinking she was taking inventory of the pantry. No one expected she'd find anyone down here, which was a stupid assumption, apparently.

Quite honestly, it was a miracle they'd successfully taken the brigantine.

And this was supposed to be the easy part.

OF ALL THE BLOODY, rotten luck.

Conal heaved himself up the last two steps and perused the deck. His skeleton crew were all tied to the mizzen mast in the center of the animal pen amidst a couple of pigs, two goats and the cow. The first mate was currently cursing at the goat busily munching on his hat.

So much for rallying a rebellion anytime soon.

To resist now would be foolish. Best to wait for a more opportune moment after they had time to evaluate their captors' strengths and weaknesses. He glanced at the one called "Stevie."

She was taller than most women. Her long, slender limbs moved fluidly, like a dancer he'd encountered once when he was in Arabia. It was hard to draw his gaze from her face. Dark, inky lashes framed the grey eyes beneath delicately arched brows, and her curves were in all the right places. Even the long vest she wore couldn't hide her form. His guess was that she had a French heritage, but since her English was flawless, was probably American.

Women weren't usually wanted, needed or appreciated aboard

a ship. There were always exceptions, like his sister, but in general, having a woman aboard brought bad luck. Chances were that Stevie was important to at least one other person in their group, or else she wouldn't be here at all. Taking her hostage would be his first move when the time was right. She was someone's lover, wife, sister, or daughter.

Surrounding the pen was a group of well-armed men. From what Conal could discern, based their mannerisms and stance, they were landlubbers. A couple had greenish tints to their faces and hugged the rail on the larboard side. Only old two salts stood with their legs braced in a confident manner. Those two were definitely seamen.

Without waiting for a pistol to poke him in the back, he strolled over to the pen. Stevie followed, keeping a wary distance. "Is your watch unharmed, Remus?" he asked his first mate.

Remus looked up and his cheeks reddened. "Yes, sir. Sorry, Captain." He added in a chagrined tone, "We just didn't expect..."

The man didn't need to finish the sentence, really. Even Conal wouldn't have expected anyone to do something this audacious so close to Harbour Town in the late afternoon, fog or no fog.

Conal scanned their captors. He'd earlier assumed they were pirates, but that seemed incorrect now. There were four other full-grown men, two of which were obviously brothers, and all most certainly had to be related in some way. Along with light eyes and hair the color of black coffee, there were similarities in build and stature, as well as in certain facial features. The only exception was one of the grizzled sailors, a short, wiry, stubble-faced man who looked to be about sixty.

In the light of day, it was more obvious the one called Gabriel was still a boy, maybe thirteen or fourteen. He was an idiot for allowing those two to take him without a fight. Pistols notwithstanding.

One of the old salts strode forward, a scowl on his face. "What's this?"

"Gabriel and I found him in the galley," Stevie said.

"Hiding?"

"Bathing."

The man's eyes widened and he spun to face the two.

"Why didn't you call for help?"

Stevie just shrugged. "Quite honestly, Uncle Bernard, there wasn't time," she said. "We found him in a vulnerable situation and easily handled it on our own."

Bernard rubbed his forehead before brushing a salt and pepper curl from his grey eyes. He spoke to one of his men. "Adrian, toss him over with the rest."

Adrian strode toward him and Conal swallowed. He was normally the tallest in the room, but this one had him by almost a half a head. He clenched his fists at his sides. This fight might be challenging.

Stevie touched her uncle's arm. "Wait, we might need him. He's their captain."

A quick flicker of relief crossed Bernard's stern features before he turned his attention back to Adrian. "Never mind. Make a sweep of the lower decks instead."

An angry shout came from the water below on the port side of the *Seeker*. "At least toss over the oars, you sons of Satan!"

Conal started to walk toward the voice, but at Stevie's raised pistol, he stopped. "What have you done with the rest of my men?"

Bernard answered. "We sent them off in longboats." He grabbed two oars, walked to the opposite side of the ship and heaved them overboard.

"You half-masted, verminous dog!" came the reply from the water below.

At least the men had oars available to them, although there was no guessing how long it would take to get to them. Conal doubted there were any swimmers among the crew sitting in the longboat. It would take some time to paddle with their hands to where the oars floated on the starboard side of the ship.

Meanwhile, Bernard moved Conal near the mizzen close to the other men, then bound his hands and hobbled his legs in irons, effectively depleting his mobility.

The pirates gathered together and the two old seamen began assigning tasks, and it wasn't long before they were in an argument.

"The anchor has to be brought up before ye can do that, ye dim-witted cur."

"I know that! But we need feet on the yards and arms on the sheets if we're going to get underway, you vermin-ridden old goat."

Not only did their captors walk the deck like lubbers, they didn't even look like pirates. There were no missing appendages except for two fingers gone on the oldest sailor's left hand. There were no visible scars, and for the most part, none of the younger men showed the effects of sun-darkened skin or scurvy.

Curious indeed.

CHAPTER 2

2 April 1718

Dear Father,
John Bonny and I have purchased a schooner and will soon embark on a
journey north to Boston with a hold full of tobacco and other naval stores.
I am happy and my hope is that you are happy for me. We shall bring back
maple syrup for you on our return trip. Be well, Father.

Your daughter,
Anne

S tevie Sauvage was now a pirate and a thief. As such, she
expected to feel more dangerous and brave.

She didn't.

Fear still had her hands trembling. The task Gampo had
charged them with had seemed impossible. It still did, even
though they had completed the first part without incident. His

promise to kill the twins if they failed was always the foremost thought in her mind.

Her uncle stood with Harvey, Gampo's second, who'd been assigned to accompany her family on their mission. The old salt eyed Stevie as he argued with Uncle Bernard about who was in charge. Finally, Harvey pointed to the ring on her thumb. "Ye didna have that gold on yer hand before. Where d'you get it?"

She fingered the signet ring and lifted her chin. She'd not let the caustic old man intimidate her. "I took it from the captain. It's our nature as pirates, is it not? Plunder?"

Uncle Bernard stopped arguing with Harvey and lowered his brows. "It certainly is not *your* nature. Give it back."

She pulled the ring from her thumb, but Harvey snatched it from her hand and shoved it on his stubby finger. "Everything on this ship belongs to Cap'n Gampo now. I'll take it. Just fer safe keepin'."

Uncle Bernard let out a disgusted snort. No one trusted Harvey. But since he was Gampo's eyes and ears, no one dared challenge him, either.

"Now, ye were sayin' that we have her captain?" Harvey asked, rubbing his hands together.

Bernard nodded and jerked his chin to the broad-shouldered man standing in braces near the mizzen mast.

"Aye, then." Harvey rocked back on his heels. "Let's weigh anchor."

The captain stood in stony silence, but his eyes missed nothing. There was an almost violent heat emanating from him, as if every muscle coiled beneath his skin was ready to spring into action given the right opportunity. She flicked her gaze to his large hands. His bindings had better be securely fastened.

One by one, his crew's hands were bound to the main capstan at the center of the deck, each tied to a different bar. Stevie's brother, Tristan escorted the captain over, and Uncle Bernard scratched his bristly chin, eyeing him up and down. "My name's

Bernard Sauvage, Captain. Best just call me Bernard. If you call out 'Mister Sauvage,' we'll all turn around."

The captain nodded a stiff greeting. "I'm Captain Conal O'Brien."

Bernard gestured to the others the captain had already had the misfortune to meet, Adrian and the boy Gabriel. "My sons." Bernard nodded toward Tristan and Stevie. "And their cousins. We mean to take this vessel to Jamaica, and it would be much less painful for your men if you assist us in that endeavor."

The captain shot a dark gaze toward her, then shrugged "I have no helmsman."

"We have full faith in your competence with your charts," Bernard replied. "Harvey and I are familiar with sailing ships and will assist in any way we can."

Harvey sauntered up and unwound a long leather whip. Stevie swallowed. It was a cat-o'-nine tails, the knots on the ends darkened with use and dried blood.

"I brought me own cat," Harvey sneered. "I'd be happy to scratch their backs with her if need be."

The captain's eyes hardened and his gaze swept over the wicked strips of leather, paused on the signet ring on the pirate's finger and then narrowed. Apparently the ring was very important to the captain. That was good information to keep in the back of her mind for when she needed it.

Stevie shifted her gaze between the captain and her family. Would he be compliant or would he fight? Her brother and cousins might be big and strong and although they brandished their weapons in a dangerous enough fashion, they weren't well-trained in the use of them. Thankfully, their hostages weren't privy to that information.

"You can put that cat away, Harvey," Bernard flicked his hand at it dismissively. "I don't believe Captain O'Brien would jeopardize the health and stamina of his crew." His voice dropped to a steely tone meant only for O'Brien's ears. "We are determined to see our plans through to the end Captain, with or without your help."

With that last sentence, Stevie stepped forward, pistol ready. After her mother died, Uncle Bernard had rescued them. She would go where her uncle said to go, and follow his instructions as best as she could. She owed him her life and her loyalty.

O'Brien turned his back to Harvey and his wicked cat. "What are your intentions once we make port in Jamaica?"

Harvey and Bernard exchanged glances. Bernard cleared his throat, then shrugged. "We have urgent business with a privateer who's awaiting our arrival."

Stevie released a breath she hadn't realized she was holding. For a moment, she feared Uncle Bernard would tell him what they planned to barter. It would have revealed a weakness better left hidden.

"And once your business is complete, what will happen to my ship and crew?" the captain asked.

Uncle Bernard shrugged again. "Once we arrive, we will have no need for either."

Very cleverly worded, Uncle.

O'Brien tilted his head and studied Bernard then Harvey. "I have your word?"

"Of course." Harvey nodded and stuck out his hand. O'Brien warily shook it best he could with bound wrists.

O'Brien's piercing green gaze captured hers and she froze. Her heart slammed into her ribcage, jarring her lungs into action and she drew in a rapid breath, unaware she'd been holding it. Mouth suddenly dry, she swallowed and turned away, afraid the guilt in her chest would show on her face at the lie.

Her cousins had finished attaching the crew to the capstan, and Harvey shouted, "Heave around, ye maggots!"

The men looked at their captain but didn't move.

Harvey shook out his cat. "Heave 'round, I say!"

The men remained motionless, eyes on their captain. Conal

O'Brien gave Uncle Bernard a long look before he nodded to his men. They braced against the bars and pushed the capstan around. With an almost musical cadence, it began to clank as the chains moved through the hawse pipes. Once the anchor was up, the men were released, and O'Brien gave them orders to prepare to sail.

Stevie released a tense breath. Thank goodness there hadn't been a rebellion from the scant crew. Her family captured the ship through sheer luck and happenstance. Had there indeed been a fight, her small band of 'pirates' would have surely been diminished and likely defeated. As fate would have it, the first part of their plan was complete. The next may not be as easy.

CONAL CURSED UNDER HIS BREATH. He didn't believe Harvey's promise to release the *Seeker* any more than Harvey took Conal's word that he and his crew would be compliant.

As it was, just breaking free of the harbor in this fog would take a bloody miracle. He'd put out enough sail to move the ship slowly forward, but even at this pace, he'd be hard-pressed to adjust direction if the situation called for it.

He glanced up, barely able to make out the figure he'd sent to the upper topsail yardarm. "Mister Remus! Eyes sharp!"

"Aye, sir!" came the reply from above.

Conal peered into the fog. He blinked. Was that a shadow or—?

"Ship sighted on the port side! Port side!" came the shout from Remus.

"Hard to larboard!" Conal shouted to Bernard, who turned the wheel furiously. Beyond the bowsprit loomed the aft end of a ship nearly the same size as the *Seeker*. Men scrambled to adjust the jibs to keep them from ramming into the other ship's hull.

The bowsprit swept across the last six feet of the near vessel's poop deck with no damage other than snapping off the ensign staff, plunging the flag into the water. The larboard side of the ship flew past them; Conal caught sight of the shocked face of a crewman through one of the open gun ports. The distance between the two vessels was barely an arm's length.

Thankfully, the rest of the way to the open sea went without incident. Like a breaking wave, an almost audible sigh of relief rolled across the deck when they finally cleared the harbor. Conal maintained the current course and crawled toward the open sea hoping the fog merely gripped the coastline and thinned farther east.

Once they finally moved out of the thick fog bank, men of the *Seeker* moved sullenly to unfurl sails and hoist them, while the young woman looked on, pistol ready but wavering.

Ah. She looked frightened. Nervous. Perhaps she'd never sailed before and was afraid of the sea. She glanced at him, and he caught her gaze and held it, testing her. The small muscles in her jaw moved as she clenched her teeth before she stepped behind one of her brothers, out of sight.

Run Little rabbit, run and find your hole, crawl inside and hide, but know that even then, I will find you.

Once Conal had her, Bernard Sauvage would have to negotiate better terms with him, which meant they would not be sailing to Jamaica, at least not without the other two ships in his fleet.

The Sauvages had released him from the irons, but bound his wrists behind his back. He stood with his feet braced wide, issuing terse commands to his men.

The *Seeker* began to pick up speed as the wind caught the square main sails. The upper sheets were still furled and lashed. The boy, Gabriel, seemed the most curious and observed the sailors closely. He enthusiastically offered a hand when he could, otherwise he stood as he did now, near the stern watching one man climb the rigging to secure a jib. Stevie sauntered over to him, and soon the two had their heads close together, deep in discussion.

"Prepare to jibe," Conal shouted. "Release the spanker." The boom began to swing toward the ship's midline. Stevie and the boy, apparently understanding neither the commands nor the resulting actions, continued to talk, backs facing the boom swinging their way.

"Jibe ho!" Conal shouted. His men were all up in the yards, their captors either guarding with pistols or doing other minor tasks. It was blatantly obvious Stevie's family of pirates had no experience working a ship of this size (if they had any experience at all). They'd done nothing but get in the way since they set sail. If he had to guess, he'd say they'd never even *been* at sea.

Even worse, those who knew what 'jibe ho' meant weren't close enough to relay his warning or help out.

Considering the circumstances, it occurred to him that if he let the events unfold without interference, the pirate band would be quickly reduced by two. The young boy was close in age to Brendan's younger brother, and as tempting as it was, Conal couldn't stand idly by and watch the lad get swept overboard. The impact of the boom alone could crack his skull open. Seeing no other alternative, he ran toward the two. If the boom hit them, they would be badly hurt, or possibly knocked into the sea.

"Hit the deck! Hit the deck!" he shouted.

Stevie's eyes widened when she turned and saw Conal charging toward her. To his horror, she drew the pistol from her belt. Didn't she see the danger she and the boy were in? Remus yelled and waved his arms from the yards, trying to draw their attention to the swinging sail, now gaining speed. There was no time to explain the why or what of the situation.

Conal grazed the boy with his hip just enough to cause him to fall backward before he lunged, lowering his shoulder to catch Stevie in the chest. Just as they hit the planks, there was a loud *crack*. The sail continued to swing over the deck until his crew secured it.

STEVIE SQUIRMED to get free from under Conal O'Brien's large, muscular body and struggled to take a breath. Gabriel rolled to his knees, his face pale. One of O'Brien's men and Adrian rushed to aid the two, but Adrian's pistol stopped the sailor short.

"Put that gun away and help!" Stevie shouted. Adrian shoved his weapon in his waistband and reached for her, pulling her to her feet. She shoved his hands away. Couldn't he see the captain was hurt? "No, not me, *him*." She pointed to Conal.

Hindered by the ropes binding his hands behind his back, Conal grimaced and finally rolled to his side, revealing Stevie's pistol on the floorboards by his stomach. A thin ribbon of smoke rose from the narrow mouth of the weapon, while a red spot of blood began to seep across Conal's shirt.

Stevie dropped to her knees and ripped the fabric, revealing a large, bloody gash. She pulled the cloth from her head and pressed it over the wound. Dear God, she killed the captain! She shifted him to see if the bullet went through.

"It just grazed his side," she said, her words reedy and relieved. Her gaze caught the green fire of the captain's and she looked away. Uncle Bernard ran up to join them. She tried to explain. "I thought he was going to attack Gabriel, so I pulled out my pistol. When I realized what was happening, and before I could lower it, he ran into me and it fired." She peeled the scarf back a little to see if the bleeding stopped. "I didn't actually intend to shoot him," she muttered. Surely they would have reacted in a similar manner.

But Conal was scowling at Bernard, his Irish brogue sharp and irate. "If ye had an ounce of sense in that head of yours, ye wouldn't let her carry a weapon of any sort."

Bernard returned the glare, pulling his own pistol out. "I'll thank you to keep your advice to yourself and remember your place in all this." Still, he nudged Stevie's pistol away from Conal, picked it up and shoved it into his pocket before staring curiously at the captain. "How did you know she was a woman?"

Conal tossed Stevie a lusty leer. "One of her more feminine parts cushioned my head when we hit."

Stevie narrowed her eyes and opened her mouth to retort.

"Hoy, there!" a cheerful voice cut through the tension. Her older brother, Tristan a bottle in his hand, strolled up to the group. "Look what I found in the captain's cabin—what happened here?" Tristan's voice raised a notch as he took in the blood on both Stevie and Conal's shirts.

"Stevie accidentally shot the captain," Adrian said darkly, taking the bottle from Tristan's hand and raising it to his lips.

She snatched the bottle from Adrian's giant paw. "Go find some clean rags." The last thing they needed was a tipsy lot.

Uncle Bernard addressed the captain. "Is there a ship's surgeon?"

O'Brien gave him a sarcastic grunt. "Yes. He's with the helmsman back in the longboat."

Stevie rolled her eyes. Of all the rotten luck. "I'm not a healer. All I know is that whiskey cleans a wound and garlic helps to prevent infection." She held up the bottle. "I have this." She looked at Tristan. "Find some garlic and the surgeon's bag." She splashed whiskey on the captain's wound.

"Arugh!" Conal roared. He locked eyes with Bernard and glared. "Get her the hell away from me!"

"Your wound can't be too dire, given you're capable of a bellow *that* thunderous," she said through her gritted teeth, returning his death glare with one of her own. Stevie set her jaw in irritation. "I'm trying to help you. Stop being so uncooperative."

He gave her an incredulous stare. "*Uncooperative?* Am I supposed to invite you to tea for taking my ship? You—"

"Watch your mouth," Bernard snarled. He gave O'Brien a swift kick, drawing a grunt of pain from the captain.

The man might be big, strong, and proud, but right now, she had the upper hand. She tossed another bit of whiskey on the gash, just to remind him. His hiss of displeasure wasn't nearly as gratifying as the earlier bellow. Whatever he'd been about to call her couldn't have been gracious. No one had ever *almost* talked to her that way before, although with her brothers and cousins always around, no one had ever dared.

"You're enjoying this," he ground out.

She gave him her most pious look, then and sloshed another splash on the wound.

The muscles in O'Brien's jaw pulsed, and he turned his attention back to Bernard, speaking through clenched teeth. "Either you get this sadistic *witch* away from me, or I swear I'll take a flying leap over the rail and end my misery once and for all, and you can sail this bloody ship yourselves wherever you desire, *with my compliments!*"

CONAL SAT on a three-legged stool near the helm while the young woman finished wrapping his wound with the linen strips she'd dug out of the surgeon's bag. It had finally stopped bleeding. He took the time to study his captors a bit more. The family hovered nearby. Hovered was probably the wrong word although the constant movement of a hummingbird almost described their actions. Pacing, glancing along the deck, watching the crew work they hadn't stilled for even a minute.

Stevie's brother Tristan was at least half a head taller than Bernard, with narrower shoulders and jaw. Conal guessed he weighed about the same as Bernard; his weight was simply stretched out a bit more by his frame. He shared the same impish mouth and silver eyes as Stevie.

Standing, Conal grimaced. He'd had worse wounds. The gash would heal but until it did, it would sting like the devil with every movement of his torso. A brief look of remorse fluttered across Stevie's features, giving him the sudden urge to needle her. "Have you been assigned to stand guard over me, now?"

Her mouth thinned and the muscles of her jaw twitched. "Apparently not. Uncle Bernard still has my pistol." She knelt in front of him, repacking the surgeon's bag.

"I have a dire need to relieve myself. Come, I'll need your assistance, since my hands are still bound behind my back."

It was rather entertaining, watching the various thoughts in her mind flow across her face like signal flags. Confusion, then shock. Her gaze flicked from his face to his belt; her eyes widened and her face turned a satisfying red.

All in all, a successful needling.

Instead of answering his question, she scrambled to her feet and darted to Tristan to whisper in his ear. From there, she took off for the helm and the shelter of the rest of her family.

He laughed. It wasn't long before Tristan loosed his bindings and moved his hands to the front of his body before re-securing them. It was a small victory, but a victory just the same. He sauntered to the rail, took care of business then wandered back toward the helm.

Gabriel stood a few feet away, absorbed by watching the old pirate Harvey handle the ship's wheel. Bernard sat on a barrel, a small, scorched, marble box on his lap. He'd taken what looked to be a journal from it and was scowling at the thing. Stevie joined him, and before long both were involved in a very focused discussion. Distracted by the conversation, the others joined them.

"It says right there they buried him in a cemetery in Savanna," Tristan pointed out in irritation. He peered closer at the letter. "Isn't Savannah spelled with the letter 'h' at the end?"

"Maybe Anne Bonny wasn't very good at penning letters," Bernard responded.

"What's so hard about simply going to the cemetery in Savannah? We just dig up the casket, empty it and then put the box and the body back in the grave," Tristan stated after-of-factly.

Bernard gave him an exasperated look. "You think we can just stroll up and ask the rector's permission to dig up a grave and he'll offer to help dig, do you?"

"We'll do it at night," Tristan said, shrugging.

"We don't even know where to find this Helshire Church," Bernard muttered. "It might be near the city center, for all we know."

"That's a strange name for a church," Stevie said curiously. She glanced around and suddenly noticed Conal eavesdropping. She turned back to the group and said something, and they all glanced at him then dropped their voices.

After a few moments, Stevie turned and spoke to him. "Are you familiar with Savannah, Captain?"

He shrugged. "I've made port there a few times."

"Do you know of a Helshire Church?"

Helshire church? He'd never heard of a Helshire Church in Savannah, Georgia.

However, there was a Helshire Church in Savanna, *Jamaica*...

CHAPTER 3

Journal entry
16 May 1718

John Bonny and I encountered the most dangerous situation imaginable. The pirate ship Fancy, *under the command of Captain Edward Low captured our ship. Low is a terrifying man with a hideous gash across his cheek and jaw. Apparently it's a wound that didn't heal entirely shut. His face has a gruesome expression even when in repose. We did our best to precipitate flight, but the brigantine was already under full sail and quickly overtook us.*
Our fate looks dim.

D rago Viteri Gamponetti (Gampo to his men), son of the youngest daughter of a French Marquis and a wealthy Italian diplomat, and a cousin to the Grand Duke of Tuscany, looked with absolute disinterest at the eight-year-old twins on his bed. They had cried themselves to sleep *finally*, about an hour ago. On the wounded sloop's deck, the boy had screamed and raged against Drago's helmsman, who held his arms while another member of the crew carried his sister aboard the *Dragon*. That was quite brave of the boy.

Senseless, but brave.

The boy's sister, however, had been temporarily shocked into complete silence as the ships drew apart. It was only after both understood that their family was powerless to save them that the silent tears began streaming down their faces. The docile little lamb had sobbed into her hands, and the boy had stood next to her, glowering at Drago while speaking to his sister in a voice that was too quiet to carry.

They were lucky to be in his cabin rather than locked up somewhere below deck where it was dark, smelly and damp. He did it out of pity more than anything. However, the way the children took inventory of their surroundings he'd be a fool to trust them in here alone, so now he sat at his desk, studying his charts.

If the children's family captured the *Seeker* and set sail for Jamaica, then Fynn Ahern and his son, Brendan would surely give chase in the *Reward*. Depending on the condition of the *Desire*, Captain Hart would likely take the *Reward's* flank. How satisfying to know his enemies so well. All three ships would easily be trapped between the Jamaican shore and Lamb's Tail Island. The artillery on the island, and the *Seeker's* guns would surely disable them.

The cargo in the captured ship's holds would offset his losses, and the ships themselves would replace the one Fynn had rendered completely useless during their last altercation. He would gain three brigantines. Two for the French King, one for himself.

"Where are you taking us?"

He looked up into the red-rimmed, grey eyes of the girl standing a few feet away. It was a good thing she wasn't armed, or he'd have been in trouble. He'd not heard a sound or caught a single movement during her transition from his bed to the spot in front of his desk. Perhaps she wasn't as docile as she appeared.

"South," he answered.

She pressed her lips into a thin line. Her nostrils flared. "South to where?"

"A place called Lamb's Tail Island," he answered, studying his chart.

"And where, *exactly* is Lamb's Tail Island?"

He inhaled and let his breath out slowly. "Off the western coast of Jamaica." He turned his attention back to his charts.

"Why?" There was a distinct undercurrent of fury rippling through her words this time.

He kept his focus on the chart. Perhaps if he looked busy, she'd stop talking. He marked the parchment.

There. She'd stopped.

She was still visible out of the corner of his eye though. She'd moved directly in front of him. He could feel her stare. In fact, the top of his head warmed as if her gaze was as heated as her words.

It was annoying.

And distracting.

Finally, he gave up trying to concentrate on the chart. "Why, what?" he asked. He could be just as annoying.

"Why are you taking us to Lamb's Tail Island?" she said, as if the question should have been more obvious, which of course, it was.

"Because I desire it."

She leaned forward and put her hands on his desk, which almost came up to her thin shoulders. "*Why* do you desire it?"

He rolled his eyes. "Because that is where your family will bring my prize ship and exchange it for you and your brother. After which, they will take you and that pathetic little sloop we're dragging behind us back to wherever you belong."

"Why did you become a pirate?"

"I'm not a pirate."

"You have kidnapped me and my brother. You took my uncle's boat. You're holding me and Julian for a ransom. How is that not being a pirate?"

"I'm a *privateer*. I have a letter of marque from the French king, permitting me to take possession of any ships hailing from countries that are enemies of France."

She folded her arms across her chest and gave him a regal stare. "We aren't enemies of France. My grandparents were French."

He leaned forward and gave her a predatory smile. "The sloop was flying an American flag, not a French one."

"Are you French, then?"

He sighed, her next question would no doubt be out of her mouth before he finished answering the last. "No. I'm Italian."

"Then why do you work for a French king?"

"Because he pays me *very* well to capture vessels like yours. I could keep the boat, but I am a benevolent man and have promised to return it to your uncle once he brings the *Seeker* to me." Hopefully she noted the malevolent tone he used. She'd been easier to handle when she was crying.

She leaned forward and mimicked the tone almost exactly. "Why do you want the *Seeker*?"

He sat back in his chair. "If I tell you, will you stop asking questions and let me get back to my charts?"

She shrugged, which he took as a 'no.'

"What's your name, little lamb?"

"Jacqueline Louisa Sauvage. What's yours?"

"Drago Vitieri Gamponetti. You may call me Gampo."

"Well, Mister Gampo—"

"No. Captain Gampo."

"Fine. Well, *Captain Gampo*, why did you choose the *Seeker*?"

Drago took a deep breath to prevent himself from shouting in frustration, which he was absolutely sure would give the little petticoat a great deal of satisfaction. "I'm doing my duty to my employer, the king of France, for one. And for two, the *Seeker* is one of three ships in Fynn Ahern's merchant fleet."

She opened her mouth, and he held up an index finger. "And before you ask, Fynn Ahern is my sworn enemy." He switched from an index finger to the palm of his hand, causing her once again to close her mouth. "He kidnapped my sister and sold her to a Persian slave trader. Or at least all evidence points to that assumption." He stared at the chart without really seeing it. "So you see, Miss Sauvage—"

"Jacqueline, if you please."

He gave her a distracted nod. "So you see, *Jacqueline*, I am *not* the villain here." He returned his attention to his chart. The silence following his statement was disturbing.

And distracting.

And annoying.

He looked up.

Her expression shifted; her eyes widened just slightly. "How long have you been looking for your sister?"

So family was important to her. He stored that information away.

"A long time." He stared out the window at the wake following the vessel. "She might be dead by now."

"How do you know?"

"I don't."

She canted her head to the side and drew her brows together in consternation. "Why don't you simply ask your *sworn enemy*?"

Drago barked out a laugh. "I tried. When I drew close enough, he sent a barrage of grapeshot through my sheets and yards, then sailed off. From then on, all we've done is exchange ballast from our bellies at every meeting."

Repeatedly, in a most expensive manner, truth be told.

He rubbed his forehead with the heels of his palms. He was nearly out of ammunition. Rather than purchase more he'd recruited help, hence the enlistment of the Sauvage family even though they didn't offer it.

"But why do you have my family doing *your* duty?" Again, her arms crossed her chest, and she presented him the same look his tutor would have given him.

Drago put his palms on his desk to prevent himself from putting them around her little neck. He narrowed his eyes and lowered his voice to what his crew would know was a dangerous level. "If you want to see your family again, you'd better mind your mouth little lamb, otherwise I'll have you strung up from the yardarm. It's much harder to talk with a rope around your neck."

She lifted her chin and threw her shoulders back. "You can't do that. If you break your end of the bargain, my family won't give you that ship you want."

"Aye, I promised they can have you and your brother back," he growled, "but I didn't tell them they'd get you back *alive*." It took a couple ticks of the clock, but she read into his meaning far enough. She clamped her mouth shut, and he nodded. "Much better, thank you."

Julian had awakened and was listening to their conversation. His sister turned and walked back to the bed, her skirts swishing in agitation.

She climbed up next to him. "A privateer sounds very much like a pirate. I don't care what you say you are. I'd wager you're a pirate from your head to your soul *Captain* Gampo," she mumbled.

He tossed down the quill and stared at her. Who taught this child manners? "Oh, you'd wager, would you? With what, might I ask? Are you a gambler?" He jerked open a drawer and pulled out a deck of cards then slapped them on the desk. "Are you familiar with Baccarat?"

A lesson needed to be taught.

At her stony silence, he continued. "It's a simple game really, between the dealer and a player. You bet whether the dealer or the player will win." He shuffled. "Usually, the game requires several decks, but since I have only one, we'll use one." He pointed to the stool next to his bed. "Bring your seat to this stool. Let's *wager*, little cat."

She paused long enough to exchange looks with her brother, then scrambled off the bed and did as she was bid.

He looked down at her. "Here are the rules: you get two cards, at most three if you want a third. Kings, Queens, Jacks and tens are worth nothing, Aces are one point, all other cards are at their face value. We sum up our cards—" He looked up. "You do know how to do your sums, don't you?"

At her stiff nod, he continued. "Total the counts of your cards, then drop the first digit and that's your score. For example, if I have a seven and an eight, my sum is fifteen. A one and a five. I drop the one which leaves me with five points. Whoever has the most points when the game is done, wins. Understand?

Another nod.

"If your sum is five or less, you may have a third card. When we are down to the last six cards, the game is over." He shuffled the cards and dealt.

She interlaced her fingers and put them on the desk. "You must remove your coat and roll your sleeves."

He snapped his head up. "The *deuce*, you say!"

She leaned forward and narrowed her eyes. "How else would I know you don't store cards in your sleeves?"

He almost laughed, but remained stoic. "Are you calling me a cheat?" He flared his nostrils and raised his voice, but she didn't even flinch. "I've killed men for less," he added.

At that, she swallowed.

He harrumphed, removed his jacket and rolled his sleeves to his elbows, then gave her a pointed stare.

She wiggled her fingers. "My sleeves end at my elbows, but I will keep my hands on the desk."

Perhaps she'd observed her brothers play enough to have such an astute sense of the nuances of card games. Julian stood next to her, hands in his pockets. Drago pointed to him. "Step back. I'll not have you assisting your sister. She's on her own."

The boy stepped back and gave him a stony look. "Of course. We want to keep the game *fair*." He looked from Drago to his sister, his meaning clear. This game wasn't fair, an eight-year-old girl against a thirty-year-old man.

Drago reached into his jacket pocket and withdrew a slim cigar. "Now, then, what shall we wager? And don't say your freedom, because I never gamble anything I can't afford to lose."

Her teeth snapped with an audible click as she shut her mouth.

He lit the cigar. "Well?" He puffed until he could send a ring of smoke into the air.

"Your berth."

He nearly choked. "What?"

"If I win, Jules and I sleep in your bed."

"And where will I sleep?"

Her thin shoulder shrugged, which he took to mean she couldn't give a cod's eye.

"It's a wager. If I win, you'll mend my trousers."

She nodded her agreement.

They played for nearly an hour. The chit knew her sums, that was certain. However, she wasn't quick. Either that, or she took great satisfaction in drawing out the game, and he had to admit it could very well be either, given what he had learned about her in this short period of time.

He won, of course. At the end of the game, he merely pointed to the Persian rug in front of his desk, then pulled out a sewing box. He placed it and a pair of trousers on the desk, then collected every sharp object or item they could possibly use as a weapon, placed them in a box and took it with him to the helm. He'd been there less than a minute before he turned around and went back to his cabin.

He'd be a fool to leave those two alone together to plot against him.

He entered to find his trousers hanging from the top of the bookshelf on the far side, and Jacqueline standing in the middle of the room with her arms crossed.

Drago made it a point to stare at her, then at the trousers. "Does that mean your word is no good? A bet is a bet, and had I lost, I imagine you'd have your little arse on my bed this moment, wouldn't you?"

He grabbed her chin and tilted it until she was forced to look at him. "And you call *me* a pirate." He retrieved the trousers and placed them back on his desk. Then he took Julian by the arm and dragged him toward the door.

"What are you doing?" she yelped, her voice tight and panicked.

"Lemme go!" Julian yelled. His face had paled from his forehead to his lips.

Drago glared at the girl. "This is not a pleasure trip for you two. You'll both earn yer keep. This one," he jerked his chin toward Julian, "has chores to do." He pointed to the mending kit. "And so do you."

With that, he dragged the boy out and slammed the door shut behind him.

"ALL HANDS! ALL HANDS! SAIL HO' to the east!" The call came from the watch high up the mainmast.

Captain O'Brien's head snapped around and he began barking orders to the men. Stevie ran to the rail. Why would another ship throw the crew into such a panic? Was it a pirate ship? A real one?

The men began to unlash additional sails. Remus scampered up the rigging to the crow's nest like a monkey up a tree, a spyglass tucked into his belt.

"What see you, Remus?" Conal shouted urgently.

"'Tis a great British vessel, sir. Tremendous sails!"

"Put out studding sails, fore and aft!" Conal ordered.

"Aye, sir!"

"Give her a rap full and spread her broad-tall wings to the gale!"

"Aye, sir!"

The ship began to move faster. Before long, she was bounding over the billowing waves of the open ocean. Still, the larger ship was giving chase.

And gaining.

A tingle of fear rippled through Stevie's stomach. A British ship sighting was never a good thing. She searched the deck for Adrian, who'd been ripped off a fishing boat by a British naval captain and impressed into the crew where he served for five years before escaping. She found him standing near Gabriel, his face pale, large fists gripping the rail.

Remus had returned to the helm and now stood at Conal's shoulder. Stevie joined the scant crew straining to see the sails the watch had so confidently identified. By then, Harvey was already tossing Bernard suggestions to ease their escape.

"Toss the stock and crew overboard," the grizzled pirate advised. "The Brits only want hands to man their ships. Let 'em hook 'em like fish from the water. They'll give the rest of us no mind then."

"Keep your forked-tongue in your mouth," Bernard snapped. "The only way we can survive this is to work together. There are precious few hands to offer for a ship of that size. If they need more men, what then?" He shifted an uneasy glance toward Stevie.

"Nor can we outgun her," Remus added darkly. "The *Seeker* has the lines of a sleek cat, but only a few guns. She's not set for a fight against a vessel like that. We're dead men fer sure," Bernard muttered. "Either the pirates enslave us once we reach Jamaica, or the British impress us into their navy. 'Tis a doomed future in the stores fer us all."

Conal O'Brien paced the deck, casting a scornful glance at the ship growing larger on the horizon. "We have but a couple hours to plan before she's on us."

"We can't outrun her without tossing the cargo," Adrian said. "And we need that cargo to barter with Gampo."

"Adrian!" Bernard glowered at his son, but it was too late. The words were out.

O'Brien's head snapped around. "What did you say about Gampo?"

A long moment of silence followed as they exchanged wary glances. Surely Conal realized they'd just exposed information that should have been kept hidden.

"He's my captain," Harvey finally growled. "An' my captain said to bring this ship and her cargo to Lambs Tail Island, so that's what we're gonna do."

"Our lives are worth more than the bounty beneath us," stated Bernard.

Harvey licked his thin, salt-dried lips. "I ain't one to risk being skinned alive for failing him, the devil. We has no choice. We has to outrun 'em."

Remus pointed. "Even if we outrun them, we're caught. Those two will have us, anyway."

Stevie looked at the horizon along with everyone else. Farther ahead were two additional warships, already positioned to cross their bow; it was only a matter of time. Fear twisted in her stomach.

Conal shook his head. "We're out of sheets. We can go no faster."

An idea began to swirl in Stevie's mind. Her brothers ran a gambling hall and were experts at both recognizing a slight of hand as well as implementing one. What if they could create a similar illusion aboard a ship?

She stepped forward under the cold glares of O'Brien's crew as she approached Harvey. "I have an idea that might save us."

"Hrumph," the captain snorted and glared at the British frigate cutting through the distant waves.

Harvey's raspy voice rose above the mumblings of the group. "I still say we offer up our hostages. Put 'em in a boat and leave 'em whilst we get away toward Jamaica."

Stevie put her hands on her hips and gave Harvey the stink eye. "At least *listen* to my suggestion."

"I hope the plan is sound," Adrian grumbled, lifting his knife and pointing it at Harvey. "Because if we fail and I have to serve in his bloody majesty's navy again, I'll personally slit that one's throat."

Squaring her shoulders, she looked at the somber faces around her. "The only way the British will leave us alone is if they don't want us."

"Why wouldn't they?" Adrian said, incredulous. He spread his arms wide. "We are a young, strong crew. We're exactly what they're looking for!"

"Perhaps, perhaps not," she answered slyly.

Her idea bordered on the ludicrous, but they were desperate.

CHAPTER 4

Journal entry
8 July 1718

Captain Edward Low is the devil in human form, of this I am convinced.
He tortured and killed all aboard, including my beloved husband. Low
made me watch as John was drawn and quartered while hanging over the
side of our vessel. I had to listen to my beloved scream even as he fell into
the sea below, which had become infested with sharks drawn to the scent of
blood.
I despise Edward Low and will not rest until I have seen to his demise in
the same manner, or worse. Of this, I vow.

S tevie's plan was the only thing that could possibly save them.
After hearing her proposal, the entire crew agreed to the
endeavor. It was drastic, to be sure. In less than thirty minutes,
half of them would probably regret their decision to take part. In
fact, a quick death might be more agreeable.

Her plan was nothing short of completely insane. Although small, there was a slim chance of success.

Slim was better than none at all. They had to give it a go.

If it failed, Captain O'Brien had stated, he would go down with his ship, fighting to the last shot rather than be pressed into the British Navy. Adrian vehemently concurred and vowed to fight alongside the man. They made a blood oath.

Stevie shuddered. Hopefully, it wouldn't come down to that.

Adrian had stood behind the captain's left shoulder, despite the disgusted looks tossed his way by Harvey. They were brothers by blood now.

Stevie and Gabriel followed the captain to his quarters, beneath the poop deck. When she entered, Captain O'Brien was rummaging through a trunk. He grabbed a silk gown and tossed it on the desk. A black wool mourning dress followed it.

Stevie held the silk one up to Gabriel. "It might be a bit short, but if you stand where they can't see your feet, perhaps at the rail or behind one of the guns, no one will be able to tell," she said lightly, as if talking to her sister rather than her sullen, twelve-year-old cousin, who looked like he'd rather pull out every tooth in his mouth than put on that dress.

"Why me?" he muttered.

He knew very well why it had to be him. "No one else aboard can pass for a female, they're all too large or too hairy." She patted his smooth cheek and then nudged his shoulder with hers. "And in all honesty, you are by far the best actor in the family, and we're all counting on you to play your part to perfection."

Gabriel straightened a little, and although he still gave her a dark look, he snatched the gown from her hands.

Stevie hid a smile and reached for the mourning gown and matching veil. "This will do just fine for me."

*

"I'LL NEVER HEAR the end of this," Gabriel muttered to Stevie as the guffaws from their family continued. The two stood on the mizzen deck, patiently waiting for the whistles and laughter to die down. Gabriel looked as natural in the gown as a baby giraffe.

Dressed in the black widow's weeds, Stevie bit back a grin. She'd replaced her headscarf with the black veil. Conal had found a dark ribbon for her to tie around her forehead to keep the veil from flying with the wind.

She had done her best to pin up Gabriel's hair and secure a hat on his head to hide its shorter length. Because of his lanky height, he needed a bosom to look older, so she rolled up his shirt and stuffed it into the bodice.

Tristan had retrieved several tankards and the surgeon's bag as instructed. She rummaged through it until she found what she needed.

Powder of Ipecacuanha.

Perfect.

She'd used a rope of dried chili peppers from the galley and made a strong tea. Next to the pot of tea was the bottle of whiskey she'd used earlier on the captain's wound. After much discussion, Bernard decided most of the crew would be spared the tea, keeping them in a condition to work the sails, rigging and guns if the plan failed. Tristan, Adrian and a scant few of the *Seeker's* crew had been selected to drink the tea as well, leaving Stevie and Gabriel to act their parts with her Uncle Bernard as their protector.

They trusted neither the captain nor his crew and fully expected them to try to retake the ship at some point. What better time than when a number of their captors lay incapacitated? They agreed that Bernard and Harvey would stay hidden with pistols aimed at the captain and first mate as insurance.

She chewed her lip. Her plan *had* to work. If it didn't...she squeezed her eyes shut and said a little prayer. The things Gampo threatened to do if they failed, combined with the weight of their current dilemma, pressed hard against her heart.

Stevie ladled a cupful of tea into several tankards. "Once you finish the tea, I'll give you a couple fingers of whiskey," she said, hoping the effects of the spirits would enhance those of the tea, but numb the men to its bite.

Tristan sniffed his cup and shot a nervous look at his cousin. Adrian stared at his for a moment before taking a sip, then quirking a challenging eyebrow. Tristan narrowed his eyes and took a drink. He was fighting viciously to prevent any outward show of weakness at the exceptionally well-spiced tea.

The hot peppers alone should have had them coughing. Adrian's forehead soon glistened with a fine sheen of sweat. He chanced a glance at the crew and his family, who were watching with undivided interest and more than a little trepidation. Adrian caught Tristan's gaze again and lifted his chin the tiniest bit. Tristan's mouth twitched in response.

She had long ago stopped trying to translate the looks, gestures and sounds the two cousins used to communicate discreetly. Born only minutes apart, they'd grown up together. It was a cross between sign language, expressions, and even unintelligible words the boys created when they were toddlers. They raised their mugs and clanked them together.

"I'd say 'to your health,' but I fear that would be counterproductive to our cause," Tristan said dryly.

"How about toasting to a long life?" Adrian suggested.

Tristan grinned. "Aye! First to finish wins. On the count of three, then?"

Adrian nodded once.

"One."

"Two."

Neither said 'three' as both tried to get an early start, draining their mugs in a couple gulps. They stared at each other for a minute in silence. Knowing them and what was in the tea, it was taking every bit of self-control for the two to remain impassive. Stevie pressed her lips between her teeth to keep from laughing. It was the first time in days she'd had anything to laugh about.

A rivulet of sweat trickled from Tristan's temple to his jaw. "I don't feel anything," he barely choked out the lie.

Adrian touched the tip of his tongue with his finger. "I can't feel my ton'."

Stevie poured a generous splash of whiskey in their cups, and both tossed it down immediately then fell into a fit of coughing. When they finally stopped, tears streamed down their cheeks.

Tristan grabbed the whiskey and refilled their cups. "I think this is going to require a bit more liquid courage."

"*Oui*," Adrian coughed.

She turned to the others, raised her eyebrows in askance and lifted her ladle. They swallowed convulsively then held out their cups, staring at the tea as if it was a snake coiled to attack.

By now, Tristan and Adrian had sunk to the deck and were sitting back to back next to a bucket, each propping up the other. Adrian had the hiccups.

Remus looked at the other men and jerked his head toward the affected cousins. "I think they have the right way about it. Toss it quick and get it done with." He grimaced as if he'd just smelled something terribly foul. He took a deep breath and gulped down his tea. The others followed suit.

Their eyes widened, and they dropped their cups, gasping for air. Remus threw an evil glare at the cousins, who by now had ceased their ego-driven charade and looked absolutely miserable.

"God, help us," Remus gasped. He grabbed the whiskey and sloshed it into his mug, quickly tossing it down as if it would reverse the actions of the tea. Tristan and Adrian, bleary-eyed, grinned in a rather crooked way, enjoying the entertainment as much as they could given their condition.

Stevie studied the two men. It would happen any moment.

Tristan suddenly went white, grabbed the nearby bucket and puked. Three seconds later, Adrian followed suit.

Remus paled. "Christ, save us," he whispered hoarsely.

THE *SEEKER'S* sails had been trimmed and stowed in preparation for her interception by the monstrous British frigate. Tristan and Adrian reclined, if one could call it that, near the aft rail, both groaning and thrashing in obvious discomfort.

Stevie stood next to Gabriel on the leeward rail and occasionally waved her arms at the frigate as it approached. With the exception of the intermittent creaks and groans of the brigantine, or the occasional retching from the unlucky partakers of her tea, a tense silence had descended upon the ship and her pirate crew as all awaited fate's whim.

Stevie took a deep breath and let it out, trying to settle her frayed nerves and knotted stomach as the frigate calmly drew abreast. Grappling hooks dangled menacingly, but they made no movement to launch them over the *Seeker's* rails.

A good sign.

A sharply dressed officer looked down at them from the rail.

"Hello, good sir," Stevie hailed. "We are so thankful to see you!"

"Truly we are," Gabriel shouted in agreement. "God has answered our prayers by bringing you to us."

"Where is your captain?" The officer's clipped voice skipped over the water. "I need to speak with him."

"Alas," Stevie responded. "My husband is no longer with us."

The officer's eyes flicked over Stevie's black gown of mourning. "Dead, is he? You have my sincere condolences, madam." He bowed slightly and touched his hat.

"Thank you, sir," Stevie replied, dipping her head and softening her shoulders.

"Your second in command, then. I wish to speak with him."

"I am sorry, sir." Stevie weakly waved her hand at a bundled body near the mizzen mast. "We had been preparing him for burial when we spotted your great ship. He, along with many of the crew, took ill. It consumed them."

"An illness, you say?" The officer looked over the crewmen who had come to the *Seeker's* rail to watch the goings-on. Most were pale and shaky and were sweating profusely or leaning against the rail for support. Tristan, looking much the same, kept batting the air in front of his face as if he sat amongst a cloud of gnats.

Adrian rose and stumbled to the rail then dry heaved next to Gabriel, who turned green and did likewise. Gabriel didn't have a strong stomach to begin with.

Another moaning sailor was on his back, his arm flung over his eyes. Gabriel inched toward Stevie, and she gave him a warning look. Right now Gabriel's boots were visible below the hem of his skirt, and he needed to stay closer to the rail to keep them hidden.

Stevie gave a warbling laugh. "I'm sure it's nothing to be overly concerned about," she rushed to explain. "Most of us are perfectly fine. We think it might be a sickness some of the men caught during our travels to the African inlands."

The officer's eyes narrowed as she and Gabriel exchanged a conspiratorial look before returning their attention to him.

She looked up at him and showed him her sweetest smile. One that hopefully looked too wide. Too sweet. "We were hoping you would be so kind as to take us aboard your fine ship and deliver us to the next port town."

Just then Tristan made a queer choking sound, staggered a few steps and fell to the deck with a thump, startling both women. Rather than come to his aide, the others standing near him immediately scurried away, leaving their gurgling mate to face his fate alone.

Gabriel gasped as he stepped back. "Oh, dear! I did not know he was ill! I asked him to help me wrap the body. He worked right beside me!"

OFFICER DANTON HAD WITNESSED many farces in his time. Some men would do anything to prevent serving in His Majesty's Navy. He'd even seen a free black man chop off his own hand with an ax to deter such a fate. The act did not dissuade Officer Danton in the least. He had been desperate for men and had taken the newly mutilated man anyway.

The widow took a jerky step away from the younger woman. "There, there, dear, don't draw unnecessary conclusions." The widow consoled the other woman without, he noticed, actually touching her.

"But he worked beside me for nearly an *hour*!" The young girl's voice held a barely restrained note of panic.

"It's nothing to worry about." The widow smiled through clenched teeth. "Would you please retrieve our reticules while I finish speaking with this kind English officer?"

The girl backed away, shaking her head. "No! I will not! I will *not* go back down there. The sounds they make—and the smell—" She pulled a handkerchief from her sleeve and pressed it over her mouth.

The widow turned from the nearly hysterical woman and smiled at Officer Danton. "She is such a sweet girl, although she has always been slightly over-reactive and speaks when she should *not*." She gave the girl a sharp look.

"What am I going to do? What am I going to do?" the young girl wailed. She began to wheeze and Danton inadvertently took a step back, even though he was yards away on his own vessel.

"I'm going to die! I'm going to die! I'm going to—"

The widow slapped the girl's cheek hard, suddenly silencing

the panicked cries. "Stop it and shut your mouth this instant!" She glanced down at her hand and then wiped it on her skirt. Once again, she stepped away from the girl and smiled up at him.

"Now, kind sir, will you be willing to accept us aboard your vessel? I assure you we will not be in the way, as there are precious few of us remaining." She stopped abruptly, as if she wished to bite back that last word: *remaining*. "We would go out of our way to avoid inconveniencing you in any way."

Officer Danton had seen enough.

"Madam, as an officer in the British Navy, it is my duty to see that this ship is manned and maintained appropriately. There are times we insist upon the service of merchant crews to aid our cause."

The ladies took nervous breaths and exchanged frightened looks. This last observation further confirmed a decision he had already made.

He lowered his brows at the widow. "I believe, madam, you are attempting to deceive me with this...this...act."

CHAPTER 5

Journal entry
27 August 1718

After being taken prisoner aboard Captain Low's brigantine, I was taken to New Providence, a pirate stronghold, then set free to live or die on my own. Since I have seen the fragile weakness of fear and flight, I have chosen to live a more vibrant life. I live by my wits alone, and although this town is run by the Brotherhood of the Sea, there is a surprising semblance of order among the disorder. The wild boisterous spirit of this island and her people suits me. I've learned how to handle weapons of every sort, and have bested several men who dared to challenge me. I still await the sight of Edward Low's ship on the horizon, even more confident now that I am ready to face that dung-souled dog.

T*hey had failed.* Conal muttered a low curse at the British officer's words: *"you are attempting to deceive me with this...this...act."* When Stevie had first voiced her plan, it had shocked him to silence. It was bloody brilliant. Risky? Yes. Chance of success? Tiny. But still, it was brilliant. Not to mention, it was the only choice they had other than to fight and probably die. They had spared him and most of his crew the vicious tea on account they needed their full faculties and physical abilities to handle the *Seeker*. He reclined, bound and half-hidden among a cluster of barrels out of sight of the British, but well within earshot.

Stevie paled. "Wh...wh...what do you mean?"

The British captain hadn't been fooled. Along with most of his crew, Stevie's brothers, her family, even young Gabriel—if they found him out—would be forced to serve on that ship and she'd never see them again. That shouldn't have bothered Conal as much as it did. He still didn't trust the wench, but he didn't wish this kind of misery on her or her family, either.

The British captain straightened his shoulders and grasped the lapels of his jacket. "You are attempting to hide the truth of your situation from me. I assure you madam, I am young, but not so green as to be so easily duped."

He signaled to his men, and they immediately set to their tasks. "I have never heard of a sickness so deadly it can kill a man who simply stands near another who is ill."

Stevie exchanged a look with Adrian, who was fingering the hilt of his dagger and glowering at Harvey. Sheer terror fluttered across Stevie's face.

The captain gestured to his men. "I cannot maintain this ship without a capable crew. My apologies ladies, but in light of your attempt at deceit and the apparent deadly nature of this illness, I cannot accommodate you. I wish you the best."

Stevie sagged against the rail, her relief mistaken for disappointment and dismay by the British crew, no doubt. She clutched her hands together. "No!" she exclaimed in a panicked tone.

"Please, sir!" Gabriel shouted. "Do not leave us!"

"WAIT!"

Both Gabriel and Stevie jumped at the high-pitched shriek, renting the air. The officer's eyes widened. Everyone turned to follow his stare.

Adrian, holding a large board in his arms, staggered toward the rail. "Wait! I want to come with you! I am strong! I can serve! I *want* to serve! I want to serve in His Majesty's Navy!"

If there was the slightest doubt in Officer Danton's mind as to whether or not he had made the correct decision, it had taken definite flight. He signaled frantically to his crew. "Call all hands! Spread broad sails!"

"Noooo!" Adrian wailed, falling to his knees. "Take me with you! Pleeeeeease!"

They cut the grappling lines free, and the gigantic ship tore away from the *Seeker* to the safety of its comrades and the open sea.

Once the frigate had become a speck on the horizon, the crew broke out in celebration. Even Conal had to grin.

Bernard was laughing so hard, he was wiping tears from his eyes. "You did good, ladies! We all played our parts knowing it was our lives on the line, but you, Adrian—" He broke off in a laughing fit that had him and everyone else clutching their sides. "Adrian, yours was far and away the glint in the gold. You cinched our fate, you did! I think the theatre might be missing a great actor!"

Adrian gave them a lopsided grin, then grabbed Stevie with one arm and Gabriel in the other and gave them both a wobbly bear hug. "I think it was these beautiful *ladies* who saved our necks, right boys?"

They clapped and heartily agreed with the exception of Tristan, who was still heaving over the side, his elbows locked around two belaying pins for support.

"What's wrong, Tristan?" Adrian said. "Stevie's tea not sitting too good in your gullet?"

"Go..to...hell." Tristan struggled to rasp, before sinking into a heap on the deck again.

Suddenly Adrian's face turned to a shade of grayish green, and he spun toward the rail.

Conal had a new appreciation for Stevie's quick mind and spirited soul. It was clear she loved her family very much. She did her best to make the afflicted as comfortable as possible on the mizzen deck, with assurances they'd be free of the tea's effects within a couple hours at the most. Gabriel, still determined to become a seaman, doffed his dress as soon as he could, then scampered up into the yards with the crew.

Stevie's gaze remained on the British frigates until they had disappeared beyond the horizon. Conal joined her for a moment at the rail. "How long until we reach Jamaica?" she asked.

He shrugged. "It depends on the winds and the currents. We sail against the current but with the wind, for the most part."

She removed the veil and fingered it with work-roughened hands. Although she was meek and easily frightened, here was no pampered young lady, that was certain. He'd wager she could outwit any of them. She had a kind of warm beauty that stirred something deep in his chest. Long, lithe limbs moved her along with a lionesque grace. One thing was certain; he'd not underestimate her again.

He took a moment to study her profile. Concern creased the smooth porcelain skin of her forehead. Her cheeks were pink from the afternoon sun. She licked her lips and drew his gaze to her mouth and he couldn't stop from wondering what it would be like to kiss her. "If we don't run into any storms to blow us off-course, we might make it within the month," he finally said.

Stevie chewed her lip.

What—or who—she was worrying about?

DRAGO RUBBED HIS THIGH. The knife wound had healed on the surface, but the muscle beneath still ached. It'd been only a few weeks since a vixen named Keelan Grey sunk a dagger into the meat of his leg, but the bloody thing hurt like she'd had done it just yesterday. The little girl had just finished repairing the trousers damaged by the stabbing.

He'd put the boy to work helping his carpenter with repairs and by midday, they'd made significant progress. Jacqueline completed his mending, and her sewing skills were put to better use repairing damaged sails.

By day's end, both children dragged themselves to a trestle table propped between the long guns. After a short meal of salted fish and hardtack, the three went back to his cabin. Drago was looking forward to a quiet evening and a few hours of sleep. Ensuring his charges were too exhausted to argue would hopefully aide him toward that end.

Apparently, the children were fascinated by the kidnapping of his sister, so it wasn't long before the subject arose again.

Julian asked, "Why was she stolen?"

Drago stared out the mullioned windows of his cabin. The sun's rays glittered off the small ocean swells on its way toward the horizon. "She was beautiful. Our family was wealthy. Although my father paid the ransom, the pirates didn't release her. Those greedy devil's spawn kept my father's gold and put her on the block."

"Could you not have saved her?" Jacqueline asked.

"If you wanted revenge, why didn't you just sink Fynn Ahern's ship?" Julian persisted.

"If they put her on the block, why didn't you just buy her back?" Jacqueline asked, walking toward his bookshelf.

Drago had asked the same questions, run through the same tactics in his mind, but he'd been a lad of fifteen at the time. They had taken him captive along with his sister and Fynn. But Fynn had used his sister to escape, leaving Drago to find his own way to freedom.

He sighed. "Although I spent a long time looking, I never found my sister among the Persian slave traders. Later I heard that rat, Ahern, kept her as his own personal...slave." There were other words that more accurately described Fynn's actions, but none suitable for the ears of children. "If I'd have sunk his ship, I might have killed her."

Jacqueline ran her hand along his bookshelf, while perusing his collection.

"Can you read?" he asked her.

She gave him an insulted look. "Of course. Can you?"

"If you want to borrow a book, you'll have to be more polite." He turned his attention to his journal, opened it to the correct page and reached for the quill. A soft sigh came from behind him.

"May I please borrow a book?"

He didn't turn, but rather simply responded. "You may. Have you selected one?"

"Yes, but it's on the top shelf."

He flipped open the inkwell, dipped the quill and began to write.

She sighed again. "Will you *please* get it for me?" The last sentence held a mixture of snide sarcasm and tempered frustration.

He smiled before putting down the quill and turning to the bookcase. A thick stench suddenly assaulted his olfactory senses, making him cough.

When his crew searched the little sloop after capturing her, they had found the children and their older sister hiding in the capstan room behind a muck-coated hawse chain, which explained the greenish-black streaks on their clothing, but the odor was overpowering at close range.

"When was the last time you had a bath?"

Her mouth opened in the shape of an "O" then she leaned forward and sniffed. "When was the last time *you* had a bath?"

"That smell's not me, it's *you*." Drago scowled at her. "You're awfully outspoken for such a young piece of fluff." He bent down and said in a soft, dangerous tone, "One day, it will get you into trouble."

She tilted her head and then gestured to her surroundings. "I'm already *in* trouble."

"I don't think pirates have to bathe," Julian blurted from the floor in front of the desk. "I don't need a bath because I've decided I will be a pirate, like Captain Gampo."

Drago clenched his teeth. "I've told you, I'm *not* a pirate. I'm a privateer. I have been for the past five years. There's a difference." He slapped a book in Jacqueline's hand and left the cabin. Once in the galley, he ordered Cookie to fill the tub in the pantry.

Drago stomped back to the main deck. After checking in with the helmsman, he gestured for Manuel to follow him to his cabin. Manuel wasn't the smartest mate on the ship. In fact, it was likely he was the dumbest. His brain had seemed to stop maturing around the time he turned ten. Drago knew this because they grew up together. They were cousins. His mother said Manuel's mind was damaged during the long hours of labor his mother had suffered. She never recovered and died a day after he was born. Manuel's useless father left and never returned.

"Wait here," Drago said to Manuel.

"Aye, Cap'n," the big man replied, and straightened.

Drago entered his cabin. How did he miss the smell earlier? There was no way those two children were going to sleep in his quarters with that stench clinging to their skin and clothing.

Both of them looked up when he entered and eyed him suspiciously. Gampo pointed to Julian. "I've ordered a bath prepared for you down in the galley. You are to go with Manuel. He will help you."

Julian balked. "I don't want a bath!"

"I don't care what you don't want," Drago replied. "You will bathe, or you will sleep in the hold with the ballast for a pillow."

"I'm not taking a bath," Julian repeated, his grey eyes flashing in defiance. He stood and clenched his fists to his sides. "I prefer to sleep in the hold."

Drago glanced at his desk, where Jacqueline sat, book in hand. She sank into the chair until the top of her head was barely visible.

So this was how it was going to be.

He'd never had children, but he wasn't used to anyone usurping his authority or ever refusing his command, and by hell's hounds, it wouldn't start now. He jerked open the cabin door.

"Manuel, please come in."

Julian's eyes widened as Manuel ducked under the doorway and entered the room. The boy's brothers were almost as tall as Manuel, however, they were not nearly as ugly or as wide. Manuel's nose had been broken no less than seven times, its shape flattened on his pock-marked and scarred face, and he was missing several teeth. His jaw was the size of a cannonball and just as hard.

"Manuel, this is Julian. Take him down to the galley and see that he takes a bath. Make sure every *inch* of him is clean before he gets out." Drago enjoyed watching the boy's face pale in terror. Manuel grinned at Julian, then walked over and reached for him.

"NO!" Julian screeched.

Manuel froze and flicked his gaze to Drago. When his cousin didn't acknowledge the outburst, Manuel blinked and reached for Julian again, this time without hesitation even as the boy kicked and screamed. He lifted Julian by the scruff of the neck as if he were a puppy and tossed him over his shoulder.

"This should be entertaining," Drago said, smiling. He offered his arm to Jacqueline. "Come, let's watch."

Jacqueline's wide eyes peeked over the top of his desk and she shook her head.

He lowered his brows. "You misunderstand, Jacquie dear. It wasn't a question. It was an order. I am the captain of this ship, and as you can see, my crew does what they are told. If they don't, then my quartermaster gets to play with his cat."

Jacqueline swallowed and slowly stood. She trembled a little as she placed a slim, pale hand on his forearm. He escorted her to the galley as a gentleman would a fine lady of the court.

Julian's yells and occasional screams echoed through the passageway, along with plenty of splashing.

"Stop it! Stop it! No! *Owwww!*"

Splash! Coughing, sputtering, cursing.

Cursing?

More splashing.

Jacqueline shrank behind Drago as they entered the galley. He understood her trepidation. At least somewhat.

Cookie sat on a stool, stirring one of two pots, one foot on the floor, the other—missing. He'd propped the stump against the far wall.

"Cookie had his leg shot off a few years ago during a skirmish with a Portuguese merchant ship," Drago said, to quell her curiosity a bit.

Cookie was what most people would call stocky. His hair had departed his head years ago. A single gold earring dangled from the only ear he had left. Cookie eyed Jacqueline and scowled. "Petticoats is bad luck."

"Indeed," Drago replied dryly.

Finally, the door to the pantry opened and Julian sulked out, fully clothed and dripping wet.

Gampo quirked an eyebrow at Manuel, who shrugged. "The imp wouldn't strip." Almost defensively, he added, "His clothes was muddy. Now everything's clean." He nodded at Jacqueline. "This one next?"

"No!" She clapped her hands over her mouth as soon as the words came out. "I mean...yes, but I—I don't need your help." She turned to Drago. "Please, Captain Gampo, don't make him bathe me!" A mortified look blanketed her face. "It wouldn't be proper," she whispered.

Captain Gampo.

Drago deliberated her suddenly polite request. Her little body virtually shuddered with every thump of her heart. After a few more moments, he finally decided he'd punished her enough. "Very well, you may see to your own bath." He ignored her sudden sigh of relief. "However, if you don't complete the task to my liking Manuel will repeat it until it's done properly."

She nodded, swallowed and eyed the big man, who was nearly as wet as her brother. Gampo had them empty the tub and refill it for her before sending Julian and Manuel back up to the main deck to dry out.

It took quite a while, but finally the little chit emerged. She'd washed out most of the muck from her dress, and her dark, sleek hair showed signs of being washed as well. After a sniff to make sure she had indeed cleaned away the stench, he nodded his satisfaction and sent her to find her brother. Taking advantage of the moment, Drago brought down a fresh change of clothes and treated himself to a bath as well.

Playing the part of a ruthless pirate was both tedious and unsavory, from the coarse language he had to use to the diminished hygiene habits, but it had been necessary to scare the children's family into doing his bidding. He took the time to shave, then reached for the newly mended trousers.

The girl had done an acceptable job on the rip made by the knife blade. He shoved his right leg through and balanced on it as he followed with his left. Halfway down the pant leg, his foot suddenly caught, and he plunged forward. Having no time to even move his hands from the waist of his pants (let alone break his fall) he hit the boards hard and let out a string of curses heard clear up to the top gallants.

After righting himself, he grabbed a wet washrag and pressed it against his skinned knee, inspected the trousers again, and cursed.

That little slip of a she-devil had stitched his bloody pant leg shut.

CHAPTER 6

14 January 1719

Dear Father,
I have finally met a worthy mate named John James Rackham in this den of pirates. He is the same Rackham who conspired with Blackbeard to maroon Captain Charles Vane on a little island so he could steal his ship from under his nose! His reputation as a trickster has been well-sealed. I have made him several pair of brightly colored britches that speak to his feats and he wears them proudly. They have become his mark of trade and he's now referred to as "Calico Jack."
He has finally asked for my hand in marriage and I have accepted under the condition that he takes me with him to sail so that I can remain vigilant for the Fancy flying her white flag with a red skeleton.

Your daughter,
Anne

I t was time to return the gowns to Captain O'Brien's trunk. Stevie entered his cabin and closed the door, then shrugged out of the black mourning gown. Gabriel had already hastily discarded the silk dress, leaving it puddled on the floor. She picked it up and draped it over the chair where she'd left her shirt and breeches. The glimmer of the bold red silk forced her to pause and finger the fine fabric again. She picked it up and pressed it against her body, allowing herself a moment to dream. She ran her fingers over the seed pearls stitched around the neckline.

It was silly, considering the danger they'd been in, but she almost wished she could have worn this gown instead of the widow's weeds for their charade. She'd seen nothing so beautiful. It was something an elegant lady might wear, or maybe even a duchess, not someone like her who hid in the hot kitchens of a New Orleans gaming house. The dress was short, but not overly so. How wonderful it would be to leave behind the men's clothing her brothers had insisted she wear on their quest. While she had to admit she enjoyed the freedom of movement the britches offered, it felt awkward to dress as a man, especially around men who knew she was a woman.

She closed her eyes, daydreaming of dancing in an elegant ballroom, her hair swept up in an exquisite coiffure, one gloved hand on the shoulder of her handsome lord the other in his large palm. Delicate notes of a waltz drift from the strings of the quartet in the corner. She and her handsome lord twirl around the ballroom floor, she in this gown, he in shiny cordovan boots, tan breeches and a dashing, deep green coat the same shade as his eyes. When he smiles at her, the dimple in his cheek shows above his neatly trimmed auburn beard, which makes him suspiciously resemble a certain captain of a certain stolen merchant ship.

She opened her eyes and swallowed hard. She daydreamed about an impossible situation. She wasn't an elegant lady; she was slightly above a servant. Or at least she was until the fire. Conal O'Brien wasn't her handsome lord or her anything. He was their prisoner, and she'd do well to remember that no matter how handsome his face or broad and muscled his shoulders.

With more determined movements, she carefully folded the magnificent gown. Any aspirations she'd ever had of getting out of the kitchens and helping Adrian run the boarding house or helping Tristan run the gaming house, drifted to the clouds along with the thick, dark smoke from the fire that had consumed everything they'd owned...everything except the marble box containing Anne Bonny's journal and letters, and the tiny possibility of finding a secret treasure buried a hundred years ago.

It was time to stop fantasizing, put on her man-clothes, and help her family.

When Stevie reached for the trunk lid to raise it, a flash of dark red on the bed caught her attention. It was a long, bloodied strip of linen. Next to it was a shirt. Both items belonged to the wounded Captain O'Brien. When had he slipped away from Uncle Bernard to come down to change? The door lock clicked behind her and the hair rose on the back of her neck.

She whirled, realizing too late that Captain O'Brien must be still in the cabin. He stepped away from the shadow of the door. Her gaze stuttered at his bare chest. In three strides he had his hand over her mouth and her back pressed against the wall.

He leaned forward and whispered in her ear, "My fingers are a mere two inches from your throat, which I can crush with one hand." To make his point, he applied a gentle pressure in the hollow just above where her collarbones met.

She shot a glance at the door. Where was everyone? Tristan and Adrian would remain incapacitated for another hour or so, and even then would probably be too weak to put up much of a fight. She looked back at the captain.

Of course, he'd already deduced the effort had weakened her family enough to enable his men to retake the ship. If her family relaxed their guard even a little, his crew could quickly overtake them—if it hadn't already happened. In fact, to force a surrender all they would probably have to do was capture Gabriel...her heart lurched in her chest.

Or *her*.

Captain O'Brien's eyes narrowed and glinted a cold grey-green, like an angry ocean. "I want some answers and you will give them to me, little rabbit. Agreed?"

Stevie nodded, taking short quick breaths; the effort pressed her chest against his. The warmth of his half-naked body radiated across her skin where they touched, and all the places they didn't. He was almost as tall and broad as Adrian. The reddish-gold of his neatly trimmed beard was a shade darker than the sun-bleached tips of the auburn curls framing his face. His cat's eyes had a predatory sheen.

He spoke in a very low, velvety growl. "You will not scream and I will not hurt you. Yes?"

For a second, she forgot the question. His voice could charm a cobra. Did he pause to think of what her brothers would do to him once this interrogation was over and she told them what he'd done to her? Did this captain always act first and think second, or was he just that desperate? She locked gazes with him, and in that moment she knew that no, he wasn't desperate; he was strong and confident, and fully expected to take back his ship.

Now.

CONAL DIDN'T BELIEVE for a moment she would keep her word, but he still had to demand her cooperation in case she was actually a female who *kept* her word. Few did. Aside from his family, the only women he'd interacted with— if you could call it that — were whores and pickpockets (the last was not by choice). And again aside from his family, women were a devious lot. He never trusted them. Never was a strong word, yes, but he meant *never*.

Either way, he was taking back his what was his.

"Do I have your word you will make no move to draw attention to us?" He increased the pressure of his thumbnail into the skin of her throat. The fingers he'd curled around the back of her neck brushed against a puckered scar.

Her large grey eyes widened even further before welling with tears, and she gave a final nod.

Terrified, as usual. Good. At least her fear would reduce the possibility of a fight, which would cause noise, which then would draw attention to his cabin. It was a small miracle he'd been able to slip away unnoticed by the two old sailors. "I will remove my hand and you will not scream." A small tear darted from the corner of her eye and splashed on his wrist. Damn it, she was about to burst into tears.

Slowly, he lifted his hand from her mouth. After trailing his fingers along the smooth skin of her jaw to her pale throat, he rested his palm against her collarbone. Her skin was warm and soft. She smelled faintly of cinnamon and sea air, and a stirring vibrated low in his belly with his next inhale. She was trembling, and suddenly he felt like an ogre for frightening her. He had no other option at the moment, right?

This was no time to go soft. He *would* regain control of his ship.

Gritting his teeth, he tilted her face up with his other hand to capture her gaze. There was one thing he had to know. One very important thing. "What business have you with Gampo?" he asked softly.

Although she quickly recovered, Conal didn't miss the look of panic that shot across her face. "We are to bring him the cargo in the belly of your ship," she whispered.

He narrowed his eyes. Her darting gaze told him she was leaving something out. "Why?"

She swallowed, then licked her lips. He followed the movement of her tongue, suddenly aware of his naked torso pressing against her chest, with only a thin chemise as a barricade.

"He...he demanded it." She straightened and tensed, giving him an accusing look. "My family...we were on our way to Savannah in Uncle Bernard's boat when we were caught in a skirmish between this ship and the *Dragon*."

That gave him pause. "*You* were in that little sloop?" That boat had drifted between the *Dragon* and the *Seeker*, providing the pirate a shield from Conal's guns. Then the main sail fell on the sloop and her crew had scrambled to haul it back up. Conal had wondered what group of buffoons were aboard. It made sense now, knowing their lack of experience. The family had hauled the mainsail back up, but not before Gampo had tossed over grappling hooks.

No wonder. Two seaman and eight lubbers with no idea how to trim a sail had been easy prey for the pirate.

Stevie's eyes flashed. "Perhaps you remember? You fired upon us and damaged our mast, then left us helpless."

"I thought you to be one of Gampo's prize ships at the time," he snapped. He hated himself for the way he was speaking to her, but the guilt from disabling her vessel and virtually handing it to Gampo stirred his anger, leaving him unable to douse the heat of his words before they left his mouth.

What was it about this woman that sent emotions exploding from him like a blast of grapeshot? One moment he was ready to shake the truth out of her, the next he wanted to kiss her.

Where had that come from?

Now, her tears almost had him begging for forgiveness. If only she'd stop crying, he could better focus on the issue at hand. "I could have easily raked the deck and caused all kinds of carnage, but didn't." He'd been about to do just that when his friend, Captain Hart had reminded him that if the sloop was a prize ship with an enslaved crew, there was a risk he'd kill innocents.

He took in a deep breath. *Damn it.* He could have killed her and members of her family in his fury. The added guilt created yet another unwanted sensation in his gut, a strong desire to protect her, and shield her from any more despair and anguish.

Stevie's accusing glare did nothing but intensify it. "You left us there as bait for him, as a distraction while you made your escape," she choked. "Do you know what kind of *monster* he is?" Her eyes glistened a silver blue and welled again with tears. A single droplet broke free and slid down her cheek.

Her lower lip trembled, and his gaze fastened on the tear creeping toward the corner of her mouth. It was sensually shaped, her mouth. The corners curved up impishly, even when she wasn't smiling, much like her eyes. Even the delicate arch of her brows had a little peak in the middle.

Dammit. Focus on the interrogation.

"Yes, I know what kind of monster he is," he finally answered. "He killed my uncle a few months ago, and there's nothing I'd like more than to see him swing from the end of a rope for it." He wiped away the tear with his thumb, using every ounce of self control to keep from licking it just to taste the salt because it came from those beautiful eyes. "And when we sail into his den, I'll give him more than just the bounty in the belly of this ship. I'll give him the sharp tip of my blade through his cold, black heart."

She gave him a look of disbelief. "He has over eighty men! We have less than twenty, many of which have never been on a ship this size, let alone sailed one."

"The latter issue I can fix, if everyone is willing." *Now where did* that *idea come from?* He needed to return his focus to the problem at hand. He would get his bloody ship back, that was a bloody certainty.

A thought began to swirl in his mind. Gampo expected the *Seeker* to sail into his hideaway—because the Sauvages should be commanding her—which meant he'd also welcome them in without firing a single shot. His guard would be down, the soft underside of his belly wide open.

There was a flicker in Stevie's silver eyes. Was there something she wasn't telling him? There must be. Lies? Half-truths? It didn't matter. He'd find out, eventually. He'd gotten this much out of her. He'd get everything else.

She didn't belong here. Although she dressed like a man, she was all woman, soft and tender. Weak. Afraid of her own shadow. A liability, yes. He could protect her, keep her safe. The best way to do that would be to leave her in Baracoa.

No, then he'd worry even more because she'd be vulnerable. Why had this urgent need to protect her locked itself in his head? He took in a deep breath and let it out slowly. "If we combine forces and serve a single goal, we can defeat him," he said.

What was he doing?

What was he *thinking*?

"We can't defy him," she rasped in a quivering whisper. She averted her gaze and stared at his shoulder while another tear broke free.

"Yes, we can," he said calmly. His cousin Brendan and Captain Hart were surely less than a day behind them. The crew driven from the *Seeker* would have immediately sought out the other two captains, who would have mustered their ships and given chase right away. He *would* get his ship back before this was all over. She couldn't know he'd soon have reinforcements, and he would not tip his hand and tell her yet, but for some ridiculous reason he had to reassure her in some small way.

If only she would stop crying, he could *think*.

She shook her head. "Threaten me all you want. Or kill me. It won't matter. My family will still do his bidding." With that admission, she simply surrendered; her shoulders dropped and she no longer resisted the pressure of his body against hers. Her legs relaxed against his thighs and her stomach stopped arching against him. She was a little rabbit cowering and paralyzed with fear, awaiting the wolf's teeth to pierce her throat.

"I must disagree," he persisted, more curious now. "I'm sure your family will drop their arms in exchange for your life." He waited for his words to sink in.

"They won't." She swallowed. Her eyes darkened to a stormy grey. "I won't allow it."

He laughed in surprise. Where had this sudden bravado come from? "How could you possibly prevent it?" His amusement dissipated at the sound of a soft click to his left. He looked down at the small pistol in her hand. She meant to shoot him again? Then she angled it so it pointed to her own head.

He gaped at her. What was she doing? "You'd kill yourself rather than allow your family to bargain for your life?"

She nodded.

"For the love of God, *why*?" One minute she was shaking in her boots, the next playing a martyr. Who *was* this woman? And why did he feel as if he could kiss away all her fear, all her worry, and all the darkness lingering in her eyes?

She opened her mouth to reply, but cried out instead as he took advantage of that small moment of distraction. It took him less than a second to wrench the pistol from her hand and release the hammer. To prevent her from doing anything else with her hands, like pull a knife, he grabbed both wrists and pinned them against the wall above her head. He tossed the pistol on the edge of the bed next to his shirt then gripped her chin in his free hand. Jesus, she smelled like fresh apples and sunshine.

"What are you not telling me about your bargain with Gampo?" He clenched his jaw at her silence, then used the one thing he knew would break her. "I'll have it from *you* now, or Gabriel later. And I'll be a lot less gentle with Gabriel."

The look of panic on her face told him his threat had hit home. She might be ready to sacrifice her own life, but not her younger cousin's.

Finally, she met his gaze. Grey irises rimmed in silver-blue studied him a long moment, and it seemed as if she were looking into his mind, listening to his thoughts. She seemed to come to some sort of conclusion and finally answered his question. "Gampo took the young ones with him. Jacqueline and Julian are only eight years old."

Another tear. Conal wanted to rip that pirate's heart out with his bare hands, just for making her cry.

"I had pulled them into a hiding spot in a dark corner of the hold, but..." She squeezed her eyes shut and more tears streamed out. "A rat ran across my foot and I made a small sound. It was out of my mouth before I had time to think, and because of me, Gampo's men found us." She swallowed. "I begged him to take me instead, but he just laughed. Unless we bring Gampo *this* ship and its cargo, he'll kill the little ones." Her chin quivered. "He said he'd hang them from the main mast of our own sloop and leave them there for us to find if we didn't bring in the *Seeker* by the end of the month."

Blast that ragged dog. "He specifically wanted the *Seeker*?"

"Not just the *Seeker*." She hung her head. "I—I'm sorry for the deception. We'd hoped you'd be less likely to resist if we told you Gampo wanted only your cargo." Her voice dropped to an agonized whisper. "He wants it all, your ship and everything it contains, including...you."

It would have been easier for him if she hadn't apologized for lying. One minute he was ready to wring her neck, and now he wanted to hold her and tell her everything would be fine. Her tears were shredding his insides. Now, a strong desire to comfort her and stop those infernal tears had taken over his stupid mind.

Before his brain could formulate another thought, he said, "I'll help get them back." He froze in shock at his own words. Before he could think, he lowered his head and kissed her. He wasn't sure why he kissed her. He certainly wasn't attracted to her. He supposed it was because it was the only way he could comfort her. To quiet her. To quiet his guilty conscience.

A kiss would have quieted *him*.

She stiffened, then with the tiniest of movements softened. Pliant, gentle, moist. Her scent mesmerized him, and he breathed her in until his lungs could hold no more. She made a small sound between a whimper and moan that made something primal flare inside him.

A desire.

A *realization*.

A realization of what, he didn't quite know, but it wasn't anything he'd ever felt when tupping a wench while at port, so it differed from the simple urge to couple with her, although the urge existed.

She tasted just like she smelled-of apples. His brain attempted to re-engage, telling him to pull away, but it was a little too late for that.

He was used to dwarfing most women, but Stevie wasn't like most women. Her eyes were level with his mouth and while she was slender and sleek, he had a feeling she was a lot stronger than she looked. Those eyes were now limpid and wide, her mouth pink and slightly swollen.

At some point, he must have released her arms because they were now around his neck and pulling his head back for another kiss. This time she kissed him back like a tempest. Tears were still streaming down her face; he tasted the salt as he trailed kisses along her jaw and down her throat. That simple movement, that tiny resonance was his undoing.

"Sweet Calypso, Stevie," he whispered against her lips. "Tell me to stop."

"No." Her eyes were closed, dark sooty lashes resting against the top of her cheeks. Her breath came and went in short, trembling pants. When she raised her lids, her eyes were liquid silver and brimming with yearning.

He should just turn and leave, but it wasn't that simple. "Stevie lass, are you sure?" he barely choked out the words.

"Yes." The word was small, almost a whisper, its impact tremendous...greater than a thirty-six-pound shot.

The raging storm in her eyes challenged him and at the same time shimmered with a vulnerability that had him struggling to stay in control. She was trembling, and when he reached out to take her hand, he noticed he was, too.

STEVIE GRASPED his wrist and pulled him toward her, all the while locking her gaze with his, searching for that flicker of doubt or treachery. She waited for a voice in her head to warn her this was foolish, wanton, impetuous. She waited for it to cry out in alarm that nothing of substance could come from this.

That day she discovered him, he'd risen from the copper tub in the weak glow of the lantern light, his wet skin had glistened a honeyed gold, muscles rippling beneath in a way that made her forget to breathe. That image had haunted her dreams at night, and alternated with the nightmare of the twins being dragged away, shrieking for help, begging her to save them. Was she lying to herself even now, blaming her current actions on the trauma of losing her siblings?

Probably.

But she didn't care. All that mattered at this moment was focusing on the way he made her feel, not her failings.

Just stop *thinking*.

His eyes darkened to a turbulent emerald green. There were no promises in them. Nothing to signal he'd feel obligated to protect her or want her to stay with him. She required none anyway, not even an indication he might want her again.

"Last chance to flee, little rabbit," he growled. The corner of his mouth twitched, but no humor twinkled in his eyes, only fire and heat.

Almost of their own volition, her hands skimmed over his chest, marveling at the sharp cut of muscle combined with the soft, silky warmth of skin and the crisp hair.

She needed him to push all thoughts of Gampo, the little ones and the danger they were all facing further out of her consciousness. The physical world around her fell away, and she sank into the rushing current of desire and let it sweep her along with him.

CHAPTER 7

Journal entry
23 February 1719

A wilder and more flamboyant honeymoon week has never been seen on
New Providence! Jack has kept his promise and allowed me to sail with
him on the Gallant *under the condition that I disguise myself as a man so*
that his crew wouldn't revolt. A woman aboard is seen as terribly bad luck
by mariners, who speak darkly of defying the ancient taboo.
I have taken delight in both dressing as a man and honing my skills with a
blade so that when I encounter that bilge-licking Captain Low, I might see
to his demise in the most painful manner possible.

I t was a long moment before either of them moved. Conal
couldn't have flexed a muscle if the sky fell on them. All his
bones had been liquefied. If he rose and dressed right now, he'd
keep what had just happened between them on a very basic level:
a simple tupping, enjoyed by both of them. He should leave her to
change at her leisure.

A soft sigh escaped from her mouth, drawing his attention to her lips, which still curled in a small, content smile. They were a rosy red from his kisses, and he had a sudden ridiculous urge to kiss them again.

Of their own accord, his fingers sought her skin. He traced the outline of her heart-shaped face and ran his fingers through her silky locks, then behind her neck and over the puckered skin. "Where did you get this scar?" he asked, needing the distraction from her mouth.

Her eyes fluttered open and their molten passion shifted, replaced by a clouded expression. Was it regret?

"It's from a burn." She turned her head and stared at the wall. "I was working in the kitchen in our boarding house, and a pan of grease caught fire. I accidentally knocked a bottle of vinegar into it and it exploded. I was burned on my arms as well. I'm...I'm not sure exactly what happened, but suddenly the fire was everywhere. If Adrian hadn't been in the hall and dragged me outside, I would have burned with the rest of the building."

She reached up and fingered the scar. "I had tucked my hair into a cap which thankfully saved most of it."

"You're lucky you came away without more damage than a burn on your neck."

She gave a small huff of disgust. "Lucky is something I am not." She finally met his gaze. "Everything we had burned that day. It reduced the boarding house and gambling parlor built by my grandfather to a graveyard of rubble and chimneys. We lost it all."

Conal raised a brow. "So that's why you tried your hand at piracy?"

She smiled then. "How flattering. Do you really think we're pirates?"

"If you are, you're terrible ones." He couldn't keep from grinning.

The corner of her mouth twitched. "That we are." She sighed

and paused, a slight frown crossing her features. He waited patiently for her to confide in him.

She traced his collarbone with her fingers and flashes of lightning zipped under his skin where she touched. "Actually, we really are descended from pirates." Her eyes danced with humor at his surprised expression.

"My grandfather's parents were Calico Jack Rackham and Anne Bonny. Grandfather was adopted and raised as John Sauvage by the man Anne married after she returned to Carolina."

Her fingers moved up Conal's neck and along the side of his face, then combed through his hair. She caressed his temples, making him want to close his eyes and just revel in the sensation. No one had ever stroked him so tenderly, at least not since he was a wee lad. He fought to focus on their conversation. "I'm not sure the lust for piracy is passed through the bloodline," he said. Did he really just use the word 'lust'?

Stevie cocked her head. A rueful smile tugged at her mouth. "No, it's most definitely not. However, when Uncle Bernard and my brothers walked through the debris, they noticed a chimney stone with a circular shape carved into it. Uncle Bernard said the carving was a compass rose. The block itself had no mortar surrounding it, and thinking that curious, he pulled it out. Behind it was a marble box containing a journal, two small jewels and a stack of letters from Anne Bonny to her father."

"What? No treasure map?" Conal asked in mock disbelief.

STEVIE PAUSED and peered at the man who casually curved around her as if it was the most natural place for him to be. Conal O'Brien would make a much better ally than adversary. Something told her if she revealed her family's objective and subsequent plan of action, the captain might be less likely to resist their efforts. She had no doubt that otherwise he and his shipmates would find an opportune moment to take back their ship. When that happened, it was likely one or more members of her family would be hurt or killed. It was imperative now for her to give the captain a good reason to wish them no harm. He'd already offered to help, after all.

The possibility of finding a treasure might be a good reason, one that she'd willingly forfeit to save her family.

Her actions and mistakes had dragged them all to this moment: the fire, the capture of the young twins, the theft of Conal's ship. She had an opportunity to shift fate more to her family's favor at this moment, and make things right with Conal O'Brien. To not take advantage of all this would be foolish.

She had no illusions about what had just happened between the two of them. The captain would agree to her terms, but not because he cared about her. He was the type of man who would fight for a cause because it was just, not because it would line his pockets.

Not once had he tried to escape or plead for his life. He stayed with his crew because it was the right thing to do. And because he was an honorable man, he'd saved her and Gabriel from being swept overboard when he could have just let the jib end them.

Yet, she'd done nothing except steal from him.

And to think, a moment ago she thought she couldn't feel any worse about the havoc she'd caused.

This was a risk, but her heart told her it was the right thing to do, so she took a deep breath and continued. "Anne Bonny mentioned her husband's ship had come across a partially plundered Spanish galleon, and they hid the wealth they salvaged just before they were captured. She begged her father to keep her letters. Uncle Bernard thinks they might contain clues or a code that will reveal the location of the hidden treasure."

Conal's face showed no flicker of greed, simply mild amusement.

She could almost hear Uncle Bernard's objections in her head. If nothing else, she owed the captain the truth. "The first clue said to go to Helshire Church in Savanna, so we traded the jewels for the little boat, some supplies, and set out." She shifted her gaze to her fingers, which were absently weaving through the long, soft curls along the side of his head again. "Then we came across you and Gampo. Currently, he has my little sister and brother, and will only exchange them for you and your ship. Unless—"

He grasped her wrist, stilling her fingers, his gaze intent. "Unless?"

The pistol he'd so nonchalantly taken from her and tossed on the bed was by her left ankle. If she was wrong about the type of man he was, then she would have to restrain him until they reached Jamaica. She'd have to shoot him in order to do that; heaven knew she couldn't subdue him herself.

She didn't want to turn him over to Gampo, but she would to save her siblings' lives. "Unless you can think of a way to rescue the young twins without sacrificing yourself or your ship." She held her breath and waited.

He brought a hand to her chin, tilted her head and looked at her for a long moment. She met his intense, moss-green gaze as calmly as she could. He was searching for a crack in her story, the hint of a lie, the crease of a half-truth. Conal's penetrating stare told her all those things. The gentle pressure of his fingertips told her he wanted to believe her. The set of his mouth told her he'd do what needed to be done if she betrayed him.

Finally, he spoke. "I'll help you and your family rescue the children from Gampo. Then, you will get back on your little boat, proceed with your little treasure hunt, and allow my men and me to go about our business with Gampo and the *Dragon*."

She exhaled in relief. "Thank you."

He arched a brow. "Then we have an accord?"

She tried to swallow. In truth, she'd weakened her family's

position irreparably when she'd sacrificed three of them with the tea in order to fool the British frigate. Even with Conal incapacitated, her family would be no match for his men should they decide to retake their ship. Did Conal realize he already had the upper hand? She mentally cringed. Of course he did.

"We have an accord," she replied.

STEVIE LICKED HER LIPS, and Conal couldn't take his eyes from her berry-colored mouth. He didn't just *want* to kiss her. He needed to kiss her.

A voice thundered in his head. *This has been a simple tupping. Get dressed. Leave, you idiot!*

He breathed her in, and it was if her essence permeated his skin through muscle and bone to the very center of his being. Suddenly, his mouth was on hers and there was no way he could force himself to go now.

Leave, you idiot.

STEVIE KEPT her word and spoke with her family. They permitted Conal to gather his crew for a private meeting in his cabin.

The men crowded in, perplexed and wary.

Conal explained the situation as told to him by Stevie.

"I knew they were lubbers," Remus growled, shaking his head. "But steal a ship the size of the *Seeker*? I'll be hanged if they don't have the biggest bollocks among us."

The others snorted their laughter in agreement. "What's the plan, Cap'n?" another man asked. "We can take them. We just be waiting on a word from ye."

"I know." Conal looked over his crew. "I've made an agreement with them. We'll help them get the children back from that pirate, Gampo."

His men murmured and nodded. They were sea dogs, all of them, but they had stout and honorable hearts. They'd rather fight Gampo than run with their tails tucked, let alone betray young innocents. "Once the children are rescued, they'll head back to Savannah to look for more clues to this magical treasure they seek."

The men laughed.

Remus chuckled, shaking his head. "They'll never make it."

At his words, Conal paused. He wanted the Sauvage family out of his hair, but not harmed, not if he could help it. "We'll have to teach them enough that they *do* make it." He pulled out one of his charts. "The rest of our crew left behind in Harbour Town would have sought out Captains Hart and Ahern and told them of our predicament. They would have made sail immediately. That means the *Reward* and the *Desire* are no more than a day behind us, if that."

"Aye," Remus agreed.

Conal continued. "Gampo left his man, Harvey, to guide us to his hiding hole. All we need to do is allow the *Desire* and *Reward* to catch up a bit and we'll have Gampo trapped, three against one. I have a plan." He pointed to the chart. "It's likely Gampo has a stronghold on a small island near Jamaica, rather than the main island."

Remus crossed his arms and nodded. "Once we have him trapped, we got 'im. The Port Royal authorities can hang 'im at their leisure."

Conal looked around at the faces surrounding him. "This accord has been set upon a very fragile foundation," he said. "If something goes amiss with the children, the family will do whatever they need to save them, including betraying our agreement. Honor the accord, but watch your backs."

*

FOR THE NEXT FEW DAYS, Captain O'Brien, true to his word, lead them through a series of maneuvers, during which Stevie did her best to avoid the handsome man. She had no idea what to say, so she steered clear of any situation that might force her to speak to him directly. Would he treat her differently? When she thought about the moments of complete bliss they shared in his cabin had been an experience nothing at all like the one time she'd been with a man before. Conal O'Brien had lit a fire in her soul, and if she wasn't careful, it would consume her.

She had to stay rooted in reality. They were two people who had used each other at a time when both were desperate to escape for a few moments. Wishing for promises, commitments or obligations was naïve and foolish. There had been no mention of attachments of any nature. She'd already been down that road, hadn't she? She'd like to think she was wiser now.

Perhaps, she should feel guilty and ashamed of her brazen actions with the handsome captain. After careful introspection, she found that she did not. What had occurred between them was magical, and if she never experienced such a gift again, then she'd at least have her memories.

When Conal O'Brien was in motion, she watched in rapt appreciation. Every movement was in harmony with the wind, the current, and the sway of the ship. When he pulled on a rope, her fingers remembered how hardened muscles had clenched and rippled under her hands. When he laughed, her mouth remembered how his lips moved with hers like two dancers turning a waltz.

Yes, it was better to keep her stupid heart detached and avoid him.

But there were times the sensation of being watched was so intense the skin on the back of her neck would twitch. The one time she didn't ignore it and turned toward the helm, her gaze collided with one of smoldering green fire. The appreciation blazing in his eyes made her catch her breath. Her body reacted in kind and for once she wished she wasn't so intuitive.

Conal O'Brien continued to shout orders from the helm. The Sauvage family raised sails, learned how and when to reef them, made adjustments to increase or slow the ship's speed. Aside from Bernard and Harvey, most of the terminology was lost on the rest of them, although they knew what 'jibe ho' meant now, of course.

The need to get away from his perusal drove her below deck, to find a place to sleep tonight. She no longer had the captain's cabin to keep her secure from the rest of the men since Conal had assumed command of his ship, meaning she was now out of a berth. She'd found a small sail cupboard and had made a bed of sorts in there. She'd been rigging a hammock when Remus found her.

"Miss Sauvage?"

She looked up from her work. The rope was being uncooperative, and she was having a rough time securing it in a way to bring the hammock up high enough from the floor. "Yes, Mr. Remus?"

He cleared his throat and jerked his head to the right. "The captain has asked me to show you to your cabin."

"*My* cabin?"

"This way, Miss Sauvage."

The cabin was off the galley. It had two doors, one opened to a passageway leading to steps up to the main deck, the other into a dining area, through which she could enter the galley.

"Bernard requested ye take this one, since both the doors have locks."

She nodded her thanks. It provided her a safer haven than the sail cupboard.

"I've already taken out most of me belongings, so I'd not need to return for anything important."

"This was yours?" She paused. Taking Conal's cabin when he

was their prisoner was one thing. Taking the first mate's berth after they had returned the control of their ship was another.

"Don't concern yourself, Miss," Remus said with a nonchalant shrug. "I've tied me hammock with the men often enough. Yer not puttin' me out. I'm happy ter bunk with my men. I like the company."

Adrian came down to test the integrity of the locks with his shoulder and was satisfied she'd be safe enough.

Stevie spent the next couple of nights staring at the ceiling in that cabin, unable to shut off her mind. Were the little twins faring well? Were they scared? Hurt? Her thoughts started to travel down darker paths to Gampo's pirate crew and the black heart of the captain himself. Her mind needed another distraction.

The problem was, there was only one other place her mind wanted to go. The memory of Conal's kisses plagued her while both awake and asleep The memories continued to torment her until she rose from her bed and paced the room. Sometimes she lit a candle and reread her great-grandmother's letters, looking for clues, a possible code, or a hidden image. It was always a relief when Tristan knocked on her door in the morning as he passed on his way to the galley for breakfast. Although Conal's men had been told the consequences of laying a hand on her, her family was still on edge, not completely trusting this tenuous agreement Stevie had made with Captain O'Brien.

Trust, in fact, was definitely in short supply in general aboard the *Seeker*. Each party cast continuous sideways glances at each other, they ate in separate shifts and slept on opposite ends of the ship.

Harvey, of course, had sputtered in an apoplectic rage when he found out about the agreement. "Gampo will have my liver fer breakfast, he will!" He pointed to her. "One signal from me, and the little lass and laddie will be strung up from the top gallant yards!"

The blood drained from her face, but before she had the chance to respond, Conal had grabbed Harvey by the throat and hiked him up against the mizzen mast until his toes dangled an inch above the deck. The captain's voice was dangerously calm and soft. "You misunderstand your new position on my ship. Either you cooperate or swim the rest of the way to Jamaica. Your choice, but I bid ye to choose with a care. Why do ye think Gampo placed only ye in charge here?"

Harvey's eyes bulged, and he gurgled something unintelligible.

Conal lowered the man back down to the deck, but kept his hand around his neck. "He could have sent a dozen men with ye. Instead, he sent an old dog with barely any teeth left in his maw to bite."

Harvey rubbed his throat and eyed Conal warily. "I've been in his service fer years, that's why."

"Too many years," Remus muttered.

Conal leaned in toward Harvey and the grizzled man shrank against the mast. "He sent you, because he knew he wouldn't need a garrison of men to commandeer this ship to Jamaica. He knew that the moment I found out you were to take me and the *Seeker* to him, I wouldn't be able to resist the opportunity to find him and kill him."

Harvey's eyes widened.

Conal looked west. "He also expects Landon and Brendan to give chase." He released the old salt and Harvey stumbled back against the mast. Conal's jaw rippled under his beard. "Gampo has prepared a trap. He plans to take the entire Ahern fleet."

It appeared that Stevie wasn't the only one with a bit of intuition.

Conal glanced her way, then to Uncle Bernard. "It's what I would do, were I in his place."

✳

IN THE PEACE of the early morning, Drago Viteri Gamponetti sat at his desk, when his cabin door opened and Jacqueline stepped in, holding the front hem of her skirt up to her waist. He cocked his head and scowled at her. "You're showing your lacy pantaloons to the wide world, little heathen."

She ignored his chastisement and approached the desk. "May we have these for breakfast?"

Her polite words triggered warning bells.

He peered over the edge of the desk, expecting something horrendous. She had gathered five eggs. "Found the hens' roost, did you?"

She nodded. "My sister ran the kitchens at the boarding house. I help her quite often. I know how to make stirred eggs. May we eat them?"

He studied her a moment before nodding. "Come with me. I'll tell Cookie I've given you access to the galley this morning."

A short time later, he and the two children were enjoying stirred eggs mixed with onions and goat cheese. The girl's efforts were impressive. He wiped his mouth with his napkin and tossed it on the empty plate. "Tell me, what were you all doing out on that rickety sloop, anyway?"

Julian used his thumb to push the last bit of eggs onto his fork. "We were going to Savannah," he said before putting the last bite in his mouth.

"Why?"

"Uncle Bernard said we needed to find something that will help us rebuild the boarding house," Jacqueline answered.

"Your uncle owned a boarding house?"

"*La Maison de la Fortune* in New Orleans has been in our family for three generations." Jacqueline paused, mentally calculating. "Maybe four generations." She counted on her fingers. "My father's father's father...well, anyway, it's been in the family a long time. We lived on the entire second floor."

Drago leaned back in his chair. "I'm familiar with *La Maison de la Fortune*. Been there many times. Why does it need to be rebuilt?"

Julian rolled his eyes. "My sister Stevie, helped make all the food for the guests. She's a very good cook. One day, she accidentally started a fire."

Jacqueline leaned forward, her eyes wide. "It caught her *dress* on fire."

"My cousin Adrian picked her up and ran outside and dropped her in the water trough," Julian added, barely able to get all the words out before he started laughing.

"Julian! It's not funny! She nearly burned her hair off!" Jacqueline's look of reproach quelled Julian's mirth, but only a bit. "There's a horrible place on the back of her neck where she was burned bad."

"It healed though," Julian mumbled. He caught Drago's amused stare and became animated once more. "Before anything could be done, the fire went up the back staircase. The entire boarding house and gambling parlor burned to the ground. *It all* burned down except the chimneys and we lost...everything we ever had."

Both sat quietly for a moment.

Drago broke the silence. "So Uncle Bernard went begging for assistance from family in Savannah?"

Jacqueline shook her head. "Not exactly."

"What does that mean? Either they are family or they are not." He stroked his chin. "He went begging, or he did not." The family owned the boarding house and a gambling parlor. Interesting. It explained the girl's knowledge of cards. He made a mental note to keep a keener eye on her if they played again.

Julian reached for a biscuit, tapped it on the table to see how hard it was and then dunked it into a cup of goat's milk. "Uncle Bernard found an old box behind a brick in one of the fireplaces. He looked at the stuff inside and said we had to go to Savannah and get help from our great-great-grandparents."

Jacqueline shrugged. "But they're dead, so I don't know how they can help," she said.

"Maybe they left your family some land," Drago suggested.

Julian shook his head. "It's not land, it's a thing, another box maybe. I don't know, but there were valuable stones in the first one, that's how Uncle Bernard bought our boat."

Drago scratched his jaw. A man couldn't help but wonder what might be in that box—if it even existed. "Perhaps there's money buried in a grave in Savannah," he thought out loud.

"I think that's what Uncle Bernard is hoping," Julian said, taking a bite of his soggy biscuit. He froze. A look of complete horror covered his features. He slowly swallowed the biscuit and gaped at Jacqueline.

"What?" She frowned, unable to decipher the look.

Julian put his hands on the table and clenched them into fists.

"Spit it out, lad," Drago said. The thoughts churning in the boy's head were nearly visible. Children were completely perplexing.

Julian sat unmoving in his seat. Finally, he leaned toward his sister and whispered in her ear. Her eyes widened and then her hand flew to her mouth before she turned to stare at Drago.

He reached for his tea and took a slow sip. "Out with it then, unless you'd like me to request Mr. Adams bring out his nine-tailed cat."

Julian's face paled further. Finally, Jacqueline spoke. "Are you going to steal it from them?"

"Steal what?"

"The treasure that's in the grave in Savannah," she whispered.

He placed his cup on its saucer. "You mean the treasure that *might* be in a grave? What makes you think I want to travel all the way back to Savannah, Georgia to dig up a grave which probably contains nothing more than a dry skeleton?"

"That's what pirates do. They steal treasure," she muttered.

Drago pounded his fist on the table and everything jumped,

the silver, his saucer and both children. "I have told you—I'm not a pirate. I'm a privateer." Such rumors led to deadly health hazards. He snatched his tea and cursed as it splashed over his hand. "I have no bloody interest in chasing after a whisper of a treasure that might not even be worth my time. All I want is Ahern's fleet of merchant ships. With your uncle's help, I will get them."

Jacqueline's eyes narrowed. Julian sat back in his chair, relieved.

Drago took a biscuit and imitated Julian, dunking it into his tea. "What's in your head now, missy?" He lowered his brows. "I can almost see words floating around it."

"How many ships are in the fleet?"

"Three."

She propped her elbow on the table and dropped her chin to her palm. "Will you keep us until my family brings you all three?" She swallowed, fighting back tears.

Ahh. So that was her worry now. He leaned forward on his elbow, mimicking her. "If they bring me the one, the other two will follow like little ducklings."

Julian sat up and tugged Jacqueline's sleeve. "Then he can search all three for his sister."

Drago nodded. He didn't expect his sister to be aboard, but he would glean great satisfaction at taking the Ahern fleet and turning the ships over to France, collecting his share of the prize and watching Fynn Ahern's merchant business go under like a sinking ship.

CHAPTER 8

Journal entry
30 March 1719

The inevitable toll of constant combat has reduced our numbers as to make it nearly impossible to man the Gallant *in a storm. This has forced us to take on smaller ships (where the outcome of battle could be easily predicted) in order to take on more men. We have captured some and given them a choice: they could feed the sharks or take a blood oath and become part of our crew and receive a share of our takings. I befriended a young sailor who signed on as 'M. Read' and we have become fast friends.*

I t was time to test their new skills. Stevie shielded her eyes with her hand and looked out at the three barrels lashed together and floating some distance from the *Seeker*. She'd fancy standing closer to the rail, but the nearness of the water made her heart pound and she felt safer near midships with one hand on a rope. Conal's crew and her family were below, manning the guns and preparing to fire at the target. Harvey and Bernard had climbed the rigging to observe and call out the closest shots.

The hair on the back of her neck rose, and she knew without turning around that Conal had moved to stand slightly behind her. "My ship is large, but not so big you can hide from me forever, Stevie."

Her stomach flipped at the soft baritone vibrating in her ears. It took a great deal of strength to maintain her composure and continue to stare at the target floating on the choppy swells. It had been a rough week, avoiding him, wanting him, remembering him, his caresses, his scent. And now he called her by her given name in a manner that sent her heart tripping.

"I've managed well enough so far, Captain," she replied. It would be foolish to think their time together meant anything other than what it had been: a moment of pleasure in a moment of time. But a small thread inside her still foolishly hoped.

She felt his breath on the back of her ear and it took all her strength to remain still. "Have you decided to trust me yet, little rabbit?" He moved beside her and gave her a long sideways appraisal.

Usually, she was the one who read the mannerisms and expressions and brought intentions to the surface. She wasn't used to the same done to her. She pressed her lips together to keep from blurting something unwise. The captain had a light, confident air about him today; that alone made her wary. She answered his question with one of her own. "Have you decided to trust *me* yet, Captain?"

His soft laugh sounded almost like a tiger's purr. "I've known precious few pirates—or women—who've been able to keep their word, lass. Perhaps you'll be the one to set a new standard for me?"

"You know I'm not a pirate," she said. He didn't trust her. That realization both saddened and angered her, although it shouldn't. She'd taken his ship, stolen his ring, lied to him about

Gampo's plans, then coupled with him like a trollop. What was there about her to trust? Heat radiating from his body had her leaning toward him before she could catch herself. He smelled of sunshine and fresh ocean spray.

He inhaled sharply. "And I know you are indeed a woman, from your lips to your toes, so my standards have been quite set for a significant period of time," he added in a whisper.

She could feel his gaze. Her heart tightened in response and she fought to keep her focus on the waves.

Which was folly.

She couldn't ignore his presence any more than she could ignore his words or the way her skin tingled when he was near. Her fingers ached to touch him; her lips ached to kiss him. Falling into bed again with Conal O'Brien would weaken her, and right now she was fighting for courage all the way down to her toenails.

Unable to remain totally aloof, she finally met his gold and emerald gaze. "What happened between us was the result of being in a desperate situation. We followed our instincts to drive away the fear and the darkness."

His gaze sharpened before one corner of his mouth hitched up. "Are you saying you seduced me in order to save yourself from cowering into a corner out of despair?"

"Perhaps." Returning her gaze to the sea without really seeing it, she added, "We're all alive, and you have agreed to help my family save the children from Gampo's torment."

He reached over and traced her hairline from her temple to the tender skin behind her ear. "Ah, so your seduction worked quite well for you, then." His touch was gentle but there was a cutting edge to his last words.

"And your seduction worked quite well for you," she countered hoarsely. "You have regained command of your ship and your men." Her voice quavered a bit, probably because both knew he would have taken back the *Seeker* by force at some point anyway.

She gave him a quick glance. "It brought us to an accord. There's no reason for it to happen again."

"None at all," he agreed. He uncrossed his arms and leaned in, tracing her jawline. "But I find myself craving it. Craving you. It's as if a part of you is inside me and is yearning to get back to you."

He was seduction incarnate. His finger was making circles behind her ear, raising bumps on her skin. It moved down the side of her neck and across her collarbone, then it was gone. It was a moment before she could breathe again.

"Come with me closer to the rail, so that we may determine which gun takes the prize for hitting the target." He pushed away from the mizzen mast and took a step toward the starboard side of the ship.

"No, thank you."

He paused. "I won't bite you."

"It's not you I fear." She stared past him at the fluttering surface of the sea. The other morning it was glowing pink and orange and she'd been convinced she'd never seen anything more beautiful. It was still beautiful in a cold, dangerous way. Today the clouds crowded the horizon, hinting at a storm thrashing the ocean in the far distance.

Conal looked from her to the water and back. "You fear the water?" His tone held a note of amusement. Doubtful she was the only person aboard who couldn't swim.

"When I was six, I fell off a raft and into the river." The muddy water had clouded her eyes, filled her nose and mouth. Her dress pulled her down until her toes sunk into the mud. Tristan had jumped in after her and dragged her to safety. The smell of the murky water had remained in her nose for nearly a week.

"I hope you're not also afraid of loud noises, little rabbit," he said, stepping up behind her, the heat from his body, warming her back.

She shook her head, and felt the heat redden her cheeks. "No, just water and snakes."

"Not rats, or bats?"

It might have been a mistake telling him how she and the twins were discovered. "The rat surprised me; I wasn't afraid of it. I've seen a snake bite kill a grown man. They're worth a wide berth."

A soft laugh danced past her cheek and the air around her thinned as he moved away. "I'll be by the rail if you change your mind." He didn't stir a breeze with his movement or take a spot of shade away with him. No, it was almost as if the energy in the air had just dissipated. An emptiness crept into her chest, and she was relieved when the first command was shouted to begin the training.

"First gunner, *fire!*"

A loud explosion was followed by a thick, black cloud of smoke that enveloped her for several seconds before the sea breeze pulled it away.

Harvey yelled, "A miss!"

"Second gunner, fire!"

This time, Stevie was ready and covered her ears with her hands and moved upwind. Now her view was unhindered, and she laughed when the barrels jumped. The shot landed directly in front of them.

"Near hit!" Bernard bellowed.

Gabriel came charging up to her from his gun. "I almost hit it! Did you see, Stevie? Did you see?"

"I did." She laughed again, loving the look of glee on Gabriel's face.

The exercises continued until Conal was satisfied the entire crew could fire the guns with an above-average degree of success.

Harvey and Uncle Bernard lowered themselves back down to the deck, arguing as usual. "It was the fourth gun that hit the target! Yer blind as an old mole."

"It missed by at least four yards. The fifth gunner hit it dead on. You can't count, you old croak."

Both agreed on one thing, however. Harvey sniffed the air and looked eastward. "We has some weather comin'."

Bernard rubbed his shoulder and nodded. "Aye, that we do."

"Sail ho!" the next watch shouted from the tops, and everyone scanned the horizon for a dot of white.

"There!" Gabriel pointed.

Conal raised the glass. "She's too far to make out her colors." He turned to Remus. "Prepare the guns in case she's hostile."

At Remus's command, the men headed back to the gun deck.

Stevie strained her eyes to see the sails. Was Conal hoping it was one of his fleet? She took a moment to study him. If indeed it was one of them, would he keep his promise and help them free the children from Gampo, or would he focus only on exacting his revenge? He didn't seem to be a man who would go back on his word, but in desperate times, people didn't always stay true to their outward character.

Conal chose that moment to glance her way and his eyes sharpened. She met his gaze and caught her breath. Her cheeks warmed and she told herself to find something to do or somewhere else to stand, but she couldn't make her feet move. The corner of Conal's mouth curled up the tiniest bit, and for some silly reason, her heart jumped in her chest.

For the next couple of hours, the ship on the horizon continued to head toward them. Conal adjusted his sails to take a more southerly tack, but the other ship had the wind to her back and her sails hauled out and full.

It was only a matter of time before she intercepted them.

Conal raised the glass to his eye and cursed. He turned to Remus. "She's flying French colors. Tell the men to prepare to fight. Bring up the weapons crates."

Remus nodded and went to relay the captain's commands. Conal strode toward her like a big cat, a sleek tiger, his gaze locked on her with such intensity, she backed up a step. Her stomach churned and her knees shook, although her mind was screaming furiously for her to stand strong.

"Stevie, go below and lock yourself in your cabin. This is no place for a woman."

She almost turned and did as she was told, then she paused as men ran about, hauling crates of pistols and swords up to the deck and securing them at the front, middle and aft parts of the ship. Sails were adjusted and the gunners ready to light the fuses.

Her heart pounded in her chest and she wanted nothing more than to hide in a safe cubby hole below. However, there was no safe cubby hole below. No place on this ship was safe from attack. Her family manned the guns along with Conal's scant crew. Gabriel's face, smudged with smoke and grit, flashed through her mind, and she returned Conal's stare. "I can't hide below when everyone else is preparing to fight."

Seeing the determined jut of her chin, he repeated, "I want you safe, Stevie."

"I want to fight, Conal." He paused at her use of his given name, then reached for her, but she stepped away. She'd not let him drag her below like a petulant child.

Conal's nostrils flared and he stepped forward to grasp her upper arms, then scowled. "You're not a fighter, Stevie! You're used to hiding in the kitchens and cooking for boarding house guests. You're a gentle soul with great compassion, but you're *not a fighter*. You are a sweet, timid little rabbit who's brave enough to sacrifice herself for her family, but you cannot fight."

Her eyes burned with tears, not at his words, but at the truth behind them. She was indeed terrified. Her stepfather had been a cruel man who spent half his time in his cups and the other half releasing his anger on her and her brothers. Withdrawing into her own quiet solitude had been the only way to live through his abuse.

Yes, all she wanted right now was a quiet, safe place to hide, but this wasn't the time to cower in the shadows and cover her eyes and ears like a child fearing what might be in the closet or under the bed. Or pounding on her bedroom door.

Conal's expression softened. He lowered his voice. "You'll be a distraction to me, lass. I'll worry for ye. You have no combat skills, and I'll be forced to focus on protecting you rather than leading my men."

She leaned in and said, "Then *teach* me."

Today, she would not hide.

Today, she would learn how to fight.

Conal's eyes widened in exasperation. "I can't teach you hand-to-hand combat well enough before that ship fires on us!"

Stevie pointed to the empty gun on the back of the poop deck, behind the helm. "You have time to show me how to fire that small cannon." Even as he was shaking his head, she was straining against his hold, facing toward the back of the ship. "You don't have enough men as it is. We barely have the hands to sail this ship, let alone bear arms to defend her. *Show* me."

CONAL CLENCHED HIS JAW, wanting to argue with her, but she was right. They needed all hands to fight off any threat the French ship might impose. He took in the determined set of her chin and her fierce silver glare. His fingers still gripped her upper arms; she was trembling, making him want more than anything to lock her safely below.

Why did he want to do that? Why was he suddenly so determined to keep her out of harm's way? Had a simple tussle in bed turned him into a lovesick lad?

Now he was being ridiculous.

He'd send any other woman below for the same reason. He looked at the stubborn line of Stevie's lips. There was a glint in her eyes, a calm determination that told him she would not stay in her cabin, even if he demanded it.

A flash of victory shone in her stare. "I'm not leaving topside, so you might as well give me something pertinent to do." She placed her hands on her hips.

Blast it all, she was right.

Well, at least if he put her on the poop deck, she'd be close to the helm, and he could keep an eye on her. "Fine, then." He turned and grasped her fingers, pulling her with him as he strode toward the aft end of the ship. "I'll teach you how to handle the demi gun."

Together they prepared the shot. He spent half an hour coaching her how to load it, ram it home and aim the gaping maw.

"Use grape shot to pepper the sails and spray the deck," he instructed. "It causes a great deal of damage to the crew and leaves enough holes in the sails to slow her down. The other, larger shot will cause more focused damage, but requires greater accuracy. For now, use the grape shot."

She nodded just as the first boom of the French vessel's guns echoed over the water.

THE *DRAGON* WAS two days out of Baracoa, Cuba when the storm hit. Drago stood at the helm and looked out over the sea at the thousands of white caps lacing surface with alarming frequency. His crew had reefed all but a few sails. Still, the wind snapped through the rigging and cracked at the lines. His ship pitched and groaned and he fought the tiller to keep her steady. The clouds nudged the horizon ahead of them; dark purple sheets of rain fell in the tiny space between the clouds and the ocean. The wind blew spume and sea spray up and over the railing, and he squinted to see past the bow.

When his second came to relieve him, his arms ached and he

was soaked through. He staggered back to his cabin and stripped off his soggy jacket and shirt, kicked off his boots and collapsed on his bed.

He awoke to a whispered argument between the twins.

"He's not dead! I can see his chest move."

"But he hasn't so much as twitched since he fell on his cot."

"Put your head on his chest and listen for a heartbeat."

"He has no shirt on! It wouldn't be proper. You do it, Julian." A wave crashed against the hull and the spray pelted the windows of the cabin, causing Jacqueline to let out a frightened squeak.

Drago opened one eye. Two pale faces hovered inches from his nose. When they noticed that he was awake, they sighed with relief.

He raised up on his elbows and noticed that someone had covered him with a quilt. His boots had been stuffed with rags, and his shirt and coat were nowhere to be seen.

Julian handed him a tankard of grog. "Cookie left this for you. It was full, but we got a little thirsty."

"We didn't drink much," Jacqueline added, wrinkling her nose. "It tastes horrible." She handed him a plate of dried beef and biscuits. "The meat made us thirsty."

"Where's my coat and shirt?" His tongue was dry and thick. Did he really sleep?

"I put them in the oven to dry," Jacqueline said.

At his horrified look, she added, "Cookie let the fire die way down when the storm hit. It won't burn them now." Still, she darted down the back hatch to the galley, and by the time he'd drained the tankard, she had returned with his clothes. He shrugged into them and wolfed down the food, then put his boots on and went back to the helm.

His second gave him a relieved nod and relinquished the wheel. The storm had strengthened. Swells loomed over the ship's rails and crashed onto the main deck. At some point, the main top gallant had ripped free and now whipped wildly in the gale.

He ordered the lower sheets let out, hoping it would give them enough speed to break free of the storm without losing the sails to the wicked claws of the wind.

When the fiercest part of the storm finally abated, Drago allowed the helmsman to take over. The setting sun peeked out from beneath the storm clouds even though rain still pelted the deck. He returned to his cabin and repeated his earlier process, kicking off his boots and stripping off his wet clothes. This time, he noticed a dry shirt and trousers on his bed. Shivering, he shrugged into the garments, nodded his thanks to the twins and collapsed.

Jacqueline touched his shoulder. "Do...you need anything?" A frown creased her brow.

"C—c—cold," he stuttered.

She looked around. "Where do you keep extra blankets?"

He was too exhausted to answer. He closed his eyes; the bed shifted. Two warm little bodies snuggled close on each side of him. He lifted a single lid and did his best to scowl, but both had their eyes closed and he didn't have the energy to tell them to get the hell out of his bed. Whether it was the gentle rocking of his ship or the cozy cocoon that lulled him to sleep, he no longer cared.

THE FRENCHMAN CAME at the *Seeker* head-on, ready to tack and show a broadside to rake them. Uncle Bernard and Harvey commandeered one of the guns on the main deck just as the first shot from the privateer hit the water, well short. Conal tacked his ship efficiently and effectively. His men up in the sheets refitted the canvas and gave his gunners access to the French schooner's bow. His second gun crew scored the first hit, aiming high with grape shot, fraying canvas and rigging.

Clouds of black, billowing smoke and flame began to erupt

from the French ship's long muzzles and Stevie shrunk back against the aft rail and prayed for the safety of her family, and Conal. Uncle Bernard lifted the thirty-pound shot and shoved it into the muzzle of the gun. Harvey's shout had him ducking and covering his ears against its thunderous roar. Harvey shouted again and Uncle Bernard grabbed a powder cartridge and fed the hungry mouth, then packed down the shot and wadding before joining Harvey to reseat the carriage and pour black powder down the touch hole. Harvey ignited it and the deck was filled with another roar, followed again by the choking black smoke.

Tristan and Adrian worked side by side at another, both stripped to the waist, faces streaked with sweat and blackened by smoke, repeating the same process as Harvey and her uncle.

The French schooner and Conal's brig danced through the waves, circling close, darting away. Conal changed tacks yet again to present the guns on the opposite side of the *Seeker*.

Tristan and Adrian ran across the deck and prepared another gun to fire. Harvey and Uncle Bernard were still in place when a shot ripped through the canvas overhead. One of the upper sails came down, sending lines whipping through the air, snapping a sailor right off his perch. He fell, screaming, to the water. Stevie froze, then ran to the rail. Was there anything nearby she could toss to the man that would keep him afloat? Her stomach lurched. He was nowhere to be seen. Gone. He was gone.

Another shot crashed through the rail next to one of the guns, sending shards of wood raining over the two old men as they bolted across the deck. Harvey went down just as the ship lurched against a swell, sending him sliding toward the jagged opening with nothing to stop his descent into the sea.

Uncle Bernard's eyes widened and before Stevie could take a step, he lunged toward Harvey, falling on the old sailor's legs. He hooked an arm around a breeching rope attached to the gun's cart and grabbed Harvey's ankle with the other.

Stevie leapt down the afterdeck ladder; a prayer left her lips in an urgent plea. If Uncle Bernard's grip slipped, both men would fall into the sea. At her alarmed shout, Tristan and Adrian sprinted to help, hauling both men away from the side of the ship to the relative safety of the quarterdeck bulwark. The young men raced back to their gun to load another shot.

Stevie knelt beside the two old salts. Blood streamed down Harvey's face. She gasped as she caught sight of the large gash on his lower leg.

"Is he dead?" Uncle Bernard flopped down on his back next to her, and gasped for breath.

"I don't think so," she replied, pressing the sleeve of her shirt against the wound on Harvey's leg.

Harvey groaned and brought his hand to the bleeding bump on his forehead. "I'm dyin'."

"You aren't dying," Uncle Bernard spat, sitting up. "Yer too hard-headed to die today, you dung-souled blighter." He reached over and ripped the sleeve of Harvey's shirt then used it to wrap the man's calf.

"That's me best shirt!" Harvey sputtered.

Her uncle eyed the grimy fabric. "That's a thankless thing to say. Would you rather bleed to death?" He flicked his hand at Harvey. "If that's your best shirt, then you're not losing anything worth grieving over."

At Conal's shout, Remus sped across the deck, jumping over debris to relieve his captain, who was already calling orders to adjust the sails yet again.

Remus took the wheel. Conal jumped down to the quarter-deck and motioned for Gabriel to join him at a gun closer aft. He was already loading it when Uncle Bernard limped over.

"We don't have the hands to reload and fire the guns any faster!" Conal yelled above the din. "We have to make every shot count! Aim for the decking beneath their guns on the main, we have to disable them!"

Uncle Bernard nodded, wiping the sweat from his brow, then

moved down to the next gun and adjusted the angle. Gabriel ignited the powder in the touch hole of Conal's gun. It jumped backwards, restrained from rolling away only by its thick breeching ropes. A deafening explosion followed, and Stevie pulled the collar of her shirt over her nose and mouth as the smoke billowed past.

A jubilant cheer arose from Conal's crew manning the braces. When the smoke had cleared, she focused on the schooner. One of the big guns now pointed up at an awkward angle, the side of its cart sunk below the boards of the blackened deck.

"C'mon." Harvey jerked at her sleeve. "Help me git up to the other gun to help Bernard. He needs me."

Stevie hefted the man to his feet. He leaned heavily on her until they reached the gun, then he reached for the powder. She ran to the ladder and ascended to the poop deck as the two vessels continued on a parallel course.

A whirring chain shot hit the mizzen mast's peak, two links sliding apart and mowing a swath through sheets and rigging. The twang of severed lines pierced the air along with cracks and snaps of yards breaking away.

Conal yanked off his shirt and tied it around his head and ears. He and Gabriel both strained on the ropes to pull a cannon forward to fire. His skin gleamed with sweat and every muscle in his chest, neck and arms bulged with the effort. Once secured, Gabriel adjusted the nose and then lit the touch hole. Both turned, covering their ears with their hands, and were lost in the cloud of thick, swirling smoke for several seconds.

The shot hit the middle of the French foremast and it shuddered a moment before it toppled backward on the starboard side of the ship, covering her gun crews. The vessel was now running ahead of them along the same course.

"Don't let her cross the bow!" Conal shouted at Remus. "For God's sake, man, turn starboard!"

All Stevie could do was pray as the *Seeker's* crews worked furiously to adjust the sails at the correct angle to push her away from the schooner. God may not think her worthy, but surely these men deserved what divine assistance He could provide?

Rather than try to keep up, the French schooner began a graceful arc away in the opposite direction, bringing the back ends of each vessel closer to each other. Stevie straightened. Here was her chance!

The smaller gun aft of the helm was loaded and ready to fire. Standing directly behind the barrel, Stevie sighted straight down its neck as the schooner broke away. She patiently waited until the boat's helm moved toward her line of sight. When it was directly in line with the gaping maw of the gun, she stepped aside and touched the powder hole with her torch.

The blast from the gun numbed her ears, the smoke cloud blinded her and the report knocked her backwards. A split second later, the rail to her left exploded and she was pelted with splintered wood bouncing off the iron neck of her gun. Coughing and gagging, she grabbed the partial rail, pulled herself to her feet and gaped.

There was now a large hole in the rail and bulwark on the other side of the demi gun. If she'd stood there when she lit the touch hole, she'd be dead.

Remus continued his starboard arc to the right. He grinned at her over his shoulder. "Nice shot, missy! Ye sent her away with her tail 'twixt her legs!"

Behind her, Harvey let out a hoot and then the rest of the crew began to cheer. Tears were streaming down Stevie's face from the smoke, and she wiped her sleeve across her eyes and tried to see through the dissipating haze.

The schooner was leaving! The vessel's helm was on fire, thick black smoke puffed from the rear of the craft.

Stevie laughed out loud. Huzzah! She was a fighter after all.

*

Moments earlier, Conal and Gabriel fired off one more shot, which took off the schooner's bowsprit before they were out of range. He jogged back toward the helm just as the two ships began the slow tack away from each other. In a few seconds, the aft parts of both ships would be closer to each other, making the guns along the sides ineffective. If the French boat had any guns back near her helm—

His heart lurched in his chest.

Conal cursed his stupidity. He'd put Stevie on an aft gun because he didn't expect to use it. It should have been the safest place for her if she was going to be stubborn and insist on staying topside. He sprinted toward the stern, sending a panicked prayer up to God to protect her. Just as he reached the ladder, an explosion vibrated through the boards beneath his feet and a great cloud of brown-black smoke rose above the aft part of his ship.

Before he could take another step, another explosion rocked the aft end of the *Seeker*, making his ears ring and sending a spray of splintered wood flying over his head to litter the deck behind him.

Dear God. Stevie!

Cold shards of fear pierced his chest. Fearing a blood-spattered boards, Conal jumped up the last few steps in time to see her sprawled on the deck. Heart in his throat, he staggered forward. He'd killed her. If he hadn't put her on that gun...

She rolled to her side and pulled herself to her knees. His limbs nearly liquified in relief. She was alive! He sent up a prayer of thanks as he surged forward. Hooking his arms around her, he hauled her to her feet, then lifted her away from the splintered rail and the rushing ocean below. "I have ye, lass." Gripping her shoulders, he spun her to face him. "Are ye hurt?"

She blinked and squinted at him. She opened her mouth, but no sound came. Shock. He felt her arms for broken bones, then leaned back to study her better, looking for blood. Some of the tension eased from his shoulders when he found none. "Stevie, answer me, love. Are ye hurt?"

She rubbed her ears and shook her head. "No, but there's a ringing in my ears and it's hard to hear you—" Her last words were lost as he pulled her to his chest and hugged her.

He'd been an idiot, putting her on that gun. What had he been thinking? He kissed the top of her head, once, twice three times. Thank God she wasn't hurt. "In time, the ringing should cease. You're not injured," he murmured, more for his own ears than hers. She began to squirm, but he couldn't release her. He let her turn in his arms so they both faced the open sea. The crippled schooner allowed the northwesterly winds to push the ship away from them.

"We did it!" She turned back and hugged him hard, laughing. "We did it!"

"If you'd been hurt or killed manning that bloody gun..." He'd never have been able to forgive himself. It took all his strength to slightly relax his hold on her. "*You* did it, lassie." He reached up and plucked debris from her curls.

At her perplexed look, he pointed at the schooner. "Ye blew away her rudder, she canna maneuver well enough to re-engage. Your shot saved the day."

She grinned, and even with splinters of wood in her hair and smudges of black across her eyes and the bridge of her nose, giving her the appearance of an ornery raccoon, she made his stomach unstable. She was intoxicatingly beautiful.

Then she did something he didn't expect, but thoroughly enjoyed.

She threw her arms around his neck and kissed him.

CHAPTER 9

19 September 1720

Dear Father,
We sighted a half-plundered Spanish galleon near an uninhabited island
near a string of larger islands called the Bahamas. She was listing badly,
probably due to a belly full of water and ballast. Jack figured she had only
a few hours before the sea would take her, so we shall board her to see if her
attackers left any scraps. We are in dire need of provisions, so it's our hope
we can salvage enough for our needs.

Your daughter,
Anne

For several hours the crew worked to remove debris from the *Seeker's* decks and secure damaged rigging, spars and sails before the sun set. They patched up the wounded and placed them in hammocks strung near the galley close to Stevie, the surgeons bag and her herbs. After preparing a meal of rice and beans speckled with small chunks of the two chickens that didn't survive the battle, Stevie joined Conal and the rest of her family at the table, finally taking time to eat as well. Gabriel had wolfed down a plate of food, then collapsed on the bed in Stevie's cabin and immediately fell asleep.

"Feels good ter get me foot high, too much blood in it," Harvey groused, his leg propped up on a stool by the trestle table in the room outside Stevie's cabin.

"I'm not going to bleed you, so stop complaining. You lost enough blood already. There's only so much in you." Stevie re-wrapped his wound in clean strips of cloth. The old pirate cussed under his breath, snatched the bottle from her hand and took a healthy gulp.

Uncle Bernard reached for a pitcher of ale and filled Harvey's tankard then his own, causing Adrian to raise his brows. Her uncle caught his son's stare and shrugged, then clinked his pewter mug against Harvey's. "To your health, you clumsy, powder-brained, spindly-legged lizard."

Harvey responded with a gap-toothed grin. "And to yours, you weak-chested, thick-pated, old dog,"

Conal reached for his cup, worried about the approaching storm. "If we had clear skies, we'd keep moving, but with that cloud bank drifting in, it's too hard to navigate now. We'll sail at first light." At the worried look on Stevie's face, he added, "If the skies clear, Remus will let me know. If we can get a solid heading, we'll journey on."

Adrian and rest of the family had pushed their trenchers away and began to study the letters from the marble box again. "I've read these front-ways and back-ways, and I still can't see how they mean anything other than what the words say," he groused.

Tristan scowled. "Wish we'd made it to Savannah so we could walk through the Helshire church cemetery."

Harvey shifted his leg. "Spent a few years in Savannah in my youth. Ain't never heard of a Helshire church, tho','" he said, taking another pull from his mug. "Whose grave ye looking fer?"

"It's nothing," Adrian blurted, gathering the letters into a pile.

Bernard put a hand over the pile of letters, stilling him. "No—perhaps he can help us, Adrian." He turned to Harvey. "Did you know of a family by the name of—what was the name in the letter?"

"It doesn't give a last name." Adrian gave a helpless shrug. "All it says is that they buried Robert the cook in the old Helshire church's kirkyard in Savanna."

The old sailor puckered his mouth and squinted his eyes, thinking. "Can't remember a Helshire Church."

Bernard picked up the letter and held it out to Harvey. "Here, you read it and see if you can make any sense of it."

The old sailor waved it away. "Can't read," he said. "But I tell ye, there weren't no Helshire Church in Savannah, Georgia, at least not when I were there."

The air in the room became too heavy to bear; shoulders sagged and expressions lengthened. They'd thought they were on the right path. Turns out they weren't.

Tristan looked from Adrian to Bernard. "Well, that's just jolly, isn't it? Now what do we do? This was the only clue we could decipher."

Harvey picked his teeth with his fingernail. "Well, like I said, there ain't no Helshire Church in Savannah, Georgia. But there *was* one in Savanna, *Jamaica*. Ain't no church there, though. It burned down ages ago and weren't never rebuilt."

Eyes widened and the air almost crackled.

"Jamaica!" Tristan said, slapping his hands on the table. He eyes held a bit of a gleam, forcing Conal to guess the reason was, that they were suddenly heading in the right direction.

The table went silent for a few moments as everyone mulled through the ramifications of that piece of information.

Bernard looked at Conal. "If we find that treasure in a

Helshire grave, we could cut you in a share to make up for losing your ship to Gampo."

Conal kept his face expressionless. He had no intention of giving up his ship, but there was no need to mention that right now. He'd keep his promise to Stevie and help get the children safely reunited with their family, but after that, he'd take control of his own helm and his own destiny. Gampo planned to lure them into a trap, but the pirate underestimated the Ahern Merchant fleet.

Harvey's ears perked up. "Treasure? What treasure?"

Bernard crossed his arms and stared hard at him. "Here's where you might redeem your soul, you black-hearted son of Satan. If you want an equal share of the treasure, you'll keep your trap shut about what we're looking for and help us retrieve it."

All eyes were on Harvey, who shifted his weight in his chair. "Well, I suppose fer two shares, I could—"

"Or—" Conal interrupted, leaning back and lacing his fingers behind his head. "You could take what little you know to Gampo. If there is truly a treasure and if he ends up finding it, I'm sure after he takes his two shares, you'll get your share, or maybe even two shares split up between..." Conal paused. "How many hands are on Gampo's ship? Sixty? Eighty?"

Harvey licked his lips and took another slug from his tankard, ignoring the stream of ale dripping down his chin, shrugged. "Aye, somewhere's along them lines." He looked around the room, his bristled brows lowered. "But I ain't no Judas."

"No one asked you to betray your captain," Bernard said. "Although I can think of a better place to throw in your lot." He stared Harvey down.

Harvey shifted his gaze to his leg and sighed. "I'm gittin' too old ter be a seaman, anyways. It's time fer me to kick back me feet and retires. I'll do me duty and see this rig to Gampo's spot, then I'm done. In exchange fer a share of the prize, I'll help ye find yer treasure with naught to say about it to Captain Gampo. Ye have me word."

Bernard pulled a dagger from his boot and drew the edge across the heel of his hand, then held it out to Harvey. The old seaman took the knife and repeated the process, then the two men shook hands.

"An accord, then," Bernard said.

"Aye." Harvey nodded. "Ye have me blood oath."

STEVIE TOSSED and turned in her bed, partially because the thoughts of her time with Conal kept warding off sleep, partially because the ship was rocking so vigorously. Remus had called the captain topside toward the end of their discussion with Harvey. The first mate said a storm was brewing, and they needed all hands on deck to secure the ship. She roused Gabriel, and he drowsily followed the men up the ladder.

Soon, the storm hit them with a violent fist of wind and hail. When she tried to help the crew topside, her chest constricted in terror. The deck was slick, and it was hard to keep her footing. Conal thankfully waved her back below with instructions to secure the galley. The wind hissed through the lines and the sea pounded against the hull like an angry hag beating a rug. The *Seeker* screeched and groaned against the onslaught. Stevie worried that the damages sustained in battle might make the ship too weak to fend off the pounding storm. She had a horrible vision of the hull breaking in half and sinking; sea water filling her mouth and seaweed pulling at her legs...sinking down, down, down...

The tempest raged through the middle of the next day. The men came and went in shifts, and Stevie did her best to make sure they got something to eat and drink when they came below. She never caught sight of Conal. Bernard told her the captain stayed at the helm with Remus.

By dusk, she could finally stoke the galley stove and prepare a warm meal for everyone, even finding enough supplies to make fresh biscuits, which the crew gratefully received. After sunset, Remus wearily trudged by the galley on the way to his hammock, pausing long enough to take a trencher of food.

"I thank ye, lassie," he said with a hefty sigh. "Cap'n thinks we're outta danger and put the two old sea dogs at the helm for a few hours so the rest of us can get a few winks 'til dawn. Ye should get some shut-eye, too."

As if his words were a spell, an intense weight pulled at her shoulders and eyelids, and all she could think of was crawling into her cot.

Stevie started toward her cabin, then paused. Conal hadn't stopped by the galley at all since the storm began. She grabbed a trencher, filled it with biscuits, dried beef and cold rice to place in his cabin for him to find when he returned.

When her knock went unanswered, she entered and headed toward his desk to deposit the plate.

The room was unlit except for the silver blue gleam of the full moon flickering through gaps in the clouds and the gallery windows, casting shadows on the walls and floor. She padded to the desk and put down the platter. A soft noise from the bed made her pause. Conal's upper body was angled across it, his feet still in his boots and flat on the floor. A puddle of water pooled around them.

She crept closer and caught her breath. The planes of his face relaxed in sleep; short stubble covered the stoney jaw. A band of moonlight slanted across his chiseled chest, the soaked shirt plastered against his skin. It looked as if he'd attempted to take it off; the strings were undone, and the bottom was bunched at his stomach, giving her a moonlit view of the fine strip of hair that trailed down to disappear into his sodden breeches. One boot was half-off.

It would be easy to pull it the rest of the way. She bent down and slowly removed it, then reached up his calf and pulled down his stocking. The other should come off too, but she was loath to wake him to do so. What would he think she was up to, sneaking around his cabin? He'd probably think she was looking for him to bed her again, which she definitely was *not*. She'd been weak last time. The charisma and energy of the man lured her in until she was powerless to stop herself. Any more of such a heady mix of man and sex would certainly be her undoing. She'd made the mistake of giving her heart away to such a man once before. Unrequited love was painful and its damage lingered.

It would not be worth the pain. She shook her head firmly. Not this time. Not the kind of pain a handsome man like Conal O'Brien would inflict. The best choice would be to leave.

Stevie rose, took a step toward the door, but something made her pause and look back. She studied the sleeping Adonis sprawled across the bed. The man was wet and exhausted. He'd collapsed, unable to remove a single boot. Dry clothing and rest would do him good. Truly, it was foolish of her to act this way. After all, she'd already seen all there was of him.

Twice, if one were counting.

The least she could do was help him remove the soggy clothes and put him under dry covers. She turned back to the bed and squatted down by his legs. She put a hand on his knee and shook it.

"Captain?"

He gave a muffled, "Mumph."

"Captain, I will help you take off these wet clothes, but you must assist me."

"Mumph-mumph."

She picked up his boot and pulled the heel up. He lifted his other foot and toed the boot off. She removed his sock. "Will you please sit up?" Stevie pulled at his arm and he complied, swaying slightly. His eyes were still closed and she wondered if he was actually still asleep. Grasping the hem of his shirt, she peeled it up. At her murmured instruction, he raised his arms, allowing her to pull it over his head. He shivered.

His skin was cold and wet. She looked around for a cloth and found a rag hanging over the back of his chair. She used it to rub his chest, stomach, shoulders and back, marveling at the broad expanse of muscle and sinew. She ran it through his hair, squeezed out as much water as she could, and brushed the strands away from his face and forehead.

She pulled at both his hands. "Now is the hardest part, Captain. Stand up and allow me to help pull these wet breeches off without falling over and taking me to the floor with you. Can you accomplish that amazing feat of balance and agility?"

He let out a great sigh and allowed her to pull him to his feet.

Here is where she faltered.

She shouldn't have, but she did. After unbuckling and removing his belt and unbuttoning his pants, she wasn't sure she could follow through with the rest.

Biting her lip She closed her eyes. This was foolish. She took a deep breath then suddenly had the solution. Keeping her eyes closed, she grasped the band at his hips and proceeded to wiggle them down to his ankles. When she opened her eyes, she looked at his bare feet.

"Step out of your breeches, Captain, and lie down. I'll look for another blanket."

Conal did as she bid him, groaning as he fell on his bed. She accomplished her task, thankful for the moonlight, as it was very easy to find the blanket in the tallboy. She smoothed the cover over him and drew it to his chin.

"Rest well, Captain," she whispered.

But when she turned toward the door, an icy hand touched the inside of her knee, shooting cold gooseflesh up her leg.

"Where are you running to, little rabbit?" Conal's words were thick and heavy with exhaustion. "Lie with me and warm me before you go, lass, I beg you. I feel as if melted snow runs through my veins."

His eyes were closed, his face relaxed, frigid fingers resting on her thigh. The chance of anything more happening between them was small. Even if it did, it would be nothing more than it was before.

Nothing more.

He didn't move. His chest rose and fell with slow regular breaths and his hand relaxed against her leg. Sighing, she sat on the edge of the bed, removed her boots, slid in next to him and shivered. His skin was so cold that if she didn't know he was alive, she could be convinced she'd just lain next to a corpse. In fact, he was shivering. Concern wiggled its way into her mind. What if he became ill? When she was young, her dearest friend had caught a chill and died from it. That last horrifying thought had her snuggling closer. Each muscle tensed then relaxed under her hands. She moved from there to his shoulders, and her breath hitched as her hands rubbed through the fine hair over his broad chest. He felt so cold. Conal shivered again, and she was glad there was another blanket over him.

Back and forth, she rubbed the cold away before moving her hands to his ribs to repeat the process and generate heat. It did no good to push her thoughts elsewhere. It was impossible while her hands touched his skin. He smelled of sea air and rain. She breathed him in, wishing there was a chance for them to end up together. Just the sensation of running her hands over his muscular frame was both satisfying and frustrating. She wanted more, but shouldn't.

Satisfied she'd been able to get the blood circulating somewhat, she snuggled back beside him. She once again eased her leg over his thighs and gave herself the tiniest bit of extra satisfaction by sliding her hand across his chest until her entire arm covered him as well. She'd stay a few minutes until his body warmed to hers, then she'd go.

His palm closed over hers. "Thank you, lass," he whispered. He turned his head and caressed the side of her face with his lips, then trailed kisses down her jaw before claiming her mouth. His kiss was smooth and gentle, his nose and cheeks still cold, she noted with a start.

It was so easy to fall into his kiss. Their lips moved together and apart as if they were performing an intricate dance. His mouth was cold, but his tongue was hot, and it beckoned to her. It was not a savage, tormented kiss like the ones they had shared before. This kiss molded her mouth to his in a mesmerizing fashion, like a sculptor pushes clay.

There would be no violent coupling tonight, but slow torture by touch and fire. His kisses were both tender and commanding. His hands caressed her as if her skin was holy and magical. All of this threatened to stress the fine cracks he'd made earlier in that iron wall around her heart. If it broke again, she'd never recover.

Ragged lust was preferable to this torment. She wanted him to saturate her mind and distract her heart with passion and heat.

Not this.

This made her feel cherished and pure, and she was neither of those things. She wasn't the quality of woman that Conal O'Brien, with his broad muscular shoulders and unflinching honor, deserved. Her virtue had been tainted. She was a pirate and a thief and a penniless kitchen maid.

She pressed a tender kiss against the pulse in his neck and tasted the sea and the moonlight. The world around them faded, until there was only her, and him.

IN THE FAINT moonlight Stevie became a silver goddess, and Conal stared in awe. She kissed his palm, then his wrist, sending a shivery jolt down his arm to the base of his spine. A wave of tenderness struck him and he watched in wonder, amazed at the sensations she drew from him with a simple touch of her lips.

Stevie was not like those he'd bedded in the past. She was ethereal, a goddess, and he watched her in wonderment and veneration. No woman had ever treated him with such reverence and trust. What had he done to deserve this?

Their gazes caught. Drops of silver flared in her irises and something urged him to tell her how he felt, but he couldn't find the words.

"You are so very beautiful," he finally murmured. It didn't nearly convey the depth of the emotions churning in his chest, but he was at a loss. "A treasure."

"You're drunk with lust and exhaustion," she whispered in his ear. "It's not I who is beautiful. It's you, golden and glistening and magical, like a Greek god."

He warmed at her words. Emotion ripped the air from his throat, an opposing tide shredded his lungs leaving her name on his lips, and her touch branding his heart.

CHAPTER 10

27 October 1720

Dear Father,
We are wealthy beyond our wildest dreams!
The bounty left by the marauders who first took the galleon is more than
we had hoped for! We found a hidden cache filled with heavy silver plates,
gold-hilted swords glittering with jewels, and chests filled with gold chains
and another small trunk with loose jewels: rubies, emeralds, sapphires and
diamonds. We shall live out our days in ease. I have enclosed a few of the
gems as a gift.
Mary Read has taken a husband, a handsome young man we took from a
small prize ship. I am thrilled for my friend.

Your daughter,
Anne

※

ACCORDING to Remus the storm had blown them several leagues off course, but the winds were now in their favor and the sails were full. The *Seeker* cut through the water like a hot blade through snow, even though the white-capped seas were still rough and choppy. They stopped in Baracoa long enough to take on a few extra supplies, make repairs to a couple of broken spars and acquire several fresh barrels of water.

Conal prepared a message for Brendan, giving his cousin the location of Gampo's camp on Lamb's Tail Island, and alerting him to the kidnapped children aboard the *Dragon*. The charts had revealed a sheltered harbor capable of hiding their ships windward of Lamb's Tail Island, allowing the Ahern Fleet the opportunity to make a quick surprise attack on Gampo's camp when the time was right.

It was likely the rest of the *Seeker's* crew traveled with either Brendan Ahern or Landon Hart. Hopefully both would come to his aid. Two ships at full capacity should have no trouble taking on Gampo; three ships could provide Gampo a reason to surrender rather than fight. In the meantime, until Landon and Brendan arrived to assist, he would scout the area and prepare a plan of attack. As soon as they loaded the last barrel, Conal walked to the harbormaster's office.

The harbormaster grinned and shook his hand. "Captain O'Brien! Good to see you again, sir!"

Conal pulled a sealed envelope from his jacket pocket. "Captains Ahern and Hart should make port in another day, two at the most, and will stop in looking for this."

McCully stowed the envelope in his desk. "I'll see that one of them gets it."

Conal took a pouch of tobacco from his pocket and handed it to the stout, white-haired man. "I brought ye a fresh bit of the Lowcountry's finest, Mr. McCully. I know ye have a sweet spot for it."

The harbormaster opened the gift and inhaled the aroma. "I

thank ye, lad!" McCully said enthusiastically. "Ah, I shall enjoy this greatly." He raised a brow. "Might ye be sailing with a Mr. Sauvage?"

An uneasy warning seeped into Conal's chest. "Aye, that I am."

Only Gampo knew he was with the Sauvage family.

"Well, then," the man pulled an envelope from under his desk. "Would ye see Mr. Sauvage gets this?"

"I will," Conal said, taking the envelope. "Do ye know who penned it?"

"I doubt it was the little ones who brought it to me. Couldn't have been over eight or nine."

"There were two?"

McCully reached into his weathered jacket pocket and pulled out his pipe. "Aye, a boy and a girl. Looked to be twins."

Conal tried to keep his voice calm and casual. "Did they appear in good health and spirits?"

McCully took a pinch of tobacco and packed his pipe, then shrugged. "I dinna note otherwise."

That was good news, then.

"I thank you." Conal shook his hand and headed back to the *Seeker*, wondering what message Gampo had for Bernard Sauvage.

CONAL MET Bernard and the rest of the Sauvage family at a tavern near the docks. They sat at a large table and were sharing platters of roasted meat, fruit and fresh bread. Harvey and Bernard poured over a rough map showing the Windward Passage, Jamaica and Cuba.

Conal pulled out a chair and handed Bernard the letter as a dark-skinned lad placed a pitcher of ale on the table. Bernard tore it open and read it quickly. Tension pulled the corners of his mouth until his lips pressed into a thin line, eyes clouding with anger.

"What does it say?" Stevie prompted. "It's from Gampo, is it not?"

Bernard nodded and rubbed his forehead. He didn't resist when Stevie tore the letter from his hand. Her eyes widened as she read.

"That wicked pirate." Her voice dripped with hatred and rage. She locked stares with Conal. "I'm going to kill him myself."

Her family stared at the normally meek woman in surprise. She shoved the letter away. "He says we have to deliver the ship within two days, or he will sell Julian into service and hang Jacqueline from the top gallant spar." She gestured at the letter as her eyes welled with tears. "He made the children sign their names in blood," she choked.

Conal clenched his jaw and let out a slow angry breath. Stevie's eyes brimmed with guilt and despair; her tears slashed at his heart. He made a silent oath to kill Gampo or die trying. He leaned forward and placed his elbows on the table. "We should see the coastline of Jamaica by sunset tomorrow. The other two ships in our fleet are likely only a day behind us. Our three ships can easily take him. Gampo will have to surrender." He nodded his thanks as Adrian slid a mug of ale his way. "We've never had a reason to attack him. We do now."

Stevie paled. "You can't fire upon him with the children aboard!"

Conal shook his head. "I'm not thinking of a battle. Between the *Seeker* and the *Reward*, we'll outnumber Gampo's men, and can stamp out any resistance easily. If the confrontation is at sea, our ships can easily surround the *Dragon*. He'll have to negotiate with us."

Harvey pointed to Lamb's Tail Island on the map. "Gampo will anchor his ship here in the shelter of this cove, then take to his house on the island." He pointed to the southern tip. "If we rows our longboats from windward, to this point, we can send one group to take control of his home and another group to cut loose the anchor of Gampo's ship, setting it adrift." He smiled smugly. "That gives us plenty of time to..." He dropped his voice. "Find what we're looking for in Helshire." Harvey traced his finger between Cuba and Hispaniola, then along the northern coast of Jamaica and around the western tip. "If we takes the Windward Passage but swings this way instead of heading to Kingston Harbour, we can sets an anchor in this cove on the near side of Devil's Bluffs. It be well out of sight even though Lamb's Tail is here, just down the coast."

It was as good a plan as any.

WHEN THE VERDANT, rolling island of Jamaica came into view, Stevie let out a relieved sigh. They'd made it. Soon, God willing, Jacqueline and Julian would be back with their family, where they belonged. Then, hopefully, the Helshire cemetery in Savanna would yield something substantial for their efforts.

The Sauvage family had run *La Maison de la Fortune* boarding and gambling houses for many, many years. They were good at it, and rebuilding the business would be their first priority when they returned to New Orleans. Only then would they re-establish the family's stability and security.

Stevie studied the last remaining longboat and canoe lashed securely on the main deck of the *Seeker*. Conal's suggestion to wait until the rest of his fleet arrived with more men and additional longboats made sense. Yet, worry swirled in her stomach. What if they were delayed? What if the same storm that had hit the *Seeker* put them farther off course, or did even more damage? What if it had sunk them?

Her insides twisted at the memory of the children being torn from her arms and carried, screaming and crying from their little sloop. They would soon run out of time. How long could they afford to wait for reinforcements?

Worse, what if those reinforcements never arrived?

THE CRESCENT MOON created just enough luminescence to light their way. Adrian and Tristan dipped the paddles into the water with long, silent strokes. It hadn't taken Tristan long to connive the *Seeker's* watch to help lower the last longboat and holding steady the ropes securing it while the three of them climbed down and sat. Believing they were simply scouting for the captain, Conal's men had been quiet and efficient.

She felt slightly guilty at keeping their plans a secret from Conal. He'd insisted they wait for the other two captains to arrive, but it had been two days. Time was up.

They simply could wait no longer.

Yesterday evening, they'd accompanied Conal and his men to scout the small island. Gampo's ship was anchored on the sheltered side, a short way from the rocky shore, his men stationed at intervals to watch and guard the long, single-story house which sat back from the water, huddled in the shade of a grove of large Guango trees.

The big question...were the twins in the house or on the ship? The logical assumption put them in the house. Gampo had placed guards around the structure. Stevie, Tristan, and Adrian hoped to approach from the backside of the island without being noticed.

They needed only to sneak into the sleeping house, find the twins and take them back. Tristan was the best choice for picking locks and breaking in. He had an uncanny ability to move with the stealth of a shadow. Stevie would follow him, leaving Adrian to stand guard.

Simple plan.

Scary, but simple.

In the wee hours of the night, with a sleeping household, it should be easy enough to execute, shouldn't it? Especially since they weren't expected to be on the offensive.

After reaching the island, the three pulled the boat ashore and hid it in the thick green undergrowth at the edge of the tree line.

"How long do you think it'll take to hike over to the other side?" Tristan whispered.

Adrian dragged several branches and placed them over the boat. "It depends—do we go over the mountain or around the island?"

"Over," Tristan answered in a hushed whisper. "He'll have placed men to watch the shoreline rather than the interior of the island. We've less chance of getting noticed if we go over. We will also be able to scout a solid escape route."

Stevie smacked a mosquito on the side of her neck, then pulled out a bottle of camphor oil and quickly rubbed some on her exposed skin. She was not about to become a tasty meal for flying fangs. Adrian and Tristan plowed ahead, unconcerned. They'd regret it later when the bite marks itched and kept them awake at night, scratching and digging.

Tristan led the way into the dense underbrush. Stevie crept behind him, her heart hammering in her ears. The plan seemed sound when they'd discussed it this afternoon, out of Conal's earshot. Now it didn't seem so easily accomplished. The air swirled as thick as the foliage. And it was way too quiet.

The light from the waning moon didn't penetrate far into the brush. It was probably only a matter of time before she tripped over a log and went sprawling face-first into a tree.

From a few yards ahead, Adrian's hushed growl echoed her thoughts. "I can't see a bloody thing. Tristan, turn up the lantern. We're far enough in to chance it, I think."

Soon, the soft glow illuminated their way. The night air was thick with the scent of damp earth, water and some sort of sweet-smelling bloom. Somewhere in the distance, the unmistakable sound of a waterfall sifted through the foliage. Thank goodness! Her throat was parched. Adrian and Tristan had the same thought because instead of continuing up the mountain, they turned and followed the sound.

A short time later, sweaty and flushed, they broke through the brush to the edge of a small pool. Here, the scant moonlight glittered on the water. A small stream fell over the rocks and down the slope. She inhaled. It was cooler, fresher here.

With a groan of sheer ecstasy, Tristan sank to his knees and plunged his head in and splashed water on the back of his neck. The others quickly followed. Stevie drank deeply. After the rumlaced barrels on the ship, this water tasted cool and sweet.

"Let's follow the stream up the mountain as best we can," Adrian suggested. "We won't need the lantern light and can save the oil for the return."

They continued their trek, keeping near the stream. It was a relief to have a clearer path rather than one blocked by thick green leaves the size of a barrel. As they neared the source of the waterfall, the terrain became trickier. The rocks were harder to climb around and over. It forced them into the brush to skirt around the steep cliff, over which the water plunged.

Stevie gasped for breath with each step. Even Adrian was breathing heavily next to her. Traversing the sharp uphill incline had her legs and lungs burning. The sooner they started their descent on the other side, the better. She paused a moment to catch her breath and to second guess their plan. What if the children could not make the return trip? She looked up to gauge the time, but the canopy above barely let a twinkle of a star through its leaves. What if dawn arrived before they made their escape back to the cove and the safety of the *Seeker*? What if they were wrong about the twins' location?

His thirst dictating his path, Tristan led them to the waterfall. They were now at the same level as its source. Perhaps that meant they were near the top of the mountain.

Tristan paused at the edge of the water above the falls. They all took in the scene in front of them. The stream flowed from a cave opening about the size of a coach.

The cave would make a good place to seek shelter during a storm or for relief from the tropical heat. As a group, they approached for another quick drink. Stevie knelt and cupped the water in her hands. A strange tingling wiggled in her stomach, making her pause to look around. What predators prowled this island? Snakes didn't move around at night, did they? It was hard to hear anything but the sound of water crashing to the pool below. She quickly splashed her face, thankful for the cooling effects. When she opened her eyes, her stomach lurched.

Standing just outside the shelter of the cave were at least a half-dozen men.

And they were armed.

With a muffled oath, Adrian grabbed a rock and threw it at the closest man, catching him completely off-guard. It hit squarely on his face and he fell backward, knocking down the man behind him. Tristan grabbed her arm and flung her back toward the shelter of the forest as Adrian lunged for another of the men who'd chosen to arm himself with a knife rather than a pistol.

His mistake.

From the shelter of the underbrush, Stevie reached for her own pistol, then hesitated. If she fired it, she'd risk alerting more of Gampo's men. The next one to emerge from the cave had so such a dilemma. He raised his arm and pointed his gun at Adrian and fired. Stevie screamed as Adrian's body lurched backward, then disappeared over the falls.

The rest of the men easily overwhelmed Tristan. Stevie sank to her knees behind the brush and aimed her pistol at the man who had shot Adrian. As soon as he stopped moving, she'd pull the trigger. He strode over to Tristan and pointed a second pistol at her brother's head, then looked in her direction.

"Either come out or watch me kill another one," he said in a cold, flat voice.

She gripped her weapon and for a moment considered shooting the pirate. The click of his hammer going back decided for her. They'd already lost Adrian. Unwilling to call his bluff, she stepped out. Another guard immediately wrestled her down and yanked her wrists together.

The man binding Stevie's hands chuckled. "Cap'n was dead right. He said they'd try this, and dang if they didn't."

Her heart sank. Their plan had surprised no one. The remaining four men shoved them toward a path heading around the other side of the cave. Tears burned her eyes. They'd failed. They'd failed Julian and Jacqueline, and now Adrian.

Conal would not give Gampo his ship, that much had been obvious to her from his expression when they'd discussed the trade yesterday. Desperate to save them, she and her family had no choice but to attempt a rescue.

Her chest tightened. *Adrian.*

Forever her protector, her cousin had sacrificed himself in an attempt to save them. She choked back a ragged sob and beside her, Tristan nudged her with his shoulder in solace. She chanced a glance at his face, and the haunted look in his eyes sent a chill of trepidation through her chest.

How would Gampo handle their duplicity? Would he kill them in order to urge Uncle Bernard to keep his end of the bargain? What if Conal still refused to give up his vessel? There'd certainly be another sea battle between the two which would surely lead to more fatalities.

She looked at Tristan, who walked looking at his feet. Her brother, the gambler, was likely calculating the chances of them surviving while in Gampo's camp. A grim expression coated his features.

*

"Dammit!" Conal slammed his fist on the rail. "What were you thinking?" It was all he could do to keep from hitting the big man in the face regardless of the repercussions of that action, since Adrian outweighed him by at least a stone. Stevie's cousin was taller and broader.

But Conal was angrier.

Adrian's shoulders slumped, and he hung his head like a chastised child. Blood soaked the left side of his collar. A trail streamed from his ear down his neck. The ear which had a chunk missing, had finally stopped bleeding.

"Stevie said you'd never give Gampo your ship," he mumbled. "She worried if we waited for the rest of your fleet, it would be too late to save the twins." His shirt was in tatters, and bruises were already showing on his face and arms from the fall. The man was lucky the pool at the bottom had been deep and the bullet wide. If it had hit two inches to the right, it would have killed him; at least he'd been smart enough to return for help rather than attempt another foolish rescue.

Conal cursed under his breath and stared at the low glow of predawn creeping above the horizon. Well, Stevie was right about one thing. Of course he had no intention of giving his ship to Gampo, but he'd never put her siblings in danger. He'd assumed she understood that. Her distrust cut deeply. Why didn't she come to him?

He ground his teeth and glared at the lush green landscape along the Jamaican shore. "There is no way we can walk into that snake's lair and make it out alive without at least Brendan's support. It'd be suicide." The faint clang of church bells carried over the water, and suddenly he had an idea.

Helshire church.

He spun and jabbed a finger at Adrian. "You..." then he gestured to Harvey and Bernard, "and you two are coming with me."

Bernard checked the priming on his pistol. "What are you planning?"

Conal turned to Gabriel. "Go fetch those letters and that map of the island. We're going to Helshire cemetery and digging up that treasure. We'll use it to barter for the lives of your family."

And maybe get Gampo out of their lives for good.

It would be better to sail around the bluffs and Devil's Point to the next cove. Then the trek on land would be shorter. It was time to relocate. "Hands to braces!" Conal shouted. "Weigh anchor, Mr. Remus—take the bunt gasket. Haul those sheets!"

The top sail yards blossomed while the crew worked at the sheets and tacks. Usually, it never failed to rouse his heartbeat or send a chill up his spine when the sails unfurled and billowed with the wind. Today, however, a tight knot of apprehension coiled in his gut. The capture of Stevie and Tristan in addition to the twins put Gampo at a better advantage. With more bodies to threaten, he could make more demands. The rock at the bottom of Conal's stomach grew heavier when he thought of Stevie in the hands of Gampo and his men. He prayed for her safety, then made a vow to God. He would get her back if it was the last thing he did on this earth. If they hurt her, he'd send them all to hell.

The chit had known he'd have disagreed with her plan, otherwise she wouldn't have slunk away like a thief in the night.

Foolish woman. Who did she think she could save?

He shook his head. The meek rabbit that she was couldn't even take care of herself, let alone execute a rescue. Rats no bigger than her fist made her scream, and she'd rather hide in the galley and cook, or unsettle the men by virtually reading their minds, rather than lathe against the grain. *She didn't have the strength.* The battle with the French privateer edged into his mind, making him pause.

Maybe she wasn't the same frightened little rabbit he'd met in the galley a few weeks ago. She was a fighter now. She had to be.

"Sail ho!"

Conal scanned the horizon. Sure enough, white sails and a sleek line peeked over the horizon. "Can you make her out?" he shouted.

"Aye sir!" came the enthusiastic reply. "She's the *Reward*!"

"It's Captain Ahern!" Remus hopped up the companion ladder and leaned over the rail. "He made it!"

"Make straight for her, Remus," Conal ordered. They had no time to lose if they were going to get Stevie and her siblings back unharmed and intact. His gut twisted when he thought of the terrible things Gampo's men would do to Stevie once they discovered she was a woman.

CHAPTER 11

31 October 1720
Journal entry

*Mary and I chanced a brief sojourn ashore to Jamaica for some provisions.
We heard rumors that Captain Barnet has been dispatched by the
Governor to capture Jack and his crew. Anne and I have decided to hide a
portion of the treasure in case our ship is taken. We found the perfect
hiding place. Should Barnet take our ship, we can tell him that we were
taken against our will, and he will likely believe us and set us free.
The best outcome of course would be to elude Barnet. If we succeed in that
then the small chest of jewels will provide stability later and allow us to
disappear and live the rest of our lives free of need and hunger. We won't
leave the jewels to Jack and his crew, it will only drip through their
fingers like water.*

No one spoke on the way to Gampo's ship. Stevie and
Tristan were thinking the same thing, anyway. Their plan
had been destined to fail from the beginning. The children

weren't in the house at all. They were with Gampo on the *Dragon*. She should have listened to Conal and waited. She should have trusted him.

The water was relatively calm on this side of Lamb's Tail Island. Dawn was pushing the night away. Stevie sat sullenly in the boat, her brother opposite her, staring at his feet, his shoulders deflated in grief. Tristan finally raised his head and stared past her to Gampo's ship. His face paled. He opened his mouth in a silent scream, the anguish in his expression making Stevie's stomach lurch. She followed her brother's gaze.

Dear God! She blinked and tried to focus and make sense of what she was seeing in the dim light.

Then she started to scream.

Hanging from the yard arm of the main top gallant were two little bodies. There was no mistaking Jacqueline's white dress and soft blue sash or Julian's matching blue shirt. Their heads were covered with burlap bags; their little arms tied behind them. Stevie choked on sobs, sank to the floor of the boat and collapsed against the side, no longer able to hold herself upright.

Gampo had threatened to hang the twins if her family failed to bring him the *Seeker*, or if they betrayed him. Yet deep down, they didn't really believe the pirate would murder children.

They were wrong.

She'd failed them. Sweet, impish Jacqueline, precocious and willful. Brave, vivacious Julian, stalwart and intelligent. She'd failed them both. She'd killed them. Hot tears trailed down her cheeks as a mountain of rage erupted in her chest.

Gampo.

He'd suffer her vengeance. If she died in the attempt, it would be fitting. It had been her fault the boarding house burned down, her fault Gampo's men discovered them, her fault the children were kidnapped. Her fault they were dead.

In the soft light of the early morning, the ocean lapped with a deadly calm at the side of the boat as the pirates secured it to the

Dragon. The men had cut their bonds to allow them to board the vessel. The look on Tristan's face told her he planned the same as she. Once on the deck, they would attack Gampo. She'd already decided to snatch the pistol from the belt of the pirate next to her. Hopefully, she or Tristan could deal a death blow before Gampo's men killed them.

Stevie was first to set foot on the ship. Before she took a second step, one of Gampo's men pushed her down to the deck and pressed a pistol against her temple while another rebound her wrists. Her plan failed even before she had a chance to execute it. They dragged her to the middle of the quarterdeck and dumped her there. She struggled to a sitting position and could only observe as Tristan thrashed and fought with the pirates, only to be beaten into submission and unceremoniously tossed next to her.

That hated man, Captain Gampo, stood with legs braced wide and arms crossed over a broad chest.

"What have you done?" she screamed at him, "Why? Why did you kill them?" Her entire body shook with grief, shock and anguish. "They were children! Sweet, harmless children."

Gampo's dark hair was tied back and the hint of stubble peppered his cheeks and chin. His nostrils flared. "They were neither sweet nor harmless." Cool silver eyes surveyed them from under half-closed lids and scowling brows. He didn't fool her. Although he gave an air of nonchalance and confidence, he was strung as tightly as a fiddle. Every muscle in his shoulders and back was tensed. The fingers he had casually curled around the hilt of a saber were a hair's breadth from the grip.

He was a panther ready to pounce. He'd anticipated their rage and hatred along with their desire to kill him. The pirate glared at his men. "Where are the others?"

The ring leader shrugged. "There be just these two. The third took a tumble off the waterfall."

Gampo glared at her. "Where's the *Seeker*?"

"Why should I tell you?" Stevie glared at him, wishing him dead.

He sighed and gestured to the hanging bodies. "Cut them down."

One of his men scampered up the rigging, and Stevie couldn't tear her gaze away as he untied the ropes and let the bodies fall to the deck. Time seemed to slow as they almost fluttered down like feathers.

A strange thing happened next.

Julian's torso separated as soon as it hit the boards and dried palm fronds poked out of the pants and shirt sleeves. Jacqueline's body had no legs. For a moment, Stevie stared dumbly at the heap of clothing the twins had once worn. She sagged against the mast and fought to steady her breathing.

Decoys.

Stuffed clothing.

Next to her, Tristan had come to the same conclusion and wept with relief even as he cursed the pirate under his breath.

"I dislike being betrayed," Gampo snapped. "Now, where is the *Seeker*?"

Tristan looked at Stevie, putting the burden of betrayal on her shoulders. From the look on his face, he already suspected she'd developed feelings for the captain. It didn't matter now. What she was about to do next would forever destroy his trust.

She swallowed. "Where are the children?" she countered, lifting her chin and praying Gampo couldn't hear the tremor in her voice.

He jerked his head in the direction of the main cabin door, and one of the sailors opened it. Two dark heads poked out. Stevie cried with relief. Gampo waved the children over. Jacqueline slipped her hand in his before she noticed Stevie and Tristan.

"Stevie!" she squealed and started to surge toward her. Gampo held fast to her hand though, and wouldn't let her go. "Please,

Captain Gampo, that's my sister and brother." She pried at his fingers. "Please let me go!"

"Why are they tied up?" Julian asked, eyes wide.

"They cheated," Gampo answered. "They didn't keep their promise."

Jacqueline stopped tugging, whirled around and stared at her siblings, appalled. "All he wants is to find his sister," she said. "Did you bring her with you? Is she on the ship?"

"What are you talking about, Biscuit?" Tristan said in a quiet voice.

"Tell them." Jacqueline looked up at Gampo. "Tell them about the man who stole Risa."

Gampo glanced down at the little girl. "Maybe later," he said, releasing her hand. "Go untie your big sister."

"What about Tristan?" Julian asked.

"I want to talk to your sister first," Gampo replied tersely.

As soon as they freed her hands, Stevie threw her arms around Jacqueline and hugged her hard. "I thought we lost you." She fought to keep her voice from shaking. There was no stopping the tears, though. "Thank God you're both alive!" She grabbed Julian and hugged him until he squirmed away.

"Pirates don't hug," he muttered. He couldn't hide his smile, though.

"Sauvage pirates do," Stevie countered with a scowl and grabbed him for another hug, which he returned this time.

"The *Seeker*?" Gampo waited.

She glanced sideways at his frigid, stoic features. How could she betray Conal? Gampo's earlier message made it very clear what would happen if she refused to give him the *Seeker's* location. She'd die defending them, but no matter how much she cared for Conal, she'd never sacrifice the little ones.

Ignoring the cold stone of guilt pressing against her stomach, she finally said, "It's anchored in a small cove not too far away."

She gestured in the general direction of the western side of Jamaica. "Beyond that point, just past Devil's Bluffs."

Conal would never forgive her.

Nor should he.

Conal, I'm so sorry.

"INCREDIBLE," Brendan Ahern muttered into his half-empty tankard.

Conal shrugged and drained his mug. "Truly it is, but that's the way of it. I have given them my word to help rescue the children, but in light of the most recent events, I think we need to provide an additional incentive for Gampo to release all of them unharmed."

The two captains and the rest of the Sauvage family, including Harvey, sat around the large trestle table on the *Seeker*. They anchored their ships in a deep cove on the other side of Jamaica's Savanna territory.

"Why don't we just go to Kingstown Harbor and tell the governor that Gampo and his pirates are hiding out on Lamb's Tail Island?" Brendan asked.

Harvey snorted. "Which pirates be ye referrin'? By rights, the Sauvages are pirates as well, seein' how they tied up the crew and pirated a ship out of Harbour Town."

Before Brendan could reply, Harvey jabbed a finger at Conal. "Although ye could lie and say they *didn't* steal it, don't think Gampo won't claim ye as part of his crew if he got caught. He'd not go to hell alone."

Brendan lowered his mug. "Understood. We can't enlist the help of the authorities here," he replied. "So if it isn't escaping the gallows, what other incentive would Gampo have to release his hostages?"

Coal shifted a brow. "Treasure."

Harvey leaned forward. "Bernard, read the captains that there letter again." He lifted the pitcher of ale on the table and quirked a brow at Gabriel. "This pitcher's a little light, lad."

Gabriel smirked and took it from him then disappeared into the galley.

Bernard handed the letter to Brendan Ahern, who read it silently. When he'd finished, he looked at Bernard with a perplexed expression. "I don't understand why you think there's treasure in Helshire cemetery. All it says here is that the cook died and they buried him there and he had a liking for roses."

"It's not what she wrote," Adrian answered. "It's how she wrote it." He traced his fingers along the words. "It says: *More importantly, Robert the cook died today.*" His gray eyes flashed with excitement. "They knew they were being pursued. Anne Bonny was in the process of hiding the treasure when she wrote this." He picked up the letter, folded it and handed it back to his father. "She took the time to mention the name of the cemetery and even describe the ironwork on the fence. There's too much detail to ignore it. It *has* to be a clue."

Conal rose from the table. "Remus and the rest of my crew will stay with the *Seeker*. Brendan, keep within the shelter of this cove until the rest of us return. Keep a watch out for Gampo." He nodded to Adrian, Harvey and Bernard. "The four of us will find the Helshire cemetery."

THE THICK WEIGHT of dread pushed down upon Stevie's shoulders as the sloop rounded the point next to Devil's Bluffs. Gampo had readied his guns and armed his men for the upcoming confrontation with the *Seeker* and her crew. She watched help-lessly from the *Dragon*.

The cove's far shoreline came into view a little at a time. She wanted to take the children and hide them below, away from the fight. Would Conal fire on them, knowing they were probably aboard? Knowing *she* was probably on board?

Surely he wouldn't. She thought back to the grape shot he'd ordered fired from the *Seekers* guns into the French privateer's sheets, rather than spraying the deck with it.

She hadn't known Conal O'Brien long, but from what she'd observed, he was an honorable man. He would do what was right, even if it meant sacrificing his ship. An ugly thought squirmed in her mind. *What would Gampo do to him if Conal surrendered?*

She cast a quick glance at the pirate. He had a determined set to his shoulders and a hard line to his jaw. Scowling grey eyes scanned the shoreline as his long tanned fingers toyed absently with the hilt of a saber tied to his waist. Cold talons of fear gripped her heart.

Gampo's bark of rage shook Stevie from her thoughts. "That son of a one-legged whore!" He stomped down from the helm toward them. Stevie pushed the children behind her and did her best not to shrink away from his approach.

"Where did he go? Where is he? Answer me or I'll send you all to hell in pound pieces!" His eyes flashed in anger and frustration.

Julian nudged Stevie. "Just give him back his sister," he whispered. "She's all he wants."

"Sister?" No other woman was on the *Seeker*. She lifted her chin as Gampo stomped to her. "Who is Julian talking about?"

Gampo looked her square in the eye. "I'll tolerate no lies from you. Is there another woman aboard the *Seeker*? She'd have hair the same color as mine and stands as tall as my nose. Did you see her?"

Stevie shook her head. "I did not see another woman, but we took the ship after most of the crew had gone ashore. Perhaps she disembarked at Harbour Town with the others."

"I want that ship!" Gampo raged. He yanked out a belaying pin and shook it at her. "I don't take well to a double cross," he sneered. He grabbed Jacqueline's arm.

Stevie came at him with her fists flying. "Let her go!" She hated him for Adrian's murder and for dragging her family into this sea of danger and death. Her nerves were more frayed than a worn rope, and twice as twisted.

Tears welled in Jacqueline's eyes. "Stop it! Please!"

A tar came up behind Stevie and flung his arms around her chest, pinning hers to her sides. Gampo spun on his heel and dragged Jacqueline with him to the helm, barking orders to his crew to return to Lamb's Tail Island.

Stevie sank next to Tristan and sobbed. Gampo would punish them for failing to bring him his prize. And Conal...she clenched her jaw. Conal had betrayed all of them. He'd abandoned them. He'd abandoned *her*.

Just like before, she'd been cast aside. Used. Useless. Unloved and unwanted.

How could she've been so wrong?. His kisses and charm had blinded her. The guilt she felt earlier for leading Gampo to the spot Conal had dropped anchor dissipated in the heat of her anger. Conal had broken his promise to help her retrieve the children and just sailed off, leaving them to their fate with an insane, raging pirate.

If by some miracle she survived this, she'd not rest until she put a pistol shot through his cold, lying, cowardly heart.

"STOP CRYING. YOU'RE NOT HURT." Drago slammed the cabin door shut and reached for a bottle of rum. He filled his cup and took a gulp, then glared at Jacqueline before dropping into the chair at his desk.

She rubbed her eyes and swallowed. "It's not their fault your sister wasn't on the other ship."

He pounded the desk. "They broke our agreement!"

"Don't all pirates?"

"I've told you, I'm not a pirate. I'm a privateer," he snapped. There was a difference, and she was well aware of it. Was she *trying* to get under his skin, or did it just come naturally to her? There was a time he yearned for children of his own. This little chit was quickly curing him of that affliction.

And now, she was crying again.

"Tristan was *bleeding*." She hiccuped and wiped her nose with her sleeve. "Why did your men hurt him?" Her eyes shot silver-blue sparks at him even as they welled with new tears.

He pointed his finger at her. "He took the first swing."

She opened her mouth to retort then closed it.

There. That stilled her tongue. If nothing else, she could be objectively fair.

Drago sighed and sat back, taking another sip of rum. This had been a risk, a long shot. Truth be known, he was surprised and impressed the family had pulled it off. They'd actually stolen a ship and sailed it all the way to Jamaica.

Amazing.

At least now the *Seeker* was nearby; the other two ships would soon join her; they always sailed together. He simply needed wait for the others to arrive. Although he'd been told Fynn Ahern was dead, he wouldn't believe it until he searched every square inch of planking on all three ships. That dog deserved to die, all right, and Drago wanted to be there when he did.

The sound of a deck of cards slapping the desk drew his attention back to the present. He raised his brows in mild surprise. "You wish to play another game?" He gestured around them. "I doubt you have anything else with which to barter. My clothes have been nicely mended, the floor of my cabin scrubbed clean, and I am now the proud owner of a white and blue dress."

Jacqueline looked down at the white pinafore covering the new soft yellow dress she wore. "The last doesn't really count, since you traded a new one for it."

"You mended the sails and Julian helped Mr. Manuel with the

damaged carpentry."

She shrugged.

He laughed. "You have nothing more to lose to me, little poppet. And I'll not let ye barter the clothes on your back."

She stared at her toes. "I have one more thing." Her voice was so soft, he hardly heard her.

He quirked a brow and shrugged, taking the cards. "Fine. Let's return to the deck and play in the fresh air." It wasn't the fresh air he wanted. He needed someone to watch his back.

She followed him out of his cabin quietly. No smirking little smile, no secrets glittering in her eyes. What was the little minx up to *now*? She was up to something, he'd be a fool to doubt it.

Drago ordered the bonds on the Tristan removed so he could lend a hand on the lines if needed. For now, however, he stood protectively over his siblings near the main mast, where Drago was shuffling cards on an overturned crate.

"Now then, what are we playing for, little skirt?" he asked.

"Freedom," Tristan said, taking a seat by the crate.

"This ship," Stevie added.

Drago held up his hand. "Jacqueline has requested to play me in a game of Baccarat. No one else." He glanced at the boy. "Julian, what is my hard and fast rule?"

Julian plunged his hands into his pockets. "Never gamble anything you can't afford to lose."

"Correct. Therefore, I will not play for my ship or your freedom."

Jacqueline perched on an upside-down bucket. "I want your promise. Promise you won't kill anyone in my family."

Drago stopped shuffling. "That's it?"

Jacqueline's eyes widened. She'd messed up, but she wasn't sure how. "Not you or any man from your crew," she added in a rush.

"So *that's* all, then?" He shuffled the cards again and set them down at the center of the crate.

Julian leaned over and whispered in her ear.

"Step back," Drago ordered. "You know I won't allow the two of you against me."

"Smart man," Tristan muttered. He gave his little sister a quick wink, and she gave him a tremulous half-smile in return.

The little skirt looked at Tristan in a way Drago could only describe as conspiratorial. He folded his arms across his chest. Time to flush the little quail out of the grass.

He looked at her. "So, if I wished, I could put your family in a longboat and release them in the middle of the Indian Ocean with no food, water or oars, as long as I or my crew refrained from killing them?"

Jacqueline gasped. "No! They would die!"

Drago shrugged.

"You must give me your word they won't be harmed," she said.

"You have already placed your bet," he countered.

She pointed at him, glaring her indignation. "But you didn't accept it!"

"Ah, then. So I didn't." He dealt the cards. "Therefore, I will agree to not harm—"

"*Never*. Never harm," Jacqueline corrected.

He cleared his throat and threw her a dark look. "I agree to never harm—"

Jacqueline tapped her finger on the crate. "In fact, I want your promise to protect my family with your *life*."

He sighed. "Agreed. I'll protect your family, if I lose."

"Yes." She nodded and folded her hands on her lap.

He sat back and crossed his arms. "What do I get when I win?" This should be interesting. She had nothing he wanted, as far as he knew. He looked up in time to catch a significant look between the two older siblings. Perhaps he was assuming incorrectly.

Jacqueline swallowed, then took a deep breath before raising her chin and looking him square in the eye. "Me."

CHAPTER 12

11 November 1720

Dear Father,
Jack and the crew of the Gallant *remain dead drunk and useless now,*
some have drunk themselves to their death, and good riddance. We dumped
all remaining spirits overboard, in hopes the crew will become sober
enough to flee the harbor.
Mary and I have completed our task ashore. Most importantly, Robert the
cook died today. Sadly, we had to bury him in the kirkyard of the
old Helshire church, which had recently burned down near Savanna.
The cemetery is surrounded by a waist-high iron fence and a tall gate
featuring twisted rails and spires, upon which is a shield engraved with a
waterfall flowing from a cave surrounded by roses. We think he'd have
liked that, since he had an affection for roses.
Please keep my letters and journal in a safe place. I hope to one day tell you
the details behind them.

Your daughter,
Anne

✳

They were almost there.

Conal trailed Bernard up the narrow, dusty path. Harvey limped along behind them, muttering to himself about being too old to walk so far with a barely healed leg. An island resident leading a burro laden with cut sugar cane had given them directions to the old graveyard. An hour later, they finally reached it.

The Helshire churchyard still stood alone, surrounded by a rusty stone and iron fence. The charred rubble of the church was now covered with a hundred years of vegetation. Conal looked up as they passed under the ornate metal arch, expecting to see flowery ironwork with a waterfall and rose blossoms; he didn't.

Gabriel and Adrian stopped and perused the iron arch as well. "This can't be the right place," Gabriel said. "Where are the roses? And the waterfall?"

Bernard frowned. "Spread out and look around."

Conal searched for a headstone of a "Roberts" or a "Robertson". He found nothing. He didn't have time for a wild goose chase. Maybe they misunderstood the letter. Perhaps it was in some sort of code they had not yet deciphered.

Oddly, it was the one man among them who couldn't read who found the marker. "What's this one say?" Harvey asked, pointing.

Bernard paused beside the old sailor and read a headstone out loud. "Let the Lamb lie near the mouth of the lion. Let roses mark the victor. Robert Cook, a Gallant man, died a pauper. May Calypso reunite him with his wife, Rose."

"What does that mean?" Gabriel asked. "It makes no sense."

Adrian pushed a shovel in his brother's hand. "Who cares? Just dig."

It took the younger men about two hours before the shovel struck something solid. Adrian knelt and used his knife to find the edges.

"It's definitely not a coffin," Gabriel muttered, deflated. "Unless Robert the cook was the size of a chicken."

A few minutes later, Adrian lifted a small chain-wrapped wooden box to Bernard and shook his head in disgust. "There can't be much in there, it's not very heavy."

Bernard used a shovel to break the chain and lifted the lid. The droop of his shoulders and the disappointment on his face told Conal everything he needed to know. Nothing was inside.

Gabriel reached down and pulled out a piece of folded parchment and a sealed bottle. He opened the parchment and stared, shaking his head. "It's a map, but..."

They all huddled around Gabriel. Conal glanced at the map and understood the boy's confusion. It was a drawing of a path through a mountain, a lake and a rock ledge all leading to the opening of a cave. That was it. There were no words stating the location, towns nearby or markers. Jamaica was a big island. It could take months to search it. It might be a sketch of somewhere else entirely. Only Anne Bonny and Mary Read knew how to follow this map. This entire venture had been a waste of time. Acid churned in Conal's gut. No treasure lie buried here; which meant they had nothing to use to barter with the pirates.

Conal cursed under his breath. "I have to return to the cove." He turned to Harvey and Bernard. "I'll send Adrian back with the longboat for you two." He had a decision to make. Well, he'd already decided, he just (regretfully) had to execute it.

Harvey plopped down on the pile of newly dug earth and lifted the bottle out of the box. He shook it next to his ear, then broke the wax seal and pulled out the cork with what few teeth he had left. He sniffed it before taking a tentative sip. "Bernard, bring yer old flea-infested carcass over here and try some of this swill. Goes down smooth as honey."

Cursing his stupidity and the false hope that there would be something under that headstone they could use as leverage, Conal took off down the slope at a trot, followed by Adrian and Gabriel.

Now he would have to do the one thing he'd sworn he'd never do while he still drew breath.

Give up his beloved *Seeker*.

"No!" Stevie lurched to her feet, heart hammering against her ribs. "Jacqueline, no! You can't put yourself as a prize. I won't allow it." Her voice shook with shock and horror.

Gampo gave her a bored look then turned his attention back to the girl. "I accept your terms," he said to Jacqueline, removing his jacket and rolling up his sleeves.

Stevie stepped toward him. "Take me instead," she said.

"No," Tristan interrupted. "I'll do it." He extended his hand to Gampo. "I'll serve on your crew for the next five years if she loses."

The pirate laughed and shuffled the cards. "That's very noble, but I've already accepted the little chick's terms."

Tristan stood and glared at Jacqueline, fists clenching at his sides. "Take it back, Biscuit. Step away from the table." One of Gampo's men shoved him back down and pressed a knife against his throat. Another stepped up behind Stevie. There would be no bargaining.

One fact gave Stevie a bit of solace. Family seemed to matter to Gampo; he'd spent years searching for his sister. Perhaps she could appeal to the pirate's softer side, if he had one. Aside from her silent prayers, there wasn't much more she could do. She directed her plea to the black-hearted brigand. "Please, for the love of God, don't take a little girl from her family." She held her breath, praying she had poked at least a small tender place in his soul.

Gampo sliced his stormy glare to her and snorted in response. Then, the heartless pirate returned his attention to her baby sister and dealt the cards.

A small hand reached down and thumped the makeshift table. "I go where Jacqueline goes," Julian said, and moved to stand behind his twin. Stevie clenched her jaw and shut her eyes to hide the raw despair that scraped her heart. She couldn't loose them both again.

Gampo studied him a moment, tilted his head in acknowledgment, then flipped his cards. "A knave and a six. Dealer shall draw another card," Gampo said. He dealt himself a queen.

Jacqueline leaned forward and grinned. "A worthless queen. You stay at six." She flipped her two cards. "I have a nine and an eight." She looked up at Gampo. "Seventeen, then drop the tens. I have a seven. I win this hand!"

Jacqueline grinned at Tristan, who returned her smile, but his eyes were worried and the skin around his mouth tight. Stevie's stomach was in knots. If she'd have had anything to eat at all, she'd be heaving it over the rail right now.

The game went on, and Tristan and Jacqueline looked hard at every card Gampo drew until there were six cards left.

Jacqueline was winning by two points, but she was chewing her lip. Tristan rubbed his forehead and mouthed a prayer. Obviously things weren't going as well as they should be, but Stevie couldn't fathom why.

Gampo dealt two cards to Jacqueline and himself. They flipped them.

Jacqueline took one look and covered her face with her hands. Gampo's smile spread across his face like blood flowing from a vein. She had a king and an ace. One point. He turned over his cards: ten and two.

"Dealer has two," Gampo said. "Player has one. Dealer has to draw another card."

Two cards left.

Jacqueline looked at Tristan then at the cards. "Four or queen," she murmured.

Gampo froze, his mouth agape. "You've been *counting* the

cards?"

She and Tristan made eye contact again. Tristan's mouth twitched.

Gampo narrowed his eyes at Jacqueline. "You've been taking me for a fool. The past few times we played, were you losing intentionally?"

Jacqueline lifted a little shoulder.

Gampo gawked at the girl. "You *have*! You've been letting me win so when the stakes were highest, I'd be overconfident in my skill to best you."

The table went totally silent. Gampo's men crowded closer to the upturned crate. Stevie's breath froze in her lungs. What would the pirate do now? Would he cry foul and end the game, then toss them overboard just for spite? The boys could swim, but she and her sister could not.

Gampo shocked her by throwing his head back and laughing heartily. "Well, I'll be a bloody dawcock." He leaned forward and put his hand over the unturned cards and let it hover there. "So, if I draw the queen, I lose. If I draw the four, I win. Care to up the stakes? Maybe throw your pretty sister in with your fate?"

Jacqueline's eyes flashed and the vein on the side of her throat pulsed.

Stevie's mouth went dry. "Take me *instead*." She shifted her gaze to Jacqueline. Although terrified, the girl was as still as an ice sculpture. Where had her little sister found all this courage and composure?

Jacqueline flicked her eyes to Tristan and back. "Only if you put in your boat as well."

Gampo sat back and rubbed his chin. Some men standing behind him grinned, others shifted their weight and gave each other sideways glances.

"I'll put up my boat with the condition that I keep it until I take the *Seeker*," he finally stated.

Jacqueline crossed her arms. "No."

He leaned back and looked around him. "She's a fine vessel. You're a fo'c's'le-head if you think different."

Jacqueline shrugged with her palms up, as if the entire world knew what she was about to reveal. "It could take you *another* twenty years before you take the *Seeker*. You've already spent that many trying to rescue your sister. Honestly, I don't think it's something you're very good at."

Several guffaws escaped from the crew before Gampo's glare silenced them.

He locked eyes with Jacqueline. "As you wish, but I'll not chance losing the *Dragon*. If you win, I'll make sure no harm comes to you or your family. If I win, then you will belong to me."

"No!" Stevie stepped forward, even as Gampo's men started toward her. "Take me instead. *Please*, Captain, she's just a child. She doesn't realize what she's doing."

Gampo never took his eyes from Jacqueline's. "I think you're wrong, Miss Sauvage. This little lamb knows *exactly* what she's doing."

He flipped the next card.

Stevie's ears went numb. A strange roar filled her head as she stared at the four of hearts.

Jacqueline's face paled. "You win," the little girl whispered.

BERNARD TOOK another swig from the bottle and handed it back to Harvey, all the while staring at the headstone. "We've missed something, I tell you."

Harvey snorted. "Ye've been saying that fer the last hour, ye wooden-headed dolt." He took a gulp then held the bottle out for Bernard to take, but the man just kept staring at the words on the headstone. Harvey sighed. "Read the letter out loud again, Bernie."

Bernard pulled the letter from his pocket and began to read:

. . .

"MOST IMPORTANTLY, Robert the cook died today. Sadly, we had to bury him in the kirkyard of the old Helshire church, which had recently burned down near Savanna. The cemetery is surrounded by a waist-high iron fence and a tall gate featuring twisted rails and spires, upon which is a shield engraved with a waterfall flowing from a cave surrounded by roses. We think he'd have liked that, since he had an affection for roses."

"WHAT'S the reason fer mentioning the waterfall, cave and roses?" Harvey asked. He gestured to the arch at the front of the cemetery. "The gate don't even have no roses on it!"

"We've missed something," Bernard muttered.

"Yes, so ye've said enough times to git it through even my block skull," Harvey responded, tossing a fistful of dirt back into the grave. He gazed at the headstone, its carvings rounded by age and elements. It stood slightly askew now, nudged sideways by the young men digging earlier. He peered closer. There was a design stamped on the lower left side of the stone.

"Hold this." Harvey handed the bottle to Bernard and crawled over the dirt pile to the headstone. He brushed away the loose soil. The top of a circle? He scampered off the pile and limped over to grab a shovel.

"What are you doing, you dull-headed ape?" Bernard asked. "Are you thinking there's something hidden under the *stone?*"

"Shut yer trap and come over 'ere nd help me dig out this bloody thing," Harvey grunted.

Bernard complied, and the two cleared the soil away from the headstone. Harvey dropped to his hands and knees and began to brush away the dirt and moss. He reached out his hand. "Gimme that bottle."

Bernard looked at the bottle then at Harvey. He handed it over. "You'd best know what you're doing. That's a bloody good bottle of truth, right there."

"If I'm right, I'll buy ye fifty more," Harvey said as he splashed the edge of the headstone with the rum.

Bernard leaned in closer. Harvey ran his fingers through the grooves and sucked in his breath. "See ye that?" he whispered. "I don't need ter know how ter read ter know what *that* is." A circle. Inside the circle was an 'x' and on top of it...a cross. A fleur-de-lis had been etched above the top center spike of the cross.

"You certainly don't," Bernard breathed, looking at the symbol carved into the stone.

"Yer Anne Bonny weren't talkin' about no flowery roses," Harvey said. "She was meanin' the compass rose." He pointed to the headstone. "What's the stone say again?"

Bernard scrambled closer. "Let the Lamb lie near the mouth of the Lion. Let roses mark the victor."

Harvey wrinkled his forehead in thought. "Is that there a bible verse?"

Bernard shook his head. "I don't think so."

"Then it's a clue. Read the next line."

"Robert Cook, a Gallant man, died a pauper."

"*Gallant* were the name of her ship, right?" Harvey asked.

Bernard nodded his agreement. "I wonder if it means there's no treasure buried with him."

"Could be, since there weren't none," Harvey growled, pulling a folded map from the sack left behind by the *Seeker's* captain. "Let the Lamb lie near the mouth of the Lion. Let roses mark the victor." Harvey repeated, placing Captain O'Brien's map next to Anne Bonny's hand drawn one.

Harvey straightened and looked out over the channel between Jamaica and Lamb's Tail Island, then tapped Anne Bonny's map. "This island is Lamb's Tail, I'm sure of it. This drawing shows the major inlets, and the rounded mountain." Harvey gestured toward the island. "Ye can't see it in the dark now, but about a quarter of the way down, there's a cave called the Lion's Maw."

Bernard's mouth dropped open. "The mouth of the lion."

"Aye," Harvey whispered in excitement. "Read the last."

"May Calypso reunite him with his wife, Rose." Bernard looked up. "There's the mention of a rose again."

Harvey jabbed the parchment. "This here map leads into the cave. I ain't ever been in it, but Cap'n Gampo has used it to hold bounty and lay low in times of strife. Rumor has it he were trapped in there once by Persian pirates when he were young."

Bernard's eyes brightened. "Danged if your jellyfish brain has finally woke up." He ran his fingers over the headstone, then slapped his knee. "We need to get back to Brendan's ship so we can use his tools." He pointed a shaking finger toward the island off the coast. "Because that treasure is hidden somewhere in *that* cave on Lamb's Tail Island."

"No!" Harvey waved the previously buried, roughly drawn map in Bernard's face. "We don't need no fancy tools!" he cried, straightening. He pointed to the finely detailed compass rose drawn on the map and then to the headstone. "We just need to look for the compass rose!"

Bernard's eyes widened. He threw his hands up and whooped. Harvey echoed his glee, then both men locked elbows and twirled a jig.

They gathered their supplies and left the cemetery. "I hope Adrian isn't too tired from rowing the longboat," Bernard panted, scrambling down the path toward the water. "Because we will need him to row us to Lamb's Tail Island."

"THIS SECRET CAVE has been used for decades by pirates and slave traders," Gampo said, carefully picking his way down the narrow stairs. "Many have attempted to navigate the labyrinth of passage-ways, sheer drops, underground lakes and other perils; few have succeeded."

The dim light of the lantern bounced off the cool stone walls as Stevie followed Gampo into the lower level of his house. After unlocking a heavy iron door on the main floor, he led them down the steps. His men prodded them to follow.

They rounded a turn and Stevie gasped. She stared into the gaping opening of a cave. The surrounding walls glistened with water. She brushed a damp wall with her fingers, then touched them to her tongue. Fresh water.

Gampo spread his arms and twirled in the center of the room. "Welcome to your new abode."

A jolt of panic shot through Stevie's chest. "You're leaving us here?"

Gampo grunted. "I don't need the distraction on my ship," he finally retorted. He nodded toward Jacqueline. "She'll be safer here as well. There are things to eat if you look. You'll have access to fresh water if you have the courage to seek it."

Jacqueline's lip quivered.

"Stop that," Gampo snapped, storm cloud eyes darkening. "I'm being more than generous and kinder than you deserve. I could have sent your family down to Davy Jones' locker after you lost." He grasped her shoulders and pushed her toward Stevie. "Your family has remained unharmed, although the temptation has been hard to resist." He sliced a glare at Stevie.

Stevie grabbed Jacqueline and hugged her tightly. That rogue of a pirate!

Gampo took a step toward the stairs, then spoke over his shoulder, this time only to Jacqueline. "You are to stay until I return to claim you, little poppet. I have a sea battle to plan and don't need the added responsibility of a child aboard, especially a girl-child. It makes the crew nervous." He paused at the first step and turned to face the little girl. "Do you remember the story I told you about a cave I was once trapped in as a young man?"

Jacqueline nodded, eyes wide.

"I'm fairly certain it was this very cave."

CHAPTER 13

17 November 1720

Dear Father,
Sadly, this might be my last correspondence. Captain Barnet ambushed us and captured our vessel without even raising his sword. Although we outnumbered them, the worthless dogs that were our crew cowered in the boat's belly. Mary and I fought as best we could, but we were two against too many. They have taken us to stand trial in front of His Majesty's chief magistrate. Since they saw us fighting Barnet's men, our story that they took us against our will is no longer believable. It's likely we will all be sentenced to hang.
Pray for us, Father.

Your daughter,
Anne

*

Conal cursed. He cursed his luck. He cursed Gampo. He cursed himself for being stupid enough to believe they would find a treasure buried in that forgotten graveyard. He cursed the silver-eyed, dark-haired, pirate heiress who'd gotten him into all this.

He shouted at Remus from the gun deck as he and Brendan finished tying the last two guns nose to nose. "Are the chains fast and locks on?"

"Aye, Captain!"

There was no time to remove all the guns from the *Seeker*, so they did their best to make them difficult for Gampo to use. Securing them together with the mouths of the guns kissing seemed to be the easiest and fastest. All that was left to do, was to sail the *Seeker* over to the sheltered side of Lamb's Tail Island and leave her for Gampo to discover.

It would be easy enough to spy on them from the island to see if Gampo took the Sauvages with him or not. It's likely Gampo wouldn't want to deal with keeping a watch on them, and would leave them behind. At least he hoped the pirate would. It's what he'd do, but expecting the brigand to have any honor seemed like a fool's hope. His gut clenched at a darker thought, that they'd been left behind because they were dead. Conal cursed himself again for wasting all that time trekking up and back to the Helshire graveyard. He checked the horizon. Only a few hours of daylight left.

Brendan cupped his hands around his mouth. "All hands! All hands to the *Reward*," he bellowed.

The men swarmed over the planks from the *Seeker* to the *Reward*, leaving Conal and Gabriel behind. They released the grappling hooks, and soon the *Reward* was sweeping away toward the cove's shelter to await the *Desire* and her turn to attack.

Conal took the helm and guided his ship out of the Helshire harbor and around the point toward the west side Lamb's Tail island. Gampo's ship hovered at anchor near the southern side. It would take time for Gampo's watch to report sighting the *Seeker*, giving Gabriel and Conal the opportunity to paddle the last remaining canoe to the island. From there, it was a matter of waiting until Gampo and his men raised the *Dragon's* sheets and sailed to the *Seeker*, before stealing into the pirate's stronghold.

Once they reached the drop point, Conal gave a shout to Gabriel, who ran along the starboard side of the ship, pulling out the belaying pins while Conal did likewise on the port side. Sails dropped to the deck like gigantic snowflakes and the *Seeker* suddenly slowed. Conal released the anchor and the ship's bow nearly stopped, allowing the aft end of the ship to swing slowly around so the bow faced the island.

A SHORT TIME LATER, Conal and Gabriel pulled the canoe across the sand and into the underbrush of Gampo's island. Ahead was the mile or so hike around the perimeter to the low house crouched against the mountain's southern side.

Conal looked back at the *Seeker*. Her long, sleek lines rose proudly above the gentle ocean waves. She swayed, strong and elegant, brave and fierce.

He would miss her.

He nodded to Gabriel, and they began walking. If all Gampo wanted was the *Seeker*, then he had her. There was no reason for the pirate to keep hostages. Conal ground his jaw. If the yellow-bellied dog hurt any of them, he'd not live to see the next sunrise.

GAMPO and his men ascended the steps and departed. A scrape, a clank, and then a key clicking in a lock echoed in the chamber. Tristan bounded up to follow. Stevie didn't expect him to be able to open the heavy iron door, but she held her breath anyway, hoping.

He stomped slowly back down. "Now what?"

Jacqueline was biting her lip and looking into the cave, her little brow furrowed. "Julian, do you remember—" She spun and looked around. "Where's Julian?"

Dear God! Stevie whirled, searching the dark recesses of the cellar. "Julian!"

No answer.

"He escaped," Tristan said in an almost jovial tone. "How about that?" He bounded back up the steps. "Hey! Anyone out there? Jules?"

They'd left the *Dragon* in two longboats. Stevie had stayed with Jacqueline. "Tristan, was Julian in your boat?"

He slowly shook his head. "I thought both the little twins were together with you."

Jacqueline paled. "He's stowed away aboard Gampo's ship," she whispered. "I just know it."

"That little scamp," Tristan growled. "I should take a strap to his hide once I get my hands on him."

Worse, what would Gampo do to him once he found him? Stevie had to admit the man could have been much crueler to the children. They'd been well-cared-for and fed. Perhaps Julian was in less danger from the pirate himself. However, if Gampo sought the *Seeker,* then they'd certainly engage in a battle. What if Conal exacted his revenge by firing upon Gampo's ship? What if he raked a swath of destruction across the deck, rather than the sails?

Stevie clenched her hands into fists. Conal *abandoned* them. His velvet touch and silky kisses had clouded her judgement, she'd been eager to believe that he'd help her retrieve the little ones. He had convinced her he was a man of honor and integrity.

Well, she'd been wrong once before. Apparently she didn't learn from her mistakes very well.

At the moment, even *Gampo's* character was more respectable than Conal O'Brien's. At least that wicked pirate was a man of his word. Strange thing...to think about a pirate being an honorable man. Would he return to release them, or would he leave them to their fate? What if he engaged in battle with Conal and lost? No one would know where Gampo had hidden them. There'd be no one to unlock the door. And Julian...what would happen to him?

She straightened. If they were to get out of here, they'd have to find a way to escape. What had Gampo said about the cave? She turned and looked at the black opening about the size of a pig. Dark, small spaces hid snakes...she almost shuddered, but didn't. Stevie squared her shoulders instead. She would do everything in her power to get them out of this cellar and to get Julian back. Conal had called her a scared little rabbit once.

He'd been right, then.

But she wasn't scared anymore.

CONAL AND GABRIEL shrank back into the foliage near Gampo's stronghold. Men were shouting and running to longboats beached in front of the house. They'd spotted the *Seeker* and were off to take her.

Conal studied the house. "My guess is Gampo has your family locked somewhere inside. He'd want them out of the way so his crew could focus on their duties."

"There he is." Gabriel hissed, pointing to a dark-haired figure striding toward a longboat.

The pirate walked like a prince, shouting orders and setting the entire place into motion as only a highly respected—or feared—leader could. Conal had never met Gampo, yet he had a grudging respect for the way the pirate led his men. Short, quick commands were quickly carried out with vigor and pride.

Within the hour, Gampo and his men were scampering up the

side of the *Dragon* and setting the sheets. A few minutes later, the ship was pulling at her tethers. Once the anchor was raised, she spread her wings and flew. Conal and Gabriel waited until the sails disappeared around the western point.

Conal expelled a breath. "At least now, if we accidentally alert any guards left behind, Gampo's out of range and far enough away to give us time to get in and get out with your family," he said, plunging through the lush foliage toward the house. He tried not to think about Stevie and her siblings lying bound and bloody somewhere inside.

They fought through the thick brush, staying hidden in the fringes rather than exposing themselves with an approach from the beach. The usual birds' songs and squawks were missing. Leaves didn't even twitch on the trees and bushes. A warning tremor skittered up Conal's spine.

Something was off.

Using hand signals, he and Gabriel attempted to scout around the house. About twenty feet away, both drew up short. So much for the plan to approach the house from the sides or back.

Gampo's hideaway didn't have sides or a back.

He had built the dwelling *into* the mountain.

"The only way in is through the front," Conal breathed in surprise. "But, it'd be suicide to try to break in that way."

Gabriel perused the structure. "Then let's not break in."

Conal arched a brow. "What do you have in mind?"

"JACQUELINE? WHERE DID YOU GO?" Tristan was on his knees, shouting into the black passage.

"In the cave!" a small voice echoed back. "Captain Gampo told us about it. There's a trail somewhere that leads out!"

Gampo had said this cave was filled with dark, dangerous labyrinths and dead ends, steep drops and deep pools.

There would be snakes.

"Wait!" Stevie yelled. She dropped to her knees and squirmed into the opening. Her skirt impeded her progress enough within the first few feet that she backed out impatiently, thankful she wore her britches beneath.

Tristan grabbed her arm. "What are you doing?"

She looked back to her brother's worried face. "I have to go with her. She can't wander in there alone," she said, dropping the skirt and kicking it away.

"We'll need light," Tristan said. He lifted a small, unlit torch. "It was in a box next to the wall. As soon as I get it lit, I'll follow."

Stevie dropped back down to her knees and scampered into the tunnel.

"It gets bigger after a little while." Jacqueline's voice sounded far away.

The uneven rock dug into her palms and knees. "Jacquie, don't move on yet. I'm following you, but wait for me!"

"I will." The little voice echoed ahead.

Stevie should have been frightened, apprehensive, probably even terrified. But now, all she could think about was making sure Jacqueline stayed safe and unharmed. She continued to grope on her hands and knees. The air cooled as she crawled along. A slight whoosh of a breeze hit her face, and she sensed more that saw the blackness expand around her. "Jacquie?"

A little hand grasped Stevie's arm. "I'm here. You can stand now."

A faint glow from the small tunnel and a lot of coughing told them Tristan finally got the torch lit. When he poked the torch out of the opening, she took it and held it high while he scrambled to his feet.

"Wow," he said as he stood, scanning the cavern.

Ahead of them were two passages. At the junction sat a wooden crate. Jacqueline reached for the lid.

Stevie grabbed her arm. "Wait! What if there's something

dangerous in there, like snakes?" When did this little girl suddenly get so reckless?

Jacqueline stepped back while Tristan took the tip of his boot and flipped up the lid, jumping back at almost the same time. He stuck his neck forward and peeked inside.

"No snakes," he breathed, then glanced up at his smirking little sister. "If there were, Biscuit, I would have twisted it into a nice necklace for you."

Jacqueline giggled then pulled out a lantern. "Gampo told us stories about this place. The first time he was here, he chose the passage on the right..."

"Fine, then," Tristan said, striding into the tunnel.

Jacqueline began rooting through the crate, pulling out another lantern, a torch and matches. "But it was the wrong way," she muttered almost to herself, and then, "Where is the rope?"

"Whoa!" From inside the passage, Tristan's voice raised an octave and actually cracked. Seconds later, he emerged, pale and shaking, then leaned against the wall and slithered down until he sat in a position resembling a neglected rag doll. He jerked a thumb toward the tunnel. "There's a tiny ledge and a deep crevice that way. I'm fairly certain going right is *wrong*, Biscuit."

Stevie turned to Jacqueline. "What other stories did that evil pirate tell you about this cave?" Gampo's cryptic remarks as he exited the cellar gave Stevie cause to worry. Persian pirates...

Her sister had a confident tilt to her chin. "I really don't think he's evil." She went back to rummaging around in the crate. "We'll need a rope and another torch," she said, pulling a coil from the crate. "Here's one."

Tristan raised a brow and gave her a pointed look. "Anything else you'd like to tell us?"

Her slight shoulder lifted. "According to Captain Gampo, there are a lot of wrong turns."

Tristan just closed his eyes and leaned his head back against the rock. "Excellent news, that."

Stevie lit the lantern. "Then how will we know which ones to take?"

Jacqueline's eyes widened and her voice lowered. "He said the *only* way out is to track the bloody hand, then follow the flight of the bats."

Tristan made the sign of the cross. "Lord, save us." He stared at the black mouth of the other passage. "*Bats?*"

Perhaps Stevie's kinder instincts she'd had earlier regarding Gampo had been slightly askew. Bloody hands and bats sounded more like a ghost story, not markers to a way out. She looked at both passages and then to the narrow, cramped tunnel leading back to their cell. Either they followed the passage, or returned to the cellar and prayed someone other than a pirate came to let them out. Eventually.

Tristan echoed her thoughts. "Well, I'd rather press on, than go back." He pushed to his feet, handed Stevie the torch, took the lantern, and gestured to the opening to the left. "After you, then." He cleared his throat at Stevie's eye roll. "I'll follow and watch everyone's back." He swallowed and scratched his ear. "In case bats or bloody hands attack from the rear."

CHAPTER 14

Journal entry
18 November 1720

His Majesty's chief magistrate, has sentenced the crew of the Gallant *to hang. Jack and his men were led to the gallows this morning. Mary and I were told that their heads were put on the harbor pikes. Mary pleaded for her husband's life. She admitted to the court that he'd been taken by us from a prize ship against his will, but the magistrate hasn't a merciful hair on his head. Mary is sick with grief.*

"Hoy there!" Conal approached Gampo's house from the beach, waving an arm.

There was no sight of a watch or even a solitary guard. It was possible they were all inside, but that seemed careless. A few yards away, Gabriel crept under the window to an area near the front door, dragging a short club with him.

Conal waved again. "Anyone? I've lost me skiff! I fell asleep, and a wave came in and took her. Can I borrow a rig to get me to the main island? I'd be grateful, and would give ye my next catch, I would!"

Nothing.

Why would Gampo depart without leaving a watch behind? Conal's heart froze in his chest. Gampo wouldn't abandon a viable stronghold. Had the pirate set explosives? He began to run toward the house, ignoring Gabriel's slashing hand.

The door opened, and an old woman teetered out. "Oh!"

Conal stopped short of driving his shoulder through the door. Eyes wide, he folded is hands in front of him like an errant schoolboy. "Um...hullo, mistress."

"Méré de Dieu!" The woman braced one hand on the door-frame, the other over her heart. "Me faire peur à la mort!"

It wasn't his intention to scare the poor woman to death. His French wasn't very good, but he'd do his best. Maybe she would understand hand gestures. "Je suis à la recherche pour les enfants." *I'm looking for children.* He placed his palm about the height of the twins.

"Oui!" The woman clapped. She continued to speak in a rush.

The best he could make out was that the children were here, but had to stay until Gampo returned. He and Gabriel were welcome to wait inside. She tottered back into the house and down the hall, leaving Conal and Gabriel at the doorway, baffled.

The two looked at each other than entered.

"This is a trap," Gabriel muttered.

Conal leaned in to glance past the small entranceway. "Of course it is, but what choice do we have? This is the only way in." He crept inside and Gabriel followed. The faint sound of a ticking clock drew him to a small parlor. He took in the marble fireplace, the mantel clock, and the portrait hanging above them.

"Empty." He withdrew.

"Captain O'Brien!" Gabriel shouted in a whisper from down the hall. He was standing in front of an iron door, peering through a small square opening at the top. "There are steps leading down.

I can smell smoke and lamp oil. Someone has been there recently." He stepped away for Conal to look.

It appeared to be a cell carved out of the rock. Conal pulled on the latch.

"Locked," Gabriel said. "I already tried." He pulled a small stiletto from his boot and squatted in front of the lock. A few seconds later, there was a click, and he pushed the door open.

"You pick locks?" For some reason, this surprised Conal. Impressive.

"Tristan showed me," Gabriel said proudly. "I am supposed to be a pirate, after all."

"That's more than can be said about your cousin Stevie," Conal muttered. "Meeker than a mouse and almost as skittish."

Gabriel gave a chagrined shrug. "Uncle Bernard has coddled Stephanie a bit since she came to live with us." He started down the steps. "Her father and Uncle Bernard were brothers. Her father died of a snake bite just after the twins were born. Her mother remarried, but the man was cruel to them."

She'd been abused? Conal ground his teeth until his jaw ached. The need to punch something had him clenching his fists. "Where was Tristan when their stepfather was abusing Stevie and her mother?" He had little patience for men who were cowards or bullies. In fact, if they took their anger out on women, both were one and the same as far as he was concerned.

Gabriel glanced at Conal over his shoulder. "Tristan had already left home to work at the gaming house. Once their mother remarried, he believed they'd all be properly cared for."

The cell was damp and dark. Conal located the lantern and raised the wick, which bounced a glittering yellow light off the walls. Stevie deserved a better life than that.

Gabriel stared at the dark tunnel. "Why would Gampo lock them in here, if they could escape through there?"

Conal shook his head. "It makes little sense, unless the tunnel doesn't lead anywhere."

Gabriel looked back up toward the iron door, thinking out loud. "Is that door to keep the residents from using the tunnel, or to keep people from entering the house through the tunnel?"

Conal crouched in front of the opening and lifted the lantern to peer in. A loud click sounded from the top of the stairs. The two looked at each other.

The old woman had locked them in.

"Now we know the answer to your question," Conal said. "It's protecting those in the house."

Gabriel turned his attention back to the opening in the wall. "Then we now know this leads to a way out." He took the lantern and crawled into the tunnel.

"The next question is," Conal grunted as he followed Gabriel on his hands and knees. "How hard will it be to find it?"

DRAGO STUDIED the deck of the *Seeker* through the glass. Sheets covered the decks like the wings of weeping angels. Nothing moved, making the ship look abandoned and forlorn. Were the men of the *Seeker* hiding below , ready to attack?

According to Stevie Sauvage, her family had taken O'Brien's ship after a good portion of the crew had been dispatched to shore. Then, they sent most of those remaining adrift in a long-boat. They'd sailed the *Seeker* here with less than twenty men. Even if O'Brien was stubborn enough to engage him, he'd be outnumbered three to one.

"Prepare to board!" Drago shouted. It was time for answers.

His men scrambled to ready grappling hooks and planks. When the *Dragon* drifted close enough, they hooked the rail of the *Seeker* and secured her. Drago boarded along with thirty men and searched the ship. He descended to the lower deck, but when he took in the guns and the way they'd been lashed together, he spun on his heel, roaring orders to return to the *Dragon*.

It's a trap.

With the *Dragon* tied to her, the *Seeker* had suddenly turned from prize to predator. Drago was helpless to defend his ship while attached. They sat still in the water like a wounded duck.

Just as Drago climbed up to the main deck and scoured the horizon, a cold fist clenched his stomach. The *Reward sped* toward him from the leeward side of the island, effectively trapping him between the *Seeker* and the shore. On her larboard side flew Captain Hart's brig the *Desire*, who was even now beginning a slow turn to show her broadside guns.

He growled in frustration as he bounded over the boards back to his ship, shouting orders to load the guns and haul up the sheets.

"Captain Gampo!"

He whirled at the sound of Julian's voice. "What are you doing on my ship!" he bellowed. This was no place for the boy. This wasn't the Royal bloody Navy. He didn't use powder boys on his vessel. Especially this boy. Jules was barely eight years old, for heaven's sake.

Julian didn't even flinch at Drago's shout. "I want to join your crew and learn how to be a privateer like you!" He ran up, holding out Drago's pistols.

Drago snatched the guns from the boy's hands and shoved them in his belt, then grabbed Julian's arm and dragged him to the side of the ship. "You are too young to sail with me, Master Sauvage. Instead, I prefer you to stand watch over our prize ship, the *Seeker.*"

Drago had fully intended to toss the boy to the *Seeker's* deck, but his men were already shoving off. There was no way he could throw the boy fifteen feet safely. Cursing, he turned and dragged Julian toward his cabin. "A change of plan is in order. You shall remain in my cabin and defend my charts."

A high-pitched whistling made Drago duck and cover Julian.

Chain shot tore through the top mizzen mast, sending shards of wood raining down on them.

"Four and six guns, fire!" Drago yelled. "Fire at will!"

A loud explosion sent tremors through the deck planks, and a thick black cloud roiled over them as his gunners returned fire. He ran toward his cabin, hauling Julian with him, and paused when he reached the door. He grasped the boy by the shoulders. "I keep my charts under my bed. I want you to hide with them and stay there, hear me? Stay there!"

The boy shook his head, wide-eyed and pale. "I want to help!"

Another volley hit his upper sheets, ripping through the lines and leaving the sails peppered with holes. He shoved the boy in the cabin. "Go! That's an order!"

They were trapped. The *Reward* and the *Desire* hovered just out of the range of his long guns, but still poised to fire a full broadside should he try to make for the open sea.

Therefore, Drago did the only thing he could; he lowered his sails and surrendered. Chances were they wouldn't fire on their own merchant ship as mercilessly as they would on the *Dragon*, so he eased his vessel closer to the *Seeker,* putting her between them.

Finally he'd have a face-to-face opportunity to call out Fynn Ahern once and for all. Even if the man was truly dead, he'd find out what had happened to his sister, if he had to draw and quarter every man on board for answers.

Drago glanced up at the damaged spars. Several were dangling like broken twigs. The *Dragon's* jigger mast had been blasted nearly in two. His men did their best to bring in the sheets where it was possible to do so. The *Reward* eased in for the kill.

Now, he waited.

STEVIE, Jacqueline and Tristan stood on the shore of something they had never seen before...an *underground lake*.

Tristan lifted the lantern high, revealing a dark, glassy shimmer near the shore and blackness beyond. He looked down at Jacqueline. "So...what now, Biscuit?"

She looked up at him, eyes wide. "He said to follow the bloody hand and—"

"And the bats, yes, I know," Tristan finished for her with forced patience. "But how do we get past the lake?" He picked up a large pebble. "And how big is it?" He reared back and heaved it over the water, then began counting. "One-one-thousand, two-one-thousand, three-one—"

Splunk. The faraway sound of the pebble finally falling into the lake made Tristan look at Stevie with eyes rounder than tea saucers.

Jacqueline peered along the shoreline, her voice hopeful. "Maybe there's a way to go around it."

Tristan held up the lantern. "Why do I feel like that might be a little too good to be true?" He expelled a pessimistic breath and began walking.

Stevie started to follow when a slight glow emanated from the tunnel behind them. "Tristan! Turn down the lantern!" He immediately did as he was bid. The torch hissed as Jacquie plunged it into the water to douse the flame.

The three of them darted into the dark recesses away from the tunnel, and pressed back into the gloom, against the cool rock. Stevie held her breath as two hunched shadows skittered along the wall of the tunnel then emerged on the ground, elongated and distorted by a lantern's glow.

Were they following them, or had they been locked in the cell too? Was it Gampo? Perhaps he sent his men to get them. Her heart slammed against her ribs in a frantic staccato. She sank down and felt around until her fingers brushed against a fist-sized rock. They would not capture her without a fight. She hefted it up. It wasn't much of a weapon, but it was better than nothing at all.

The figures paused. Rather than lift the lantern to see better, they lowered the light closer to the ground.

Stevie sucked in a breath. They were *definitely* tracking, looking at the footprints in the rocky sand.

"Well, I can still smell smoke from a torch, so they've been through here recently," one said.

"But to where?" the other answered.

She knew those voices! *Thank you, God*. She sagged against the wall. Conal and Gabriel! She sank to her haunches and sighed in relief, still shaking. She was momentarily confused. Why was Conal *here*? Hadn't he sailed away, leaving them to their fate with Gampo's pirates? Had he not abandoned them to save his ship?

A dawning realization told her she had been wrong.

Conal hadn't abandoned them. He was *here*.

Suddenly, Jacqueline released Stevie's hand, then hopped out into the light and squealed with joy. "Gabriel!"

Gabriel twirled then held out his arms. "Jacqueline! Where have you been? We've been looking for you everywhere!" He squatted down to look at her. "How did you fare against those wicked pirates?" He lowered his brows. "Did any of them hurt you?"

Jacqueline put her hands on his cheeks and shook her head. "Turns out they weren't pirates. They're *privateers*. So it wasn't *quite* as scary. And Captain Gampo isn't as good of a card player as he thinks he is." She glanced at her brother over her shoulder. "Isn't that right, Tristan?"

Tristan stepped into the arc of golden light. "That's right, you little gambler."

She hugged her cousin. "I missed you, Gabriel."

Tristan put his hands on his hips, a scowl darkening the already shadowed planes of his face as he glared at Gabriel. "Why aren't you with Uncle Bernard?"

"Well..." Gabriel began to bring his cousin up to date. Soon

Tristan and Gabriel were whispering, talking with their hands as much as their mouths.

A low growl near Stevie's shoulder jerked her attention away. "I have half a mind to wring your pretty little neck."

She whirled to find Conal looming next to her. Her Adonis. Golden, strong and darkly angry. Green fire sparked from his eyes. Guilt coated her chest. He knew she had betrayed him. She dropped her head. She deserved his ire.

He pulled her closer and carefully cupped her chin in his large hand and tilted her face up. Dark green eyes swirled with emotion. Anger? Pain? His voice was certainly pained. "Are ye hurt?" he rasped, sounding as if he had a slender grip on every word.

Hurt? The vision of Adrian tumbling backwards over the falls still slashed her heart. Julian was missing. Gampo was preparing for battle. Yes, she was hurt. Maybe it wasn't a visible wound, but the pain was just as excruciating. Even so, it was nothing compared to what others in her family had been through.

With a muffled oath, Conal put his arms around her and gruffly pulled her closer. "God's blood, Stevie. I feared I'd lost ye. I was afraid that Gampo—"

"I'm fine," she whispered hoarsely. Mostly, anyway.

The safe shelter of Conal's arms soothed her, and she breathed in deeply. The familiar scent of sea, sunshine and leather smelled heavenly. His skin tasted slightly salty on her lips and with a start, she realized she was kissing his neck. He pulled back and looked at her with such intensity, her stomach quivered and her knees shook. His eyes had a wild, almost panicked sheen; his hands skimmed over her shoulders and down her arms.

"Do ye have any idea what you've done to me?" he croaked, fingers gripping her hands almost painfully.

A jolt of understanding hit her like a punch to the chest. The man was on the verge of *shattering*.

He closed his eyes and sucked in a long breath. "Finding you gone nearly tore me in half." His voice became an anguished whisper. "Thoughts of ye drowning in the sea, being shot or...or...hurt by Gampo or his men...Good God, lass, I've died a hundred times already, just from the worry!"

He'd worried about her, which meant he cared about her on some level, which was strangely pleasing. He seemed glad to see her again. This went beyond a simple physical attraction, but how much beyond? Like the bond between a brother and a sister? Maybe something more?

Dared she hope?

He cupped her face and kissed her. Softly. Tenderly, as if he might break her. Stevie's heart pounded against his chest. The power in his kiss seemed to both energize and weaken her. The confusing dichotomy was oddly satisfying. Conal O'Brien drew her to him like a moth to a candle. She wanted just to be near him, and suddenly she didn't care if her wings were singed in the process. She was stronger, braver next to him. This feeling...she didn't want to forget it, ever.

Conal broke their kiss and leaned his forehead against hers. She closed her eyes and memorized the sensations fluttering over and through her body. Into the deepest, safest place, she locked these impressions. The smell of sunshine on water, the low timbre in his voice, and the jeweled glitter of his eyes all sheltered safely where she could later pull them out and relive them. If...*when* he took back his ship and sailed away, she'd at least have that small part of Conal O'Brien to cherish, remember and relive. She now had another memory to savor for later.

After everything she and her family had put Conal O'Brien through, he'd still worried about her, when she deserved to be cast aside instead. Why? It was baffling, and suddenly she needed to know.

"Why would you care what happened to me? I've stolen from you. I've lied to you." She squeezed her eyes shut, unable to put a voice to her worst sin.

I betrayed you.

Conal jerked back as if she had slapped him. "Do ye not know?" He peered at her, then cradled her face in both hands. "Ye've stolen from me, aye. You've stolen my heart, lass. I dinna have a choice but to follow where ye take it." He kissed her nose, her eyelids, her forehead, her lips. "I beg ye... next time, tell me when ye take off with it so I can follow." Those jewel-green eyes imprisoned her gaze. She couldn't look away if the cave exploded. "But will ye lie to me again and tell me ye don't love me?"

Love him? Painful awareness clenched her heart. Of course she loved him. She'd lost her heart to him ages ago. She touched his cheek and looked into his eyes for a long time. Threads of gold flared through his irises, now the color of soft moss. She stole his heart? What did that mean? Love? As a brother or something more? Better.

It couldn't be possible. Conal couldn't love a woman like her. He deserved a lady with the grace and integrity of a queen, not a kitchen maid with a penchant for disaster and piracy.

But, this man...he was a man easy to love. The vision of him the day she'd taken him hostage floated through her mind. Shoulders back, hands bound behind him, legs braced wide, standing with his men, russet hair brushing his shoulders, green tiger's eyes flashing in defiance. Voice hard and controlled. He never begged for mercy, never tried to bargain for his freedom. He chose death before servitude to the Royal Navy. Protected his men. Saved her life.

The one moment, the easy moment, when she'd lain in his arms, sated and vulnerable, when he could have reversed the fates and taken her, used her to bargain the return of his ship, he'd offered to help instead. He'd aided them, when he should have hated them. Killed them.

A wave of shame swept through her. She'd thought he of betrayed her. Betrayed her family, because it was something she would have done. Something she *had* done.

Conal was a man of honor from his toes to his soul. She should have understood that. Believed in that. Believed in him. He deserved so much better than she.

He stroked her cheek with the outside of his fingers, which trembled now as they moved over her skin. "Ye dinna answer me question, love." His voice faltered. "Do ye love me?"

Her heart shattered into a million pieces. She owed him the truth, even though it was worth nothing. "I think I'll always love you, Conal." The next sentence came out more as a whisper, an afterthought, something he wasn't really meant to hear. "Even though I know you could never love a woman like me."

A look of horrified surprise flashed across his chiseled features. "Devil take me if I don't. I woulda thought it was obvious. I dinna know what kind of woman ye think ye are, but I'll tell ye this, I want ye to be *mine*." He grasped her shoulders and returned his forehead to rest against hers. "I love ye, Stevie Sauvage. With every breath I take, I love ye more and more."

The press of his forehead against hers seemed to transfer his calm, his determination and his confidence into her. Even so, the energy that flowed in him around him and through him created a frenzy of emotion that swirled and spiraled in all directions like an explosion. She inhaled to steady herself, but his scent was intoxicating and it made it impossible to think, move, or speak. "I don't deserve the love of a man like you, Conal O'Brien."

He clasped her hands in his large palm. "The woman who'd sacrifice her life for her family? The gunner who fired the shot that saved our ship? The woman whose wit saved the lives of every mate from British impressment? Lass, ye are worth your weight in *diamonds* to me, and even then their glitter is worth less than your smile. Can ye not ken that I love ye with all that I am?"

A rush of pure happiness surged through her. She felt it in her mind; she felt it in her heart; she felt it clear to her toes. "I love you, just as much." She smiled and kissed him. He loved her.

He *loved* her!

CHAPTER 15

25 November 1720

Dear Father,
They have hanged the rest of the crew.
Mary and I have suffered a brief reprieve. We are both with child, and the Magistrate is obligated to stay our execution until the babies are born. I beseech you, on behalf of my unborn babe, to use whatever manner possible to stop our execution. If it can't be stopped, at least fight to have it delayed until your only grandchild is born.

Despite whatever capacity I have lived my life to this point, I remain,
Your daughter,
Anne

B rendan Ahern signaled the *Desire* and when she signaled back, he released a tense breath. When he'd deposited the wounded in Baracoa after their last battle with the *Dragon* several months ago, he wasn't sure they'd recover. As was their usual procedure, Landon Hart, and the *Desire* had stopped there, received his message from the harbor master and brought his recovered family members along. It was time to end this feud once and for all before it got further out of control.

Brendan shouted commands up to the tops, and soon the *Reward* was coming alongside the *Seeker*. Men stood at the rails, grappling hooks at the ready. The *Desire* had moved to a position off the sterns of the *Seeker* and the *Dragon*, where she could attack without putting any of their ships in harm's way, should she need to go on the offensive.

Brendan had Gampo trapped, and the pirate had no choice now but to negotiate. The best option for the Ahern Fleet would be to take the pirate's schooner and deposit him and his crew back on Lamb's Tail Island to ponder the next course of their lives. If Gampo had no vessel, then he'd not be such a nuisance— for a while, anyway. Problem was, eventually he'd acquire another, and then they'd be back in this same situation.

If only Brendan could negotiate an accord with the man, one that would end the dissonance between Gampo and the Aherns, their travels would become easier. If he couldn't, then he'd have to make a more drastic and perhaps fatal decision.

Brendan and his boarding party clambered onto the deck of the *Seeker*, across to the larboard side of the ship, and studied the deck of the *Dragon*. Gampo stood on the aft deck, by his helm, a gleaming saber in his hand. His crew clustered around the main mast. They held no pistols or swords, but by the way they stood with their backs to the mast, they probably had a cache of weapons in the center of their group, in case things went awry.

"Prepare to board the *Dragon*," Brendan said.

The atmosphere was eerily quiet. The water slapped half-heartedly against the hulls of the ships. Even the gulls must have sensed the tension and fled the area.

"Why have you attacked my ship?" Gampo shouted.

"Do not act like you've been the one wronged," Brendan shouted back. "You have attacked us multiple times unprovoked."

"You lie!" Gampo returned. "I sent a shot across the bow signaling for you to halt, and you responded by blowing away my main mast! You and your father are both scabrous pieces of filth! By-blows from a trollop! No honor among any!"

Brendan couldn't care less about what Gampo thought of him, but no one would call his mother a trollop and live to repeat the slur again. He clenched his saber and flung an order to Remus. "Send out grappling hooks and planks. I'm boarding."

GAMPO OBSERVED the young captain leap aboard his crippled schooner. He would not allow a battle between the crews if he could help it. He jumped down the companion ladder and strode to the midships deck, stopping before his crew.

"Manuel, step forward," he said.

His cousin shouldered his way through the men and gave Drago a salute. "Aye, Captain."

Drago scanned his crew. "I will settle this with the *Reward's* captain personally. You are not to raise a weapon in my defense regardless of what happens." At the objections of several men, Drago held his hands up for silence. "This is my fight, not yours. I'll not draw you into a battle leading you to your deaths." He locked his gaze with his cousin. "Manuel, if any man on this crew raises a weapon in my defense, you are to toss them overboard. However, if they are attacked, then you are to help them fight."

Manuel saluted him again. "Aye, Captain."

His cousin stood head and shoulders above the next biggest member of the crew; his loyalty was even bigger. There was no doubt among the men that Manuel wouldn't hesitate to carry out his captain's orders. When no amount of grumbling changed Drago's mind, they grudgingly agreed to stay out of any confrontation that might occur between the two captains.

Drago spun on his heel, intending to head back to the helm, when *Reward's* captain strolled onto the deck, a saber glinting in his hand. "You and I appear to be at odds on what constitutes the truth," the young man snarled. "Foremost, I demand you rescind your earlier remarks about my mother and father."

"You would have me lie?" Gampo slapped his sword against the side of his boot. How dare this son of a blackguard act as if *he'd* been wronged? "Who are you to demand anything of me?"

"My name is Brendan Ahern." He brought his sword up in a salute. "I'm the eldest son of Fynn Ahern and captain of the *Reward.*"

"A shame ye admitted yer the son of that motherless dog. He was a Judas, worth less than a sack of entrails, and if you're willing to fight for his black honor, then you're no better than he."

"What wrong did my father commit to give you such a worthless opinion?" Ahern stood just beyond the range of Drago's reach, jaw clenched and knuckles white around the hilt of his saber.

"You don't know?" Drago sneered. "He lied to you too, then." He spat on the deck next to Ahern's boot. "Fynn used to be my friend until he betrayed me. Fynn became a slaver and a thief, and it looks like you are following in your worthless sire's footsteps. The devil himself couldn't desire better company. "

With a roar, Ahern lunged. Drago parried the attack and locked hilts with him. "You lie," Brendan hissed. "My father was never a slaver. He escaped his own bondage and freed my mother as well."

Brendan Ahern was a young man with the strength and endurance of youth. How old was he? Twenty-five? Even so, Drago still had him by about twenty pounds and more than a few years of experience. The young man was agile, but he wasn't as well-trained. It would be nothing to disarm him. He could've done it the moment Brendan charged, but he needed answers.

Drago lowered his shoulder and shoved young Ahern away. They circled, glaring at each other. Years of searching with no reward pressed upon Drago's shoulders like a yoke of failure. He was cursed. Fate had punished him by taking away the one person able to provide answers to his questions. Blasted inconvenient for Fynn to die before Drago had a chance to face him. He needed to know...why had Fynn kidnapped his sister? Where did he take her? Where was she now? Was she alive or dead? Did she suffer? His chest constricted. Was she still suffering?

Drago pointed his saber at Brendan. "Your father bribed a guard and then stole my sister. When I searched for her, I was told Fynn *sold* her to a Persian prince. What do you call someone like that, if not a bloody slaver?" Years of anger surged through Drago's veins, and he charged. His blade flashed. He nicked the young man's chin, then his shoulder. It was a dragon against a dog. He lashed out with his blade over and over, leaving a trail of fire on Ahern's flesh, backing Fynn's son aft, toward his cabin and away from the crew. Drago's father's voice echoed in his head.

"You're fifteen, Drago—almost a man. I'm counting on you to protect your sister and bring her safely home."

It should have been a short, simple journey from the small island of Elbis to the nearby seaside village of San Vincenzo. However, it had been anything but simple. Their ship had been attacked and taken. Drago had tried to defend Risa, but the pirates were too many. He could not return home without his sister. How could he face his father after he'd failed so completely?

Drago had become a wealthy man in his own right, over the last few years. When France gave him a letter of marque, he became a privateer and his fortunes doubled. He'd searched for her. A man who watched over slaves bound for the block gave him information leading Drago to Persia. No one on the Persian docks had heard of Risa or the prince who'd purchased her.

That was when he vowed to find Fynn Ahern and strangle the truth from him. Who had the rat *really* sold Risa to? What had he done with her?

Brendan barely blocked Drago's onslaught. Again they locked swords, again they broke apart to circle. "I'm telling you, my father was not a slaver," Brendan snapped, his chest heaving. "My mother would have never allowed it, even if my father had paused to give it the slightest thought."

This young man would not give Drago the information he needed. Obviously, Fynn had kept the more lascivious side of his nature from his family. There was nothing more to do now, other than surrender and hope the son had more honor than the sire.

A soft click grabbed Drago's attention. He glanced at his cabin door to his right. Julian stepped out, holding a long stiletto he must have found under the bed. That second of distraction was all Brendan needed to bring his saber to Drago's throat.

"Yield," he said.

Drago dropped his saber.

"No!" Julian jumped toward Brendan, brandishing the knife.

Instinctively, Brendan spun away from Drago, toward the sound of Julian's shriek, blade flashing.

Cold horror pierced Drago's chest as the blade swung toward the boy at a level that would likely take off his head. Drago flung his body between the sword and the child, knowing if he felt the sting of steel, then he'd saved Julian's life.

If not, the boy was dead.

A FAINT FAN of light crept toward Stevie and Conal. She should stop kissing him, but it was impossible. After hearing a light giggle from a few feet away, she broke the kiss and made do with entwining her fingers with Conal's as they turned toward her little sister. Jacqueline grinned. "Will he be your husband, Stevie?"

A soft warmth radiated from Conal's eyes. His gaze never wavered from Stevie's face. "I soon hope to be."

Jacqueline clapped her hands. "I'm so glad. She really needs one, she's already twenty years old."

They laughed and Stevie felt the blush crawl up her neck. "Let's find the boys."

They found Tristan and Gabriel by the lake. Her brother stood in a small puddle, still dripping.

"The lake is too deep to walk across," Tristan said gruffly. He pulled off his shirt and wrung it out while taking two steps closer to Stevie.

"The water is cool and fresh, though." Gabriel said, flanking his cousin. He, too, was sopping wet, although he seemed quite content about it.

"It's harder to swim in the dark." Tristan muttered. "It's spooky. I'll bet that lake is a hundred feet deep."

They took a few moments to inform Conal and Gabriel of Gampo's cryptic instructions on how to find the exit.

Jacqueline's excited voice bounced off the walls of the cave. "I found it! I found the bloody hand!"

Stevie whirled. The little girl's impish voice sounded very far away. Gabriel's eyes widened and he looked for Tristan, who was already trotting to the lake with the lantern. Conal took off toward a faint torch light clinging to the cave wall several hundred yards away. Jacquie was climbing *on* the cave wall. Over the water! Stevie began to run.

Jacqueline was perched on a rock ledge running along the lake's rim. The water gleamed fifteen feet beneath her. She had Conal's torch in one hand. The other clung to the jagged wall of the cave. "Look!"

She raised the torch and sure enough, it illuminated a rusty brown handprint on the rock. She swung the torch to illuminate the area in front of her. "Here's another one." She craned her head around toward them. "This is the way we need to go!"

Stevie could barely focus on her sister's words. A giant roar filled her head and she couldn't drag her eyes from the glassy darkness reflecting Jacqueline's flickering torch light like the fires of hell.

"That's fantastic, Biscuit," Tristan said gently. "Come on back here and let us lead the way."

Jacqueline expelled a puff of air, offended. "I've come this far just fine, Tristan."

"And you've been very helpful, still..."

"Look at this." She leaned forward with the torch. Just past the handprint was an opening on the side of the cave wall. The problem was that the ledge ended at Jacqueline's toes, and the floor of the cave threshold was at least twelve feet away.

"I'll be..." Conal whispered. "That's it!"

"Fine, then, Jacquie," Tristan continued calmly, he began to slowly wade toward her, but his gaze darted from his sister to the now rippling dark water below. "Just retrace your steps back and we'll figure out how to get there from here." He tapped the side of his leg with his fingers in a jerky staccato.

"We need the rope," Jacqueline stated. "I can see a spike here and another one on the other side of the cave. If we attach the rope, we can use it like a stair rail to get up there."

"Excellent, little one," Stevie said, taking the cue from Tristan and keeping her voice soft. "I have the rope, so if you very carefully step your way back, then I can go up and attach it."

Jacqueline nodded and began to retrace her steps. Stevie held her breath each time the child's foot went from one narrow rock to another.

Until the ledge crumbled.

Jacqueline had time for one short, tiny shriek before she

plunged into the lake. Darkness surrounded her as the torch hit the water.

"Jacqueline!" Tristan yelled, surging forward.

Conal grabbed his shoulder. "You stay here, let me go."

But Jacqueline's head had already disappeared. Stevie bounded into the water at a dead run.

"Stevie, no!" Conal yelled.

CONAL HAD TAKEN off his boots the second he noticed the little girl up on the ledge. In his opinion, this could end only one of two ways. Either the girl continued until she scampered into the cave opening—which was the best possible outcome, although unlikely to happen—or she'd reverse her track and lose her balance. The rocks giving way under such a feather weight had taken him by surprise, however.

He'd waded out into the lake only a few feet when the dark, smooth surface broke into small ripples. His original idea was to wade into the lake under the child and either see her to the cave, or be there when she slipped. It seemed like a good plan until the snakes began swimming from their nest. Tristan had eyed them as well.

The snakes, longer than a grown man, were swimming near the edge of the lake. The splash and screech of the little girl was enough to startle them away from the wall of rock. Stevie, however, her eyes on the bubbles her sister left behind, was heading straight for them.

Conal reached down and grabbed several stones. He could throw them and try to scare the snakes away, but what if he startled them and they struck Stevie or Jacqueline? As he contemplated, more of them oozed out of crevices along the wall.

"Stevie!" he yelled. "Stop! You're heading for the snakes!"

"Snakes?" She paused, then surged to Jacqueline, who'd just

come up sputtering for air. Around the little girl, half a dozen snakes slithered across the top of the water.

Stevie started splashing them and yelling, "Go away! Go away!" She didn't hesitate after that, just kept splashing and yelling. A cold tendon of fear clenched Conal's spine. He found himself frozen. If he moved to help, he risked driving the snakes toward the girls.

The men were helpless and could only watch as Stevie splashed on through the chest-deep water near the edge of the lake, toward her sister, through the swarming snakes which fanned out from them like palmetto fronds. Jacqueline had managed to grasp a rocky handhold along the sheer face of the cave wall and clung there, coughing. Stevie reached her and pulled the child into her arms.

"Hold onto my shoulders," she said, pushing the little girl around back. Jacqueline latched her arms around Stevie's neck and clung like a turtle shell until they reached the shallows. Tristan and Conal jumped to help pull both away from the lake, doing their best to hide the fact that they'd been nearly scared witless.

"Well, then," Tristan said, glancing back at the spot where Jacqueline fell. "All that splashing certainly must have scared away all the snakes. Should be perfectly safe to go back and climb up to the passageway our little Biscuit found." He gave Stevie a weak smile, then elbowed his cousin. "Gabriel, you go first."

Stevie squatted down in front of her sister. "From now on, you stay close."

Jacqueline coughed. Her shoulders sagged as she looked down at her clothes. "I hope I didn't ruin my new dress. Captain Gampo would be sad if I did."

"A dress can be replaced," Stevie said. "You, however, cannot be. Promise me you'll be more careful."

The girl nodded. "I will."

Stevie stood and took charge. "Good, then, let's go." She

pointed to the ledge. "Gabriel, try to find a way for us to get up there."

Gabriel nodded, squaring his shoulders at being selected for the task. He looped the rope over his shoulder then splashed into the water. It wasn't long before he had secured the rope in a way that allowed him to scale the ledge up to the cave opening. Tristan and Conal went next.

Conal studied Stevie as she placed her feet firmly against the rock wall and pulled herself, hand over hand, up the rope toward him. There was a determined angle in the way she held her head. Although her lips pressed together in effort, her eyes shone with a brightness illuminating her entire face. She no longer hid in the shadows like a frightened little rabbit.

She had become a tigress.

He reached down, grasped her forearm and pulled her up the last step, then sucked in a quick breath when she smiled her thanks and stopped his heart. Her beauty almost left him speechless.

"I did it!" Cheeks flushed and breathing from the effort, she grinned in giddy jubilation, and he found himself laughing in response. Her joy was his, and he reveled in the sensation.

"Well done, love," he spoke low, and a strange knot formed in his throat. "Well done." His pride in her efforts and bravery grew. This woman had struggled through many difficult situations. Yes, she'd been afraid, but she hadn't let fear trap or paralyze her. Although it still hovered around her, she hadn't allowed it to take control. Not this time and, he'd wager heavily, it never would again.

Once everyone was up, they gathered just beyond the cave entrance. Between them, they had two lanterns and one remaining torch. Tristan collected the rope and looped it over his shoulder. He picked up one of the lanterns and held it high, illuminating a sharp incline ahead of them.

"Looks like we are going back up," he observed. Jacqueline

took his hand and he gave it a squeeze. "You and I shall lead the way." He took a step, then paused to remove the rope. He looped it around his waist a couple of times, then tied it. He did the same around Jacqueline's waist with the other end. "Now we're a team."

Jacqueline pointed. "Let's go. I see the next handprint."

The group began to climb the steep, rocky trail. Stevie paused and put a hand on Conal's forearm. "Wait a moment, I have to give you something." She pulled a long, thin chain from around her neck. Hanging next to a small gold cross was his family's signet ring. She removed it and handed it to him.

In all honesty, he'd forgotten about it entirely. He could've requested it back from Harvey the moment the old sailor had agreed to help them find the Sauvages' treasure. He could've taken it by force when they were in the graveyard. His mind had been on other things, other more important things.

"Thank you." How did she get her hands on it? "Didn't Harvey take this for Gampo?"

She grinned. "He did. After the battle with the French privateer, I stole it back." She secured the cross and gold chain around her neck. "I'm a pirate, after all."

"You certainly are, lassie." Conal pulled her closer and kissed the top of her head. "You certainly are."

She grasped his shirt collar and pulled his face down and kissed him. The sweet taste of spring-fed lake water greeted his lips. Her body carved into his at all the right spots, as if they were two puzzle pieces, fitting together perfectly.

Their breath became one. Time stopped. The movements of the kiss were no longer his, nor hers. A swirling sensation radiated through his chest. For a moment, Stevie was a pulsing, bright light. He breathed it in and out until it surged through him and enveloped them both.

Never in his life had he experienced anything like this. He traced his lips up her cheek to her eyelid, then to her forehead.

What kind of spell had she put over him? With a jolt of surprise and joy, he answered his own question.

"So this is what it feels like," he murmured.

She pulled away enough to look at his face. "What?"

She'd known the answer before she'd even asked the question. He saw it in her silver eyes.

"Love," he whispered.

CHAPTER 16

Journal entry
8 December, 1720

Sadly, Mary was removed from my cell today. She'd had a fever for days and I begged them to take her to a healer, with whom I am well-acquainted. It's my hope that she will recuperate while among our friends and find a way to escape the island. I suffer no such maladies, and therefore they will not allow me to join her. I fear I am doomed to my fate.

Julian was shouting.

That was a good sign. It meant the boy wasn't dead.

Fire was creeping across Drago's ribcage, though. That was a bad sign. It meant Brendan's blade had sliced him open. He lifted his eyelids to find Manuel restraining the kicking and screaming eight-year-old boy in his massive arms.

Brendan Ahern stood nearby, face ashen. "God's breath," the young captain whispered, staggering back. "I almost killed him."

"If you had," Drago gasped as the pain flickered across his ribs, "I'd have had your heart for supper."

"And I'd have helped you cut it out," Brendan responded, wiping his sleeve across his forehead.

"I yield," Drago said. "Name your terms."

"I'll leave that to my father," Brendan said, helping Drago up to a sitting position against one of the guns.

Drago's heart lurched in his chest. "Hart told me Fynn died during our last scuffle." Was the young Ahern lying, or just biding his time until Hart and O'Brien joined him?

Brendan scowled at Drago. "He almost did. He lost a leg and then the fever set in. I left him and my mother in Baracoa with the hope he'd be able to recover. Captain Hart retrieved them before joining me." He crouched in front of him and peeled away Drago's coat and shirt in order to examine the damage. "I'd have brought them myself, but they weren't ready to depart, and I couldn't take the chance of losing sight of you for very long."

"So Hart lied when he said your father was dead?"

"No, he and Conal really believed Father was dead. We hoped to convince you so you'd quit attacking our ships." He shrugged. "As it is, my father's lucky to be alive. I wasn't sure he'd make it."

Manuel must have released Julian because the boy skidded on his knees to Drago's side. "Captain Gampo! Are you hurt bad?" His eyes were welling with tears.

"Stop that, boy," Drago rasped. "Pirates don't cry."

"We're n—n—not pirates," Julian choked. "We're p—p—privateers."

Drago gave him a grim smile. "So, *now* you're finally convinced?"

"Yessir." Julian spun to face Brendan. His face twisted in anger. "All he wants is to find his sister! Can't you just tell him where she is? That's all he wants, you son of a yellow-bellied cod!"

Drago grinned then grimaced. "Well, now, that's some mighty

fine cussing, lad. But it's probably best not to raise this man's ire, since I've surrendered my ship to him."

"Why?" Julian cried. "How will you find Risa if he takes the *Dragon*?"

"*Risa*?" Brendan's head snapped up, and he shot a glance at the boy before he returned his attention to Drago. "Risa?"

Manuel had ripped off his sleeve and was pressing it against Drago's side. "Poor Auntie Risa," he muttered. "Stolen away."

Drago merely nodded.

Brendan slowly straightened. "What...is your sister's full name?"

Manuel pulled a whiskey flask from his vest and doused Drago's wound. "Poor Auntie Risa," he repeated sadly.

Drago winced as Manuel drizzled another splash of whiskey on the slash in his side. "Madre di Dio, Manuel! Enough!" He snatched the flask from his cousin's hand and took a swig before he answered. "Marisa Sophia Margarita Gamponetti."

Brendan Ahern was quiet. The silence grew, and Drago looked up at him. What had taken the squid's tongue?

Brendan's lips moved, but no words came out. It was easy to read his lips: *Gamponetti...Gampo.* He shook his head, then looked Drago straight in the eye and said something that hit Drago's gut harder than a cannonball.

"Marisa Sophia Margarita Gamponetti. That's my mother's name."

THE ROCKY TRAIL contained sharp stones, deep holes and ruts. It was impossible to avoid every hazard in the dimming light of the lanterns.

Tristan slowed. "We're nearly out of oil in this one. I'm turning down the wick, stay close."

They were climbing roughly hewn steps. Mother Nature

might have made these passages with her quakes, underground springs and streams, but at some point in the past, Man had attempted to fine-tune her work. Stevie's legs were burning. Tristan led the way swinging Jacqueline up to his back, ducking under and stepping over a variety of rocks and formations as they progressed ever upward. The light from the lantern dimmed, but there was still enough to see the trail twist out of sight ahead of him.

He disappeared, and a moment later they heard a surprised shout. Conal had been holding her hand, pulling her behind him. He looked over his shoulder at her, then up to where Tristan had disappeared. She released his hand.

"Go on ahead and check on them," she said. She was winded, but Conal hadn't even broken a sweat. She'd only slow him down.

He nodded and took off at a jog, taking the stone steps two at a time. When she and Gabriel finally wheezed their way to the top, she understood Tristan's exclamation.

They'd entered a huge, round cavern. The faint light didn't reach the ceiling or into every corner, but there were vague outlines of darkness spaced at regular intervals around them.

Conal turned in a circle, taking in the sight. "It appears several trails merge into this chamber."

"How do we find the right one?" Tristan asked, walking toward one of the dark shadows.

"Have a care, Tristan," Stevie warned. "Remember what happened last time you walked blindly into a cave opening?"

Her words stopped Tristan in his tracks. Her brother cautiously put one foot down at a time, walking toward the shadow more slowly now. "These aren't all tunnels," he finally said. "This one appears to be an alcove hewn into the rock. There's an altar or something in front of it."

"I found another," Gabriel said. "There's a tall, narrow stone in this one." He moved to the next dark opening and disappeared, plunging the cavern in total darkness. After a few seconds, he returned. "This one appears to be a passage."

Some alcoves had rocks or statues in them. There were at least two other tunnels. "What now?" Stevie asked. There was no telling where the other passages led. Unless they found another bloody handprint, they risked getting lost in this labyrinth.

Before anyone could answer, distorted voices drifted into the cavern. Everyone fell silent. Stevie turned her head and listened. It was impossible to tell where the voices originated, but it was easy to tell they were heading toward them as they became louder.

"Everyone, find an alcove and hide!" Conal whispered, pulling Stevie with him. "Put out the lanterns!"

Tristan untied Jacqueline and pressed her toward a smaller fissure. "Don't be afraid, Biscuit, I'll be in the alcove next to you."

She wiggled her body through the opening and disappeared. "Tristan, it's so dark in here...I can't see my hand in front of my face." Her voice was tiny.

"Just stay quiet, little lion. No pacing and no roaring."

The child giggled, her earlier fears calmed by Tristan's jovial demeanor.

"Jacqueline," Stevie whispered into the crevice. "You are not to come out until you are told. If there's a fight or an argument, you must stay quiet. No one can find where you're hiding. Understood?"

"Yes, Stevie," she whispered, her voice drifting through the cavern.

All lights extinguished, Stevie, and the others pressed their bodies deeper into the crevices and alcoves of the strange cavern. A solid silence fell over the group as low voices once again drifted through the cave.

Stevie slipped into an alcove with Conal. He pressed her against the cool rock wall. Her shoulder brushed his, and he found her arm, slid his fingers down and entwined them with hers. He gave her a reassuring squeeze, and she returned it. With her other hand, she withdrew the small knife she kept hidden at the small of her back, behind her belt. The faint whisper of steel against leather told her Conal did the same.

The voices came from a different direction, which meant these people had entered the cave from another opening.

"That's it, I've had enough of this chuckle-headed lout's miserable sense of direction. Gimme the lantern," a scruffy voice groused.

"And you think you can see a false floor any better? That was a craftily made trap," snapped another voice.

Stevie grinned in the dark. She'd recognize those two old salt's voices anywhere.

Tristan was already easing out of his hiding spot. "Uncle Bernard?"

Harvey barked out an oath. "What? Who's that? I gots a pistol. Don't think I won't blows yer eyes outta yer head, whoever ye are. Come out and show yourself!"

"Shut up, you feckless, hen-hearted rake, it's Tristan," Bernard said in an exasperated tone. "Good to see you, boy, any luck finding the others?"

"As a matter of fact, yes," he replied as the rest of them emerged. Tristan turned up his lantern. The additional light revealed a large, round cavern with four passageways. Interspersed were a total of twelve alcoves, half of them filled with stone statues in various shapes and conditions, from the unblemished to the nearly destroyed.

Stevie gaped at the immensity of the cavern as she crawled out from behind the tall rock, which was actually a statue of a Greek warrior.

Tristan's yelp of surprise echoed off the cavern walls. "Bless the saints, you're alive!"

Stevie eyed her uncle and Harvey. Both were covered with rubble dust, cuts, and bruises. Bernard's sleeve was torn off, and

Harvey was holding his britches up with one hand and wearing only one boot. Her gaze shifted to the hulk limping into the lantern light.

"Adrian!" She ran to him and threw her arms around his neck. "We thought you were dead! They shot you! You fell over the falls!" She kissed his cheek and hugged him until he grunted in pain.

Adrian patted her with one hand and grimaced. "Yes, the experience was painful but not fatal, although I'm not sure I'll survive much more abuse from these two old curmudgeons. Thank God Tristan's here to distract them."

Stevie stepped back and took in her cousin's blackened eye, bandaged head and bruised arms. His knee was bleeding through an open slash in his britches. Tristan and Gabriel joined her and clapped him on the shoulder, as overjoyed as Stevie to see him alive.

"What in heaven's name happened?" she asked.

Adrian opened his mouth to speak, but Harvey answered. "These devil-cursed caves are filled with treachery and traps. This dull-witted buffoon plowed his way right into one of 'em. It were a layer of canvas covered with dirt and small stones stretched across a fissure the size of a long gun."

Adrian winced as he bent over to look at his knee. "It was cleverly done. If we'd been more cautious, we might have noticed a smaller well-worn trail running along the wall."

"It was the compass rose on the wall beyond it that lured our gazes from our footing," Bernard added.

"Compass rose?" Conal asked, looking from Bernard to Harvey.

"Yessir, ye left us too soon, mate." Harvey gave Conal a gap-toothed grin. "Me an' this old dog figured out the clues in them letters." He nodded toward Bernard, who then brought them up to date on their theories.

"We've been following etchings of compass roses on the cave

walls and boulders. They appear at passageway junctions like this one, as well as along the route," Bernard said.

"Now we know the ones along the route are also warnings to be wary of traps or hazardous footing," Adrian added. He straightened and looked around at their group and took in a heavy breath. "No sign of the little ones, then?"

"Oh dear, we almost forgot about Jacqueline!" Tristan darted over to her hiding place and raised his lantern to illuminate inside. Jacqueline peeked around the edge.

"Now here's a smart girl who knows how to follow directions," he said, smiling.

"I heard voices, but I couldn't tell if they were arguing or not," Jacqueline said. "I sat on a piece of flat wood while I waited. It has pieces of metal wrapped around it. I wonder what it looks like in the light." She glanced around her little cave.

Tristan brought his lantern closer for her. "What do you see, Jacquie?"

"It's a short, fat barrel," she said.

Harvey had shuffled up and shouldered his way past Stevie and Tristan to peer inside the tiny grotto. "It's a bumpkin, cut in half," he whispered.

They looked at one another. "Could it be the treasure?" Tristan asked.

Harvey stepped back and studied the walls around the crevice. "Can't be. Ain't no compass rose."

"Yes, there is," Bernard responded. He stared at the statue blocking the grotto entrance. "Look at this."

Jacqueline squeezed out of the tiny space and joined the rest in front of the statue. "She looks sad."

The statue was of a Greek woman. In one hand, she held a child, in the other, a compass. Her hair blew forward and nearly covered her face, as if a strong wind pushed against her back.

"Well, I'll be a baboon's uncle," muttered Harvey. "It's Calypso."

"May Calypso reunite him with his Wife, Rose," Uncle Bernard recited.

"What's a Calypso?" Jacqueline reached up to touch the baby's head. Harvey grabbed her hand.

"I don't trust anything is this blasted cave. Touch Calypso and the entire thing just might collapse on us."

Everyone collectively took a step back. Conal answered Jacqueline, "Calypso is a sea nymph. She's the daughter of a Titan and is known to be a concealer and a seductress. When a man, Odysseus, was washed up on her island, she kept him hidden there for years. She had his child. Odysseus pined for his family, and finally the Greek gods demanded she release him. By then, Calypso had fallen in love with Odysseus. Even so, she couldn't defy the gods. Although it broke her heart, she helped him build a boat and then sent him on his way with provisions and a strong wind."

Jacqueline tilted her head. "So that's why she looks so sad."

Stevie looked down at her sister. "Jacqueline, you're the only one who can easily squirm in and out of that little chamber. Will you try to push the bumpkin out?"

The girl grinned and wiggled her way back inside, and was able to move the barrel out of the grotto. A short time later, they were all gathered around the small modified bumpkin, the size of a small ammunitions box.

Adrian picked it up and shook it. A large mass thumped against the sides. Bernard reached into his sack and pulled out his tools, then proceeded to pry it open. Inside was a beautiful pale, yellow, silk gown. Gold brocade lined the bottom of the skirt, the waist, neck and sleeves. Emeralds and pearls were attached by gold threads in intricate patterns around the neckline and sleeves. White silk piping outlined every seam and edge. A jeweled belt was wrapped with it.

"A belt and a dress?" Tristan looked perplexed. "It's valuable, to be sure, but how would this gown make Anne Bonny and Mary Read 'wealthy beyond their wildest dreams'?"

Adrian lifted it out of the barrel. "It's heavy."

"Of course it's heavy, ye driveling ape." Harvey ran his hands along the lines of the gown, over the white piping. "It's because there are stones sewn into all the seams."

Everyone stood still and quiet in the cavern, each digesting this new information. It was a full-skirted, formal gown with a long train. Yards and yards of seams. Filled with jewels.

Stevie was the first to break the silence. "We have to find Gampo and retrieve Julian." She gestured to the gown. "There's enough wealth to pay a ransom for him and rebuild our boarding house."

Bernard looked at Conal. "If Gampo won't relinquish your ship, we'll build you two new ones." He clapped, then rubbed his hands together. "Adrian, replace the dress and reseal the lid; we can use the rope to create a makeshift harness for it. We'll take turns carrying it." He glanced at Harvey. "Now, what do you think *you're* doing?"

Harvey paused in the act of threading the jeweled belt around his waist. "If yer pickle-headed son hadn't ripped off me belt, I wouldn't need ter use this one."

"If I hadn't grabbed your belt, old man, you would be in pieces at the bottom of that hole back there," Adrian said dryly.

"Aye, well, it's either this or traveling with my bare bollocks exposed in the breeze." He patted the belt. "I'm happy to take this as my share, if yer happy ter not have ter view my arse."

"That works for me," Adrian muttered.

Tristan gawked at Harvey. "We haven't even figured out how much is there. You're probably shorting yourself quite a bit, you know."

Harvey shrugged. "I don't need no more than this to see myself fat and happy fer the rest of me days. B'sides, I ain't going to let Gampo gets his claws in me. Accuse me of mutiny, he will."

He stared at Bernard a long minute. "It'd be best fer us all if ye told him I were dead."

Bernard nodded. "Agreed. Now let's move along. It'll be easier finding our way back than it was getting here."

The group followed Bernard, Harvey and Adrian. Stevie paused to take one last look at the curious chamber tucked away in the center of an island mountain. Jacqueline took her hand. Stevie looked down at her sister. "It's an amazing sight, isn't it?"

Jacqueline nodded, perusing the figures forever captured in stone. "Calypso's story was sad. I wonder who the rest of these statues are and if they all have sad stories." She tilted her head up and smiled at Stevie. "I wonder if Captain Gampo knows, since he's been here before. I'm going to ask him."

They walked into the tunnel, but after a few yards, Jacqueline stopped. "This is the wrong way."

Adrian paused, but the rest kept walking. "Why do you think this is the wrong way? Your Uncle Bernard and I just passed through here."

"Look around," Jacqueline said. "There are no bloody handprints."

Tristan and Gabriel stopped in their tracks. "She's right. Turn around."

Harvey and Bernard paused. "What bloody handprints?"

"Captain Gampo told me he'd been through the caves when he was younger," Jacqueline explained. "He said to follow the bloody handprints and the bats."

"We saw no bloody handprints on the way here," Bernard said warily.

Adrian glanced down at his torn clothes and bruises. "That explains our difficulty in getting here."

The handprints Stevie could handle. Bats, however...she tried to suppress a shudder as Jacqueline pulled her hand so they could return to the chamber. The group split up and explored the other two passageways, and it wasn't long before the next bloody hand-print was located.

Satisfied now that they'd found the right tunnel, they continued along.

"How long do you think, until we find the way out?" Jackie asked.

Tristan studied the walls and ceiling with a nervous twitch. "When will we reach the bats?"

CHAPTER 17

12 December 1720

Mr. Cormac,
I have received your correspondence and the subsequent request for a
continuance on behalf of your daughter, Anne Bonny. While I rarely show
mercy to Pirates and Thieves, I am not without strong Moral Character. I
have deemed it appropriate to delay your daughter's execution until after
the birth of her child.

I have arranged her transfer from here to the gaol in New Berne in the
Providence of Carolina, where she will remain until the child is born. At
the most appropriate time, we will expect her to pay the penalty of Death
by hanging, for her crimes of Piracy and Murder.

Ultimately, the authorities in New Berne will be responsible for seeing
Justice is done.

I Remain,
His Honor, M. C. Marlowe III
His Majesty's Chief Magistrate

Port Royal, Jamaica

✳

The sun was hovering low in the sky, throwing glorious pinks, corals, purples and oranges across the clouds. The ocean glittered with bright sparkles of sunlight and mirrored the sunset, making it twice as beautiful. A calm southeasterly wind skimmed over Drago's skin. The breeze brought wafts of island fruits and sweet Ixora blossoms. He took a moment to close his eyes and breathe it all in, one last full breath before—.

"Where is he?" Fynn's voice boomed from the starboard side of the ship. "Where is the dog who cost me my leg?" Fynn and Risa had finally arrived. "An eye for an eye, I tell ye. I will chop off his leg and he can watch while the sharks make a pretty meal of it —that is, if they can stomach the taste."

Brendan rose from where he sat next to Drago and walked toward the rail, where his men were hauling up the longboat. Drago craned his neck, trying to catch a glimpse of Risa, but several barrels and the wheels of a long gun blocked his view.

Finally, the creaks and groans from the blocks ceased as the boat was hauled in and secured. A scrape and a step followed a step, thump, step, thump. Fynn approached with crutches and his new wooden leg. Other footsteps joined in, lighter ones, stronger ones. He could make out Brendan's voice greeting his parents.

A shadow blocked the fading light of the day. Drago looked up, his chin narrowly missing the tip end of a gleaming saber. Captain Landon Hart.

"I should run you through for what you did to Keelan." Hart's voice was low and chilling. "As soon as you are healed, I will demand satisfaction." He lowered his blade. "As much as I'd love to drive this sword through your heart, I'll not challenge a wounded man."

Drago stared into the icy blue eyes that glared at him. "Precisely what do you think I did to her?"

Hart's jaw clenched, and he squatted down to look him in the eye. "Your men kidnapped her and sold her to a lunatic."

"They did that on their own. I did not order it." Drago shifted to sit up straighter, which was a painful mistake.

"One of them put out word that you'd give a reward for her return."

"So I heard."

Hart growled and leaned forward. "It almost cost her her life."

"I was trying to save it," Drago said, leaning his head back against the mizzen mast. "That lunatic you spoke of hired those two to kidnap her. When I found out, I went to the warehouse to get her. I saw you there and assumed you were an associate of Garrison. He's insane."

"Midway through our duel, you found out who I was, yet you continued to chase after Keelan." Landon's eyes narrowed.

He sighed. "I did that for two reasons. If I had her, I could get to Ahern through you. She slipped away, but Garrison was on his way to claim her. He was running down the alley toward us, so I yelled threats to both her and him in order to scare away the louse-eaten dog." He forced himself to lean forward toward Hart, "I don't take kindly to those who use my name to further their private affairs and bribe my men. As it is, I'll never be able to set foot in Charleston again. The entire city wants me to hang."

Hart sat back and was silent a moment. "And the theft of my cargo?"

"Ah, that," Drago sighed again. Tiny details. "French privateers still have to make a living."

Hart gave him a dark look and left.

Drago's men had been released to tend their duties and begin repairs, but at the moment, most of them perched in the yard arms, watching.

"WHAT DID YOU JUST SAY?" Fynn's voice pierced the relative quiet of the deck.

A feminine shriek quickly followed, causing Drago to start. Footsteps, running. Drago looked up and then laughed with glee.

It was her. It was Risa!

She had aged, yes. Tinges of grey graced the temples of her shiny black hair. But her eyes were the same. Although at the moment they were wide with disbelief. He couldn't see much of her face because her hands covered her cheeks.

"Drago! Dear God in heaven, is it really you?" A short sob jumped from her chest.

He opened his arms. "Yes, Risa, it's me." His sister fell on him, laughing and sobbing and kissing his face. It hurt like the devil, but he didn't care. Finally, she placed her palms on his cheeks and stared at him. Then she said the strangest thing.

"I thought you were dead."

Puzzling. "Dead? Why would you think I was dead?" She was the one who had been missing all these years. His thoughts froze for a second as he recalled the times he had fired upon Fynn's ships. Thankfully, he'd never raked the decks. All his shots were designed to slowd own and cause costly damage, but what if he'd killed her during one of those fights? He could have. According to Brendan, she'd been on the *Reward* with Fynn when the man had lost his leg.

Risa picked up his hand and stroked her face with it, tears streaming down her cheeks. "They threw you overboard! I grieved for you. When did you begin using the name of Gampo? We did not understand that Gampo was *you*."

"I...it's a long story. I was told they had sold you to a Persian prince. You boarded a brigantine with Fynn. I tried to follow, but I had no money, and they needed no hands. I even tried to stow away, but was discovered and tossed from the ship. All I could do was watch him steal you." His voice broke, and he took a moment to swallow a sip of whiskey and regain his composure a bit. "I learned the ship's destination and followed it when I was able. When I couldn't find you there, I thought perhaps Fynn sold you to someone else or kept you as his slave."

"Well, I'll be a sottish, stump-winged blighter." Fynn limped up and leaned heavily on his crutches. "Drago, ye have a heck of a way with family."

Risa smiled at Drago. "We have many stories to tell each other, you and I," she said. "But for now, I want to get you to a bed so we can tend your wound." She gestured to Hart, who stood with his jaw slightly slack. "Landon's wife, Keelan, is very good with healing herbs."

"Keelan? You don't mean Keelan Grey." That vixen who'd sunk a knife into his leg in Charleston? He shot a glance at Hart, who'd straightened and narrowed his eyes.

"She's Keelan Hart now," Hart said tersely.

"And a lovely young woman," Risa added.

Drago released a lungful of air. *A lovely young woman.* What a pile of pig dung. Keelan Grey—now Keelan Hart—was the devil's handmaiden as far as he was concerned. Better to sail around her than through her.

Risa was apparently not quite as savvy about the woman. He glanced up at the wary visage of Hart. The two were obviously made for each other. He'd rather not spend much time in the presence of either of them.

"Fine, but make sure she's escorted by Manuel and comes *unarmed*," Drago muttered. "Check *all* her pockets."

TREACHERY AND TRAPS. That's what Harvey had said earlier, and it was in everyone's mind as they picked their way through the tunnel. Thankfully, the passageway had leveled off, and the trek was less hazardous and exhausting. They had three lanterns between them now illuminating the rock walls. They'd found only one other bloody hand a few paces ago, so at least they were still going the right direction, hopefully.

What if Gampo's advice was errant? What if he'd intentionally lured them into danger, rather than freedom? Stevie glanced at her little sister. Jacqueline seemed to trust the pirate's word, but children could be manipulated so easily.

"Ugh! What's this?" Tristan had paused at a sharp crook in the passage. He lowered his lantern. Droppings covered the floor.

Harvey held up his hand, and they all stopped. "Bat guano. Means we're nearing the cave entrance. Stay close and quiet." He took the lantern from Tristan's hand. "I'll lead on."

As if to confirm Harvey's statement, a sudden slapping echoed through the cave. Tristan cringed. Several bats seemed to appear out of thin air and flew above him. He shrieked and covered his head with his arms and crouched down. "A bat! A bat! A bat!"

Suddenly, the cave exploded with chatter and motion. Hundreds of bats released from their perches on the ceiling and swarmed through the cave.

"I told ye to keep quiet, ye bone-headed blowfish!" Harvey snarled.

Conal pressed Stevie and Jacqueline back against the cave walls. "Stay low and still," he said.

Tristan shrieked again and dove to the ground, arms wrapped around his head, followed immediately by Adrian. The others took their cue from Conal and flattened themselves against the cave walls.

It wasn't hundreds of bats. Harvey's lantern was only a few yards away, but the flying creatures completely obscured it. There had to be thousands of them. They stayed in the center area of the cave for the most part, but still, it was a few minutes before the last straggler had flapped around the corner and departed.

Harvey scowled at Tristan. "Is that a head on yer shoulders, or a dead jellyfish?" Looking chagrined, her brother rose from the floor along with her cousin. He and Adrian were both covered in dung.

"Ugh." Uncle Bernard gagged and stepped back. "Stay away from me," he said. "In fact, you two can step in at the rear, well downwind of the rest of us."

They moved on around the curve of the cave to the most glorious sight of the day, the week, the month, and the century. Through a small rocky opening, the western horizon bathed the island and sea in the muted pastels of the day's end.

They'd made it out.

THE FRESH, humid air tasted sweet. Perhaps it was from the scent of ripe mangoes drifting on the breeze. Conal paused. The cave opened up on the western side, about two-thirds up the mountain. The horizon, the channel of water between Lamb's Tail and the island of Jamaica were all visible from this vantage point. The sun was roaring its descent in pinks, oranges, purples and golds as it sank.

Now there was another pretty sight. Conal smiled. The *Dragon* sat paralyzed in the water, the top mast crippled, her spars dangling at all angles, sails shredded. She was surrounded by the *Reward*, the *Desire*, and his beloved *Seeker*, who looked no worse than when he'd left her.

Brendan and Landon had done it. They'd finally captured Gampo, and with any luck, the pirate was dead.

"We made it!" Jacqueline said, pausing to take in the view. "Oh, Captain O'Brien, look! Have you ever seen anything prettier?"

But Conal was watching Stevie as she turned her smiling face toward him. "No," he answered softly. "I haven't."

She blushed and took Jacqueline's hand. "Come, Jacquie, let's rinse off in the stream. I'm sure you're thirsty."

Eager to wash off the bat guano, Tristan and Adrian were already trotting toward the pool at the base of the waterfall cascading down the mountain from yet another cave opening.

Harvey was grumbling. "Now we have ter row back to the *Seeker* in the same longboat as a couple of—"

Stevie put her hands over Jacqueline's ears at the same time Bernard cuffed Harvey on the back of the shoulder, stopping him mid-sentence.

"That'll be enough, you old codfish. You should be grateful that with these four big, strong young men with us, we won't need to work an oar."

Harvey hitched up his britches and tightened his bejeweled belt. "Well, then. Seein' as how Captain Gampo and his ship have been taken, I don't mind accompanying you to the *Seeker*. I've a mind to sail with her back to America and see about settling down and mayhap getting married."

Bernard snorted in laughter. "There isn't a woman mad enough to take a scupper-brained fool like you."

"Look who's a-talkin'. I'm surprised ye were able to string that many words together without losing track of the thought."

It wasn't long before they uncovered the longboat from its hiding place, and Tristan, Gabriel, Adrian, Bernard, and Harvey, who was sitting on the bumpkin cask, were pulling long, smooth strokes toward the cluster of ships just off the leeward side of the island. Conal led Stevie and Jacqueline to the canoe he and Gabriel had hidden earlier. With Jacqueline sitting on the floor in the middle, Conal pushed them out past the breaking waves, then climbed in and followed the longboat toward his ship.

"I hope that wicked Gampo hasn't harmed Julian," Stevie said, pulling her oar through the water.

"He didn't," Jacqueline said confidently. "He wouldn't. He's training Julian to be a privateer."

Stevie harrumphed. "I'm afraid Julian won't have time to train as a privateer. Now that we've found Anne Bonny's treasure, we have to head back to New Orleans and rebuild our home."

"And Tristan's gaming house," Jacqueline added.

"That, too," Stevie replied, smiling over her shoulder at her little sister.

Conal's chest tightened. Was Stevie going to return to New Orleans too? It was obvious her family was tightly-knit. They lived together, worked together, took care of each other, just like he had done aboard the *Reward* for his uncle, aunt and cousins as a lad. If he asked her, would she marry him? Stevie still had young siblings to care for. How could he ask her to leave them? As badly as he wanted her as his wife, how could he expect her to make such a sacrifice?

The Ahern and O'Brien families made their living sailing the seas. The *Seeker* was his home, the Ahern merchant fleet his family. His younger brother, Ian, would soon join him to learn the skills needed to captain a profitable merchant ship. Conal had a duty to teach him. His sister, Keelan, sailed aboard the *Desire* with her husband, Landon. If only Stevie would do the same with him, he'd be a happy man.

The sun was barely kissing the horizon. Stevie stared out over the water. Was she thinking the same thoughts as he? Did they make her just as sad?

A shout drew Conal's attention to the longboat. They were designed to hold twenty men. That one, however, sat low in the water, as if it carried sixty. Not a good sign.

Harvey and Bernard yelled at them and waved their arms while Gabriel, Adrian and Tristan began rowing faster toward the *Seeker* which was still a quarter league away, at least.

"The boat's sinking!" Stevie gasped as Bernard baled a bumpkin barrel full of water over the side.

Both began to paddle madly toward the foundering longboat. Even as the men shifted toward the bow, the stern dipped below the waterline. After that, it was only seconds before the bow reared up and capsized.

"No!" Jacqueline screamed. "Hurry, Captain O'Brien! Stevie paddle faster! Tristan is a terrible swimmer! Faster, Stevie!"

By the time they reached the overturned longboat, her passengers were clinging to its sides. A long, gaping hole was now visible near the stern where planks had rotted and broken away, allowing water to seep in.

Thankfully, some crew from the *Desire* ad taken notice of their dilemma and had launched a longboat to stage a rescue.

"Where's Tristan?" Jacqueline's face was pale as she scanned the water. "Gabriel, where is Tristan?" she yelled.

"In here." A muffled voice came from inside the capsized boat. Seconds later, Tristan's head broke the surface, and Adrian grabbed his shirt and pulled him closer.

"I lost it," Tristan said, thumping his head against the wood.

"Ye had one job, ye squid-eyed piece of shark bait. *One job*!" Harvey's voice shot over from the other side of the boat.

"Lost what?" Jacqueline asked.

"The bloody dress," Adrian muttered. "We needed the barrel to bail water, so we took the dress out of the bumpkin."

"Once it got wet, it got slippery and heavy," Tristan mumbled. "I couldn't keep ahold of it."

Conal looked over the side of the canoe. The water was a clear, bright blue, but beneath them it was dark. The water was deep here, and a coral reef was the likely cause of the discoloration, but he couldn't even make out any shapes below. The dress was gone.

"All that, for nothing," Harvey lamented.

Things were looking up for Conal. Not that he wanted misfortune for Stevie's family—far from it. But if they had no funds to rebuild their business, they'd have to be open to other ways to make their fortune, such as learning how to work on a merchant ship. Could he persuade them to move to Cuba? Baracoa could use a decent boarding house. The rooms at the taverns there were small and sparse.

By this time, the other longboat from the *Desire* had arrived, and the sailors began to pull the men from the water. They reached Bernard first. What about Harvey's belt? They still had that, didn't they? He'd have to warn the men to look for a fight. The Sauvages might demand Harvey relinquish the belt to divide it among them. If Harvey argued the point, then there'd be a brawl. This thought dispersed, however, the moment his crew pulled Harvey's bare arse from the waves.

The old pirate had once again lost his belt.

CHAPTER 18

8 March 1729

Dear Father,
It is my hope that my escape has faded in the law's memory over the past
eight years. Your grandson has grown into a delightful boy with your
sparkling grey eyes and bright wit.
I have married a man from New Orleans named Jacques Sauvage, and he
has adopted your grandson so that he may grow up without the darkly
notorious surname of Bonny or Rackham hanging over his head.
Jacques is not without means and in fact is quite wealthy. I have arranged
for official papers to be delivered to a parish in Virginia, documenting my
marriage to a Mr. Burleigh.
I apologize for the duplicity, but I feel it is imperative in order to secure
the safety of my family and your grandson.

I will always remain,
Your Daughter, A

A depressed silence settled on the Sauvage family's shoulders and pulled at their hearts. Doom and dread seeped into their bones, making it impossible to move beyond a sloth-like shuffle on the *Seeker's* deck. Stevie couldn't be angry with Tristan. Guilt resurfaced like a bubble of air from the ocean's depths. Hadn't she been the one to put them all in this position in the first place? They'd been lucky to have this chance to bring back their fortune. Maybe the treasure was a gift they weren't meant to keep. Perhaps God was telling them they needed to forge a different path.

She let out a rush of breath. For three generations, the Sauvage contingent had operated *La Maison de la Fortune* Boarding and Gaming house. What other path did they have? What other way did they know? Based on their experiences over the last few weeks, sailing wasn't a strength, either.

Tristan sank to the deck and dropped his head in his hands. Jacqueline stepped behind him and put her arms around his neck then rested her cheek on top of his head. "It's okay, Tristan. Don't be sad."

Tristan's voice held all the weight of a condemned man. "I let everyone down, Biscuit. We worked so hard to get the treasure, and I lost it. I lost it all."

"You didn't lose it all, Tristan," Jacqueline said quietly.

"Yes, I did. Everything sank. The dress, the belt, everything."

Stevie sighed. "Tristan, you can't take all the blame. If I hadn't caused the fire, the boarding house wouldn't have burned down."

"And if the boarding house hadn't burned, we'd have never found the marble box with Anne Bonny's letters," Bernard said.

"And if I hadn't let a rat startle me, Gampo's men wouldn't have found where I hid the twins," Stevie retorted. Uncle Bernard was up to his tricks to make them feel less terrible. Well, she wasn't about to let go of the guilt that had been pecking her conscience the past few months. She deserved to feel terrible. She deserved her family's wrath and disappointment.

"If Gampo's men hadn't found the twins, we'd never have had a reason to sail the *Seeker* to Jamaica with Harvey," Gabriel chimed in.

The warmth of Conal's hand enveloped hers. He raised it to his lips and kissed her palm, causing a shiver to sweep down her spine. Startled, she turned to look at him. His hair was loose and flying with the sea breeze. Deep green eyes bored into hers, and for a moment, she forgot where she was. He looked the way she envisioned a Viking king: tall, strong and brave.

"And if ye hadn't been forced to bring the *Seeker* to Gampo, we'd never have met. 'Tis fate and fortune that brought us to where we are, Stevie, my love. It was all meant to happen just the way it did."

He was right. How empty would her life be right now if she were still in New Orleans, making beignets and tea cakes in the boardinghouse kitchen? He brushed her lips with his and she grasped the front of his shirt and kissed him back. Yes, they were still destitute, but right now she was wealthy beyond compare. She was rich with the love of a wild sea captain who'd given her his heart.

"And if I hadn't been aboard, ye all would have never known to search the kirkyard of old Helshire church," Harvey said in a stout voice. "And I broke the code of the compass rose."

Uncle Bernard pulled off a water-logged boot. "No one cares, you sorry excuse for a seaman," he retorted.

When she and Conal broke their kiss, she glanced at her family. They were smiling.

Jacqueline patted Tristan's shoulder. "See? It's okay, Tristan. We didn't lose everything—"

Tristan brushed her hand off his shoulder and raised his head. "Yes, we did, Jacquie," he snapped. "Why don't you understand that? Because of me, we lost *everything*. Just stop trying to make me feel better, would you?"

Tears sprung to Jacqueline's eyes. "Mamma always told us if we had each other, that's all we'd ever need." Her voice was soft, but her words could've shattered rock.

Stevie caught her breath. The rest of the family paused. Uncle Bernard looked at each of them and nodded. "Your mother was right about that, God rest her soul. We do have each other. I'm not sure what our future holds, but whatever it is, we'll find out together." He clapped Gabriel and Adrian on the shoulders, reached over and squeezed Stevie's hand before giving Tristan a cuff on the head. He reached down and picked up the little girl. "Sometimes we have to stop and listen to the words of innocent hearts, and remind ourselves there are more important things than treasure belts and golden gowns," he said.

"And stones and jewelry," Jacqueline added.

"And stones and jewelry," Uncle Bernard confirmed.

"I know it's not the same as a golden gown," Jacqueline said, reaching down inside the neck of her dress, "but I'll share my shiny pebbles with everyone, as long as I can give this necklace to Stevie for a wedding gift. Did you know Conal was going to be her husband?"

"What wedding?" Adrian asked, walking up to the group.

"What necklace?" Uncle Bernard added.

Jacqueline pulled up a gleaming, teardrop-shaped ruby pendant surrounded by at least ten large diamonds. "This one." It hung on a thick gold chain. The little girl handed it to Stevie.

It was heavier than Stevie expected and she almost dropped it. The ruby caught the flash of the fading sun, which transformed it into brilliant rays of light, the diamonds adding a sparkle that seemed to radiate fire. Stevie forgot to breathe. This could save them. This could save her family.

"It's for Captain O'Brien and Stevie's wedding," Jacqueline answered Adrian.

Suddenly, gazes shifted from the pendant to Conal and Stevie.

"What wedding?" Adrian asked again. "When did they decide to get married?" He tossed an accusatory glare at Conal. "We're basically brothers now. How is it you mentioned none of this to me, after all we've been through together?"

"I..." Conal started.

"I think I should have a yea or nay in all of this," Tristan mumbled. "I *am* the oldest in the family."

"Uncle Bernard is oldest," Jacqueline stated. She glanced over at Harvey, who'd been standing quietly in his state of partial dress. His shirt hung to his knees, and he had only one boot, which he had yanked off in frustration upon gaining a foothold aboard the *Seeker*. He still held it in his hand. "Unless we count Mister Harvey," Jacqueline added with her brows furrowed. "Then Uncle Bernard is the second-oldest."

"Fine, then." Conal's voice sliced through the conversation like a honed saber.

Talk ceased as Captain O'Brien stepped forward and faced Tristan. The way the breeze lifted the hair from his shoulders gave him the appearance of a great eagle ready to swoop down and attack his prey. And for a moment, it appeared that Tristan was wondering if *he* were the prey. Conal's eyes glittered with an intensity that almost made the entire deck quake.

"I respectfully request your sister's hand in marriage." Conal shifted his gaze to her. "If she'll have me."

If she'd have him? If *she'd* have *him*?

He'd told her he loved her in the cave, but this was different. This was binding. This was a lifetime. This...was...a lifetime. And he'd just asked her to share his. Her throat closed and she couldn't speak.

"If she has chosen you, I'll give you both my blessing," Tristan said, studying her intently.

"Ye better answer the captain, lass," Harvey groused. "If ye don't, he's likely to have us all tossed overboard as a pretty meal fer the sharks, just fer spite."

Answer?

Jacqueline suddenly grabbed Stevie's hands and dragged her toward Conal, laughing. This was funny? No. This was serious. Her baby sister couldn't possibly understand that this was very serious.

Conal's big, warm hands encompassed hers. She looked at their hands. Hers...with long, thin fingers, slightly pink from the sun. His...a golden bronze, strong and firm. He drew hers up to his mouth and kissed each knuckle. Was this a dream?

"Dinna break me in half and reject me, lass. I told ye that ye'd already had my heart." His next words were whispered for her ears only. "If ye give me yours, I promise I'll protect it 'til I die."

Reject him? She stared at him. How could he not know? "Conal, I lost my heart to you before we were halfway to Jamaica."

"Then ye will marry me?"

"Yes."

Suddenly, she was engulfed in a bear hug and lifted from the boards of the deck. Laughing, Conal swung her around. He silenced her shriek of surprise with a kiss that curled her toes. Her family took turns shaking Conal's hand and giving her big, hard hugs.

When she knelt down to hug Jacqueline, her little sister took the thick gold necklace and dropped around her neck. "Happy wedding," Jacqueline said.

Stevie kissed her on the cheek. "I need a maid to assist me. Will you do me the honor?"

"Yes!" Jacqueline squealed, clapping her hands and hopping up and down. She ran back to Uncle Bernard and jumped into his arms, making him laugh.

"Biscuit," Tristan said slowly. "Will you show us your shiny pebbles now?"

"I will." She wiggled out of Uncle Bernard's arms. "Captain Gampo bought this dress for me specifically because of the pockets. He said they'd probably hold a small seal, although I've never seen a seal, so I don't really know how big that might be."

With growing curiosity, the family gathered closer as Jacqueline reached into the pockets sewn into the side seams of her dress. Gampo was right. They probably could have held a small seal. Jacqueline's arms disappeared to her elbows as she groped. She pulled out a small leather pouch and handed it to Bernard.

He emptied the pouch into his hand. Roughly hewn emeralds glinted in the fading light of the day.

"The others were in a cloth pouch, but when I picked it up, the bottom fell out." Jacqueline reached into her other pocket and pulled out a handful of loose diamonds and handed them to her brother. "Here, Tristan, take these so I can fish out the rest."

"By all that's holy—," Tristan breathed, as the little girl poured a fistful of glittering diamonds into his waiting palm.

A bony *thud* echoed across the deck.

Harvey had fainted.

CHAPTER 19

22 March 1729

Dear Father,
It is with a heavy heart that I must sever all communications with you
going forward. This is for your protection, as well as my son's. May God
bless you and keep you healthy and safe.

Remember, we still have additional assets (mentioned in my earlier letters)
hidden, but available near Savanna. Please do not hesitate to seek them
out if you are ever in need. You will know how to locate them from my
letters and journal.

I thank you for all you have done for me and my son. We send you our love
and deep affection.

I will always remain,
Your Daughter
A

They all stood in the common room in Drago's house, Stevie's family as well as Conal's. Landon and Keelan Hart had joined them. Outside, in the shade of the front porch, Drago reclined on a chair next to a small table that held a platter of fruit and bread, a bottle of wine and a pitcher of ale. Jacqueline and Julian sat on the floor at his feet, playing cards. His wounds were healing well, and he was in good spirits.

Almost a week had passed since they'd returned to the *Seeker*, and it was hard to believe what had transpired while Conal had been away from the ship. Uncle Fynn was alive, Gampo wasn't dead, and Aunt Risa was Gampo's *sister,* of all things.

Apparently, Brendan had grudgingly agreed to allow Conal and Landon to believe that Fynn had been killed in the confrontation they'd had with Gampo near Baracoa.

"It was my idea," Fynn had said. "I needed time to heal from my wounds." He thumped his cane on his new wooden leg. "Besides, I thought that we were being attacked by those Tripoli pirates from way back."

At Stevie's curious look, Conal explained, "Years ago, a group of pirates captured Fynn's ship. They forced him to be a crewman and was a slave for several years. He finally escaped, but in doing so, as well...stirred their ire. That earned Fynn a black mark, and they've been pestering him ever since. He thought the *Dragon* was part of their fleet, which is why we always tried to avoid her, or if we had to engage, cripple her and flee."

"But Gampo wasn't one of the pirates from Tripoli?"

"No. Gampo had been told that Fynn had kidnapped his sister and sold her. When Gampo couldn't find her or confirm they had sold her, he sought out Fynn to confront him and demand her return."

Fynn stepped closer. "I hoped if Gampo thought I was dead, he'd stop attacking our fleet, but he didn't." He chuckled. "His head is thicker than a stone."

"Which makes his almost as thick as yours," Risa said, slipping her hand around his elbow. She smiled up at her husband.

Fynn attempted one of his dark scowls before giving up and leaning down and pecking her on the cheek. "How is the young buck?"

"He's resting more comfortably now that Keelan has finished with him," Landon said, a smile tugging at his mouth.

Conal chuckled. His sister had been merciless with the man while treating him. Although after all the facts had been sorted and discussed, they decided to leave it in the past. They were all bygones now, and everyone was happier for it.

"Thankfully, Brendan's blow didn't go very deep." Risa studied Stevie. "Drago seems to be very fond of your young siblings, and they of him."

Stevie dipped her head. "I'm very grateful to him for saving Julian's life. If he hadn't reacted the way he did..." She closed her eyes briefly.

"But he did," Conal reminded her. "Everything turned out well for all."

Risa lifted her chin in pride. "My brother, he is a strong, healthy man and will heal soon enough," she said.

Drago's voice filtered in through an open window. "Julian, my boy, hop down to the cellar and bring up a couple more bottles of this wine, then tell Manuel to tap a hogshead of ale for the men," Drago said. "It's not every day that we have a wedding on Lamb's Tail Island."

"Yessir, Captain Gampo!" Julian scampered off.

"Now, I believe it is time," Risa said to Stevie. "We must go."

Conal bent down and gave her a light kiss. He'd see her soon enough.

"C'mon, boy. We have time for another ale." Fynn clapped Conal on the shoulder and headed for the porch. "Keelan?"

"No thank you, Uncle Fynn," Keelan said, laughing.

Keelan Hart had become a friend and would soon be Stevie's

sister by marriage. Although petite, Keelan was quick, strong and fearless. She'd treated Drago and his wounds over the past week, and although the man had threatened her with every punishment under the sun, she hadn't been fazed in the least by his gruff demeanor. Conal had made an off-handed remark suggesting his sister might have been enjoying the torment she wreaked.

"Mrs. Hart, would you join us?" Stevie asked. She wanted Conal's sister to help her dress for the wedding.

"I'd be delighted!" Mrs. Hart jumped to her feet. "But I insist you call me Keelan. We're about to become family, after all." She tossed a grin to her brother, who returned it with a nod.

Risa beamed. "I'm so happy for you and our Conal." She gestured to her. "Come, my dear, let us go upstairs and begin. It's been a long time since I've helped a bride prepare for her wedding day."

CONAL TURNED up the lantern in his cabin until a soft glow chased away the darkness. The beach on Lamb's Tail Island still flickered from multiple roasting pits and tall torches shoved into the sand. Laughter and music drifted over the water to the ship. The revelry would likely continue until dawn.

He and his bride had sneaked away in one of the canoes. If anyone noticed, they had the good sense to ignore them. Now, they were alone on the *Seeker* as the ship breathed gently at anchor with the calm, clear tide of the bay.

He faced his new wife and sucked in a breath. Her grey irises were tinged in the same dark blue as the midnight sea. The red silk dress clung to her in all the right places. He'd accepted the gown as payment for something a while back, and thinking he'd swap it for a new pair of boots had stored it. It was a good thing he hadn't traded it because he could think of no one else who would look as stunning in it as his bride.

He lifted the lantern glass and held a taper to the flame. Someone had entered his cabin earlier and placed a dozen candles in various locations. Flower petals littered the floor and had been scattered across his bed.

It was probably Keelan. His sister was bold and secretive enough to have accomplished such a task unnoticed. He smiled.

God had determined that his path would cross Stevie's; he'd forever be grateful for it. Tonight was his wedding night. Two months ago, he'd have bet his last pair of boots he'd never marry. Now, he could barely contain his desire to share his life, his ship, his dreams with his wife.

Conal held the last taper to a nearby candle wick just as the soft *click* of a hammer echoed in his ear. Taking a chance, he turned his head slightly and his cheek brushed against the cool, smooth metal of a pistol barrel.

"Don't even flinch," the voice behind him whispered in a low and lethal tone.

He froze. "What do you want?"

"I have demands. If you don't acquiesce to my demands, I'll be forced to take more extreme measures to see to your compliance."

"And what are your demands, exactly?" he asked in a stilted voice.

"Take off all your clothes."

His mouth twitched into a smile. Whirling, he grabbed Stevie around the waist and spun her in circles while she laughed.

"You first," he said, dipping his head to brush a kiss on her cheek.

"Oh, no, Captain." Stevie shook her head. "I insist—" Her words dissipated as Conal kissed a sensitive spot behind her ear. "I...insist—oh!"

"You insist what, little rabbit?"

"I...I'm not a rabbit, I'm a...pirate."

"Then you have me at your mercy, Lady Pirate." He nibbled

her neck where her pulse had begun to throb erratically. "Or should I refer to you as the Pirate Heiress?"

"Both. I...insist..." She sighed and traced her fingertips from his chest to his nape and curled her fingers into his hair. "I insist...that you don't stop."

"I am your captive," he murmured, trailing kisses down her neck. "I have no choice but to comply."

"And my treasure," she whispered. "I love you."

He cupped her beautiful face in his hands. "And I love you, Stevie O'Brien."

For Drago's story, get the next book: The Heart of a Spy

THE HEART OF A SPY

The Hearts of Adventure Sweet Romance Series

Book 5

HE STEALS FOR THE FRENCH CROWN.

SHE HEALS FOR THE CATHOLIC CHURCH.

HE WILL HEAL HER HEART.

SHE WILL STEAL HIS.

*NOTE: This is the *sweet version* of the novel *If You Give a Spy a Scheme*, (Book 5 of *Pirates & Petticoats Series* By Chloe Flowers).

"Dramatic, engrossing, suspenseful, exciting."

French Privateer and former pirate, Captain Drago Gamponetti is given one final mission from his employer, the king of France: reclaim religious relics from a New Orleans cathedral. Trouble begins when he's forced by a mysterious, veiled, novitiate nun to swear on the Bible to protect the very items he was instructed to steal.

Church healer, Eva Trudeau hides more than her face behind the veil. The convent has been her safe haven since she crawled, beaten and bloody, to its door nine years ago. When an old enemy re-surfaces and threatens to drag her back into the dark underworld from where she'd escaped, both she and her dark pirate captain stand to lose everything they've fought so hard to protect...including each other.

What readers have to say:

Set against the backdrop of the famous Battle of New Orleans, This story will have you turning pages into the wee hours of the night. If you love pirates, history, humor and a bit of romance you will love this newly released book by Chloe

Flowers. The author has a way with historical fiction that enthralls and entertains.

SNEAK PEAK

THE HEART OF A SPY

He steals for the French crown.
She heals for the Catholic Church.
He will heal her heart.
She will steal his.

T he silent, brooding Captain Gamponetti with his storm cloud eyes and catlike grace settled Jacqueline and Julian in the back of the cart, then handed Eva up to the bench. She tried not to flinch at his touch. Instead, she propped her sack of herbs and salves between her feet while he settled in and gathered the reins, giving them a flick of his wrist to spur the old mule into motion.

She'd roused Sister Beatrice long enough to inform her of their planned trip to the caves. Eva shot a sideways glance at the man next to her, a mountain of muscle and bone. At least if she didn't return, the sisters would know where to search for her body. While she had no true outward cause to be so wary (other than his presence and Kalia's premonition) remaining cautious was more for self-preservation than anything. Truly, the man merely delivered words and sentences in a crisp, terse manner. Still...

Stop it.

Those ominous statements only added to this discomfiture. Allowing them to churn in her mind didn't help at all. Her duty was to treat and heal the girl. But even so, she would be on her guard every moment.

Eva pulled the hood lower over her head. Keeping her scarred face in the shadows came instinctively. The hoods and veils were less to protect herself these days. She'd learned if she kept her face hidden, it saved others from being affected by the sight. Their reactions no longer surprised or mortified her like they once did. Just a numbing punch to the gut.

Children cried.

Ladies spoke in hushed whispers as they stared from behind their fans. *"What a horrible thing to happen to a young girl. I wonder how she was maimed."*

"It's likely she's a prostitute. I've been told older women in a brothel will attack and scar the younger ones, so they don't steal their customers."

"Oh, how do you know she's a...a..."

"No chaperone, no protector, what else would she be?"

Five summers ago, the young man who'd promised love, marriage, and a life outside the convent, had recoiled in horror when she finally found the nerve to remove the veil. He soon disappeared from her life and left her with a shattered heart. The malicious, bloody shards still jabbed at her lungs when she allowed the memories to invade. Long ago she'd accepted the fact she was too damaged for any kind of romantic relationship. Hugo, in a drunken rage had seen to that.

At least now she was valued. Aside from God, her friendship with Sister Beatrice was as close as she would ever get to love.

"Are you expecting the waters to heal the girl?" The captain's dubious tone broke the quiet, startling her.

Another quick glance revealed a grim set to his jaw. The healer in her wanted to ease his worries and keep him calm by any means possible. The rest of her wanted to shake bells and shout warnings to the villagers.

Fighting the unease best she could, she kept her voice calm and soothing. "The cave waters are cool and will reduce her fever, which I suspect comes from her bladder. She must drink a medicinal tea and a *lot* of it over the next fortnight, to dispel the sickness."

He shifted uncomfortably on the hard wooden seat, shoulders tight and coiled. "Have you healed someone with this type of infirmity before?"

"Of course—"

"Did the treatment work? Did they live?"

"*Capitaine* Gamponetti, I may be young for a healer, but I assure you—"

"She's such a little piece of fluff, but she's as stouthearted as any of my men." He jiggled the reins, giving the mule the opportunity to keep up his pace without getting a crack on the rump for lagging. "I haven't been around many small girls, but I believe she's stronger than most." His voice bore a hint of pride; daring her to argue.

"I know you're worried about her and I promise I'll do everything I can to help her."

"But what of the burns on her arms?" The steadiness of his words did nothing to disguise his concern, nor the stern resolve in the angle of his frown.

"Your daughter probably played beneath a Manchineel tree after the storm."

He released a long breath, glanced at her, then dipped his head trying to peer inside her hood. She couldn't stop herself from ducking. The observer's expression after that first glance was always the hardest to take.

He scowled. "They're not my children, although I am responsible for them at the moment," he finally said.

His explanation gave her pause. Some tightness eased from her shoulders. He had a kind heart then, surely. Although he appeared composed at the moment, she sensed a hidden menace lurking beneath the surface, like an alligator submerged in the murky waters of the bayou. Waiting.

"Where are their parents?"

"Dead."

Eva nodded, understanding. Thankfully, the abbey had room, should the children need a home. The nuns never turn a child away; she was living proof. A question ripped at her stomach. *Dead by whose hand?*

"Are you related?" she asked, hoping with all her heart the answer would be yes.

He shrugged. "No, but their family is very special to me. I'm an unofficial guardian of sorts. Their uncle, cousins and brothers operate a hotel and gaming house in New Orleans, which was destroyed by a fire. I offered the twins a place to stay while it was being rebuilt." His mouth twitched. "To keep them out of the way."

"Are you with the British troops?"

He shook his head. "I have my own schooner."

"He's a privateer," Julian piped up from behind her.

Even as Eva sent up a brief prayer of thanks, a shiver ran down her spine. Privateers were nothing more than pirates with permission to plunder, some spurred by loyalty to their sovereign, others by greed. Worse, in times such as these, said permission wasn't always sought. Letters of Marque were not always obtained, nor were they often authentic. Privateers were thieves and marauders, the lot of them—a people and a lifestyle she avoided with determined vigor. And she'd done so quite well, up until tonight.

A wisp of hair tickled her chin, and she tucked it away. She should have grabbed her long veil. It draped diagonally across her face and over her shoulder, covering the puckered, maimed skin on her cheek.

She peered discreetly at the man next to her. He had a restless aura about him, loose limbs ready to snap into action. Charcoal eyes carried a hint of leashed violence. Which kind of privateer? A devious one might not concern himself with children, although it would take a true demon of a man to deny minor assistance to a child, such as taking her to a healer.

Well, the man couldn't be completely black-hearted. Miss Kalia's strange insights might be helpful here. Her mind returned to his schooner. There was indeed a reason he knocked on her door tonight, beyond the girl's sickness. Perhaps beyond the prediction.

Providence.

She'd prayed and prayed for guidance and assistance. God had answered her prayers and sent someone to help her and the Ursuline nuns. They were in dire need of a protector to save their relics from being stolen. A responsibility that could cause an unambitious man to shirk away, but surely once properly presented, might not be so immense a quest for a privateer. Once she explained everything to the captain, he'd understand that, too. This quiet moment offered her the opportunity to voice a plea. How to start?

"I believe, *Capitaine* Gamponetti, the divine hand of God has sent you to me."

Silver-hued eyes held a hint of humor. "Pardon my lack of conviction Sister, but I doubt God's hand would send a man like me to someone like you."

A man like him? Perhaps her observations had been correct, then. Not that it mattered, overmuch. The only thing concerning her now was whether she could trust him a reasonable amount.

A direct approach might be best. "Oh, but I honestly believe He has, *Capitaine*. You will deliver the children back home to New Orleans soon, no? I am a novitiate of the Ursuline order there, and I have a desire to return to the convent. When it is time for you to depart Jamaica, I would happily act as the children's chaperone." Surely he'd relish the opportunity to divert more of his attention to his ship, rather than split it with keeping a watchful eye on the young twins.

He repressed a snort and cut her a short dark glance. "Had you been acquainted with the two of them while both were in stout health, I doubt you'd make the same offer."

"Are you saying they're rascals?" His warning made her smile. Just the fact that he made an attempt at levity allowed her to relax somewhat (as much as a person could relax with a coiled panther seated four inches away).

The corner of his mouth tipped up. "They are rascals of the highest degree and much too smart for their own good. The two of them together are especially dangerous."

She laughed. "I shall endeavor to stay alert when they're near. How long will the twins be with you?"

He twisted and cast a concerned stare over his shoulder.

Eva followed his gaze. Julian was sitting with his back against the box seat, his sister leaning against his chest. He tightened his arms around her as the cart rolled and jolted over the bumpy trail. Still, she remained asleep, her head lolling on his shoulder.

Gamponetti's lips flattened. "They were to stay with me until early spring. I had been preparing to journey south to Cartagena. I have a trade route to run and a timetable to keep."

Had been. Would they delay or leave earlier? "Have your plans changed?"

The captain shrugged once more. "I might return the children to their uncle in New Orleans before I depart, depending on Jacqueline's health."

Eva caught her breath. Here was the opportunity she needed. "I should very much like to accompany them. As I have a need to return also, I would be happy to look after them during the journey." She'd repeated herself. She had already offered herself as a governess of sorts. Now, she must sound desperate. Which of course she was, but she didn't want to raise his suspicions.

He remained silent. Too late. She'd raised his suspicions.

Drat.

The hesitation sent a mixture of trepidation and relief to her chest. He might consider it, but was not yet convinced it was a good idea. She must think of a way to persuade him to take her along. Perhaps appealing to his ego would help. "I have talked with every merchant ship's captain in Port Royal, begging for passage back to New Orleans, but all were too cowardly to assist me."

One had gawked at her like she had an octopus on her head. "I ain't sailing into them waters, Sister. Not with them British blighters—pardon my language—not with the British and their war with the States. Too dangerous. Only a fool or a madman would even try."

Gamponetti shifted, giving her a full view of both narrowed gray eyes. "Why are you so eager to return?"

Before she could answer, the captain's shoulders straightened and his attention whipped around to focus on the right side of the trail ahead. Broad leafy shadows crossed the moonlit path. Nothing moved, no sounds.

No noises at all.

No beetles buzzing, no night creatures rustling in the underbrush, no chirping tree frogs. Her lungs tightened. Jamaica wasn't without its dangerous beasts, both human and animal.

"What is it?" she whispered, gripping the edge of the cart seat, staring wildly into the dense flora.

"We're being watched." Easing a pistol from his belt with one hand, he pulled the reins with the other. The mule's ears twitched; he stopped abruptly, attention forward, listening. The captain spoke in a low voice. "Easy."

A lone figure stood on the trail a few yards ahead of them. "Why you be travelin' dis time o' night, Sistah Eva? You gots troubles?"

She slumped with relief. Next to her, the captain stilled, his hands gripping the reins as if they kept him from falling into a burning pit of lava. "I'm taking a sick child to the caves, Miss Kalia," she replied.

"Girl-child then. Who wit you?"

She swallowed. The premonition. "*Capitaine* Gamponetti."

Miss Kalia grinned then cackled a short laugh. "Ah, yes, yes. Last time him saw I, him come from de red house. Long night wit de rum. Bad day next, eh Drago?"

The captain had turned to granite beside her, likely embarrassed (as well he should be) that Miss Kalia had seen him leaving a brothel. Eva chewed her lip. It was possible she misread the man. Allowed desperation to dictate her earlier impressions.

The old woman approached the wagon, swaying like seaweed with the tide, perhaps due to aching joints, but on a night like this, it was bewitching and unnerving, like an adder mesmerizing prey. The moonlight subdued her brightly patched skirt into shades of grayish-reds, greens, blues and yellows. Colorful feathers poked out in every direction from the silver hair piled high on her head. A streak of white paint trailed from one ear, ran along her jawline, across her chin, ending at her other ear like a gruesome grin. Eva fought the strong desire to squirm closer to the pirate for protection. Except that would give her as much reassurance as jumping from an alligator's jaws into a jaguar's mouth.

Kalia hummed as she peered over the side at Jacqueline. "T'ought so. Eva, see I in a vision just now. Surrounded by t'under and frost, perched next to a jaguar black as night. Woke I wide up." Before Eva could respond, the woman scampered up into the wagon bed, bringing with her a strong tang of wood smoke.

Julian didn't take his eyes from her but still leaned away as she bent over his sister. She placed her palm against the girl's cheek, her brown hand contrasting sharply with the pale skin, even though it was still flushed with fever. She tilted Jacqueline's head back, pressed her chin down to open her mouth. Sniffed her breath.

Unsure what to say or do, Eva dragged her gaze from the old woman to the captain. How long have they been acquainted? His storm-gray eyes followed the crone's every move.

Miss Kalia hopped down and slipped to Eva's side. The old woman grasped her hand and pressed a cluster of herbs against her clammy palm. "Her need dis. It make best tea for dee girl." She nodded toward Captain Gamponetti and lowered her voice until it was barely there. "Him must to drink *dis*." She caught Eva's gaze and held it, as she slid a small flask under the herbs. "Den dat what you want by him, you get."

Eva shoved both into her bag, afraid to refuse them and unsure of what else to do or say.

The old Jamaican woman stepped back from the wagon and lifted both hands in farewell. Or some sort of blessing?

Maybe a curse?

A white witch. A "good" witch, if there was such a thing. Sister Beatrice would say there was not. But Eva had seen too much to denounce anything outright. There was no telling what spell Kalia incanted or bestowed upon them. The pirate jiggled the reins and clucked the mule forward.

As they passed, Kalia spoke again, but this time to him, her voice both smoky and chiseled, eyes black and white. "Change in de wind, Drago. Time come near for you to make a choice. Choose wrong and die. Before de tree flowers bloom, you betray an ally...aide a foe...break a vow. Light beckons you, but de dark always a seductress." Her wild stare locked with Eva's. "Which voice will him follow? Him heart or him head?"

Tension radiated from the captain in waves of heat. Kalia had slithered past his stoney, rugged aura to poke the tiniest gap between courage and unease. The muscles in his jaw tightened, but he did not look at the old woman as they passed.

"I...I don't know how to answer her question." Eva peered over her shoulder, but the witch had disappeared. An awkward silence followed. The jungle remained paralyzed for several minutes while they plodded along the path.

He could have taken Jacqueline to Kalia. She peered at him again, now understanding why. A rigidity thrummed through his broad shoulders; he had a flare in his nostrils, a fierce glint in his eyes.

Then it hit her; *Kalia terrified him.*

Her curiosity flared. "Have you known her long?"

The captain expelled a slow breath. "Everyone knows Kalia. And Kalia knows everyone." A wry smile seeped up to his eyes. The edges crinkled, and a dimple settled in his cheek, giving him a roguish, but more pleasing appearance. Much like an unapologetic child holding a stolen cake. "In truth, I found there's no way to avoid her even when it's your intense desire."

She'd learned much the same. A strange sense of balance lodged between them. The vulnerability the old woman raked from the captain made him less threatening. "The people here have great respect for Miss Kalia. It would be foolish to dismiss her or her methods. To do so would also betray the islander's trust," she said.

The captain slapped the reins again and muttered, "Kalia's black medicine attracts too much attention, especially from the white man. They do not understand it. White men fear what they don't understand."

"It's not black medicine." She corrected him. "Obeah is a very ancient healing practice." She shifted the tea and the tonic to the bottom of her sack, trying to ignore the twinge of foreboding they sent through her chest.

"Call it what you will, the white settlers and plantation owners fear it," he muttered.

How should she approach the last premonition? He had to be familiar with the old woman's visions if indeed he knew who she was. How would he react? Surprise? Disbelief? There was one way to find out.

"Miss Kalia stopped me at the market two days ago and told me a man would come to the abbey with a sick girl-child," she blurted it out before she could stop herself. He would think her a ninny, talking about an old woman's premonitions as if they were gospel, which they were not.

Yet, a flicker of surprise shot across the captain's face. "She did?"

So he was familiar with Kalia's visions. "Yes and here you are."

"Indeed." His brows dropped in thought, or perhaps concern.

She couldn't, *wouldn't* confide what Miss Kalia had said next. That was something she dared not repeat.

"Him not what him seem to be," the old woman had whispered. *"But den, so not are you."*

ENJOY THE NEXT BOOK!
The Heart of a Spy
For more information go to www.chloeflowers.com

MORE BOOKS BY CHLOE FLOWERS

CONTINUE THE SERIES WITH THE

PIRATES & PETTICOATS NOVELS

This trilogy follows Keelan Grey and Landon Hart on their adventure of discovery and a love of a lifetime. Two hearts have never battled more fiercely to be together...

You Give a Smuggler a Secret

If You Give a Rake a Reason

If You Give a Hellion Your Heart

PIRATES & PETTICOATS STANDALONE NOVELS:

If You Give a Pirate a Treasure

If You Give a Spy a Scheme

PREFER SWEET ROMANCE INSTEAD?

Read Chloe Flowers' *The Hearts of Adventure Sweet Romance* Series!

The Heart of a Tempest

The Heart of a Siren

The Heart of a Bride

The Heart of a Pirate

The Heart of a Spy

BRIDAL VEIL FALLS
THE TOWN OF HAPPILY EVER AFTERS

COMING SOON: A NEW SWEET CONTEMPORARY SMALL TOWN ROMANCE SERIES SURE TO CAPTURE YOUR HEART AND TICKLE YOUR FUNNY BONE.

✳

Chloe's Website: www.chloeflowers.com

RECIPE

CITRUS BEACH PIE

7 ingredients, one delicious pie, what's not to like?

Makes one pie

For the crust:
1 1/2 sleeves of saltine crackers
1/3 to 1/2 cup softened unsalted butter
3 tablespoons sugar

For the filling:
1 can (14 ounces) sweetened condensed milk
4 egg yolks
1/2 cup lemon or lime juice or a mix of the two

Fresh whipped cream and coarse sea salt for garnish, maybe a little citrus zest for color!

Preheat oven to 350 degrees.

Crush the crackers finely, but not to dust. You can use a food processor or your hands. Add the sugar, then knead in the butter until the crumbs hold together like dough. Press into an 8 inch pie pan. Chill for 15 minutes, then bake for 18 minutes or until the crust colors a little.

While the crust is cooling (it doesn't need to be cold), beat the egg yolks into the milk, then beat in the citrus juice. It is important to completely combine these ingredients. Pour into the shell and bake for 16 minutes until the filling has set. The pie needs to be completely cold to be sliced. Serve with fresh whipped cream and a sprinkling of sea salt.

ABOUT CHLOE

Chloe supports the National Breast Cancer Foundation.

Chloe Flowers is an award-winning author and the recipient of the University of Akron, Wayne College *2018 Writer of the Year* Award. She writes small town contemporary women's fiction, and historical women's action and adventure romance novels about scoundrels, pirates, and spunky, independent heroines.

Chloe keeps bees, and identifies her hives by the different flowers she paints on them. Her pets have always been named after her favorite characters or action heroes: Indiana, Luke, Gimli, Thelma, Rocket, Al Giordino, Severus, Mushu, Mérida, Jack...Dead Pool (he's a goldfish).

Chloe's biggest fault is the apparent inability to say "no" whether it's in response to a call for aid or a double-dog-dare to hike home through 30 acres of a snow-covered forest at midnight...during a full moon. It was early morning during said adventure when she came upon a group of sheriff's deputies searching for a lost girl. So, of course she offered to help (turns out, they were searching for her).

She is a member of the Romance Writers of America, Northeast Ohio Romance Writers and RWA Contemporary Romance Writers, The Beau Monde Romance Writers group, where she served as secretary 2017-2019.

She has given workshops and presentations on creating a critique group, how to provide effective critiques, story structure, marketing and self-publishing lessons to writers groups, library patrons and school children.

Chloe has a weakness for good red wine, Calvin & Hobbes comics, pie, dark chocolate and brown-eyed guys with beards, which is probably why she digs pirates, men in uniform and treasure hunters and writes about action and adventure and of course romance, which is the greatest adventure of all.

w.ingramcontent.com/pod-product-compliance
ning Source LLC
ersburg PA
30828260626
300003B/885